Frances Ive has been a journal
    She has had many articles ~   ... national
newspapers and consumer magazines and has written
several non-fiction books. *Finding Jo* is her first novel.

Five Press 2021, www.fivewrite.co.uk

Copyright © Frances Ive

Cover image of the Himalayas courtesy of Alan Parry

Finding Jo

Frances Ive

five press

Chapter 1

I open my eyes and an unusual emotion surges up inside me - pure joy. It's coming from deep within and has nothing to do with anything or anyone else.

I never like the landing, particularly the bumpy ones like this. The engines roar, we slow down and draw to a halt. The scramble for bags and clamour to get out of this tin box begins. I step outside and am greeted with an assault on my nostrils. It's only 5 a.m. and already it's hot.

I have been up all night and crossed continents to get here. Puffing and blowing I wait for my bag which arrives surprisingly quickly. I yank it off the conveyor belt and wander through customs trying not to make eye contact so I don't get hauled over and searched.

Unscathed and looking through the crowd waiting to greet passengers, it dawns on me that no-one's here for me. Why would they be? I feel a bit empty inside. What greets me outside the terminal is a cacophony of noise – jabbering voices, taxis hooting, planes soaring upwards - and hordes and hordes of people.

Dawn has just broken but life is in full action already. Scattered randomly as far as the eye can see are old Mercedes and even older British models I recognise from a dim distant past. And then a deluge unleashes.

'I take you Miss?' 'Come with me.'

'Best taxi.'

'Best prices.'

Lots of drivers with heads nodding at me and shouting,

'Come, come, come.' They must be desperate for business. I choose the least pushy of them all.

1

'Do you know the Cumberland Hotel?' It sounds like downtown Bournemouth.

'It's in Delhi,' I add for clarity's sake.

He doesn't speak but wiggles his eyebrows around which means neither yes nor no to me, but as I'm desperate to get there, I climb in. It's more like a front room than a taxi. All over the windscreen are little garlands of flowers, bracelets, key rings and numerous pictures of what I presume are members of his family.

If he deviates off the main road, I'll jump out, but of course I don't know where I'm going, so that might not work. I'm a bundle of nerves jangling, uneasy and a bit queasy. The driver pays little attention to me though.

The taxi starts up, sounding like a tractor and we're on our way. Cars criss-cross the highway as if there are no rules, and all the time a wave of humanity weaves in and out of the traffic on foot – kids, adults and animals The pace is slow, but treacherous.

A car is coming right for us but it swerves out of the way at the last minute. My driver bangs his horn and swears – the tone is universal. My hand flies to my mouth and I start to pray, not a habit I'm used to. I don't want to die here when no-one knows where I am, and after I've let them all down. I suppose they'd find my passport and word would get through eventually, unless it gets stolen.

'Stop it,' I say aloud to myself.

My mind is captivated as I watch the daily rituals in awe. Willowy men with loads on their back, women almost bent double with baskets on their heads, going about their daily grind. Men, women and kids pick up their beds from the ground as the day starts, and set off to do whatever they do.

Among the masses are people wheeling bikes, donkeys, dogs, cats, chickens, and kids, some without clothes. And in the middle of it all people are setting up stalls selling strange looking juices and cooking food. Who buys it?

There's a large cloud sitting over the city, a pollution cloud, I assume. I've read about it, but now I can physically see it.

2

My driver's phone rings for what must be the fourth time and he careers along, one hand on the steering wheel, one on the phone stuck to his ear. He's so animated that his other hand is waving around so there are no hands on the wheel. It's chaotic enough on these roads without him adding to the danger.

I've seen one particular sign at least twice before, so we must be going round in circles. I lean towards the front and try to say firmly,

'The Cumberland now. I must go there now.'

He nods and twitches the one eyebrow I can see, bangs down the phone and two minutes later the 'Cumberland Hotel' sign looms in front of us, which rather proves the point.

He picks up a grubby piece of paper, writes on it, and hands it to me - '3,900 Rupees'. Sounds a lot to me. I try to calculate quickly what it would be in pounds, but I'm tired and my brain is woolly. I just want to get out of here, into the hotel and under the shower. He grabs my bags, I shuffle through my money, not knowing what I'm looking for and finally hand him 4,000 Rupees.

I have no idea if I should be tipping him, if it's enough, or if I've been fleeced. In fact, as he drives off it occurs to me that I've paid him £40 and this is India, which is supposed to be incredibly cheap.

The hotel looks clean enough, hardly luxurious, but there is an en-suite shower and toilet and a big bed, which is all I really want right now. I dump my bags in the room and go back downstairs, stealing a glance at my watch. It's only 7.30 and it's hotting up. The huge fans in the restaurant whoosh cool air around and ease the oppressive heat.

I plonk myself down at a table, keeping my bag close to me. Everyone goes on about being careful with your belongings when travelling. I peruse the menu and choose the bread, eggs and yoghurt and a cup of tea and ease back in the bench seat.

My tired mind is throwing up random ideas and concerns. What am I doing here and what am I going to do? Perhaps I am completely

3

insane, setting off on this adventure and leaving them all in the lurch?

I'm so hungry that I feel weak, and I can't get rid of this sense of motion all the time as if I'm still in the plane. I need to sleep, to eat, to cry but not necessarily in that order. My breakfast arrives and despite the eggs being the smallest I've seen in my life, I wolf it down. It's probably the best meal I've ever had.

Back up in my room the screeching of the traffic, the whirring of the fan and the buzz of voices outside the window make sleep virtually impossible. The tiredness is coming in waves, but my mind is wide awake.

Rob's head is peering at me.

'Where are you Jo?' he cries with big tears running down his face. He looks haggard.

I must get away from him but my legs are rooted to the spot. When my legs do respond they are like heavy weights and won't move quickly. Somewhere in the distance I can see Matt and I want to scream.

I start to scream and then hear shouting and cars and open my eyes. I've actually been asleep for a few minutes. The room moves around still as if I'm drunk, but it's that moving plane sensation. There's a hint of nausea in my stomach.

I ease myself up and wonder why I've waited so long for a shower. It's sure to invigorate me. I grab my wash bag and venture towards the shower which is just a spout stuck in the ceiling, and the water runs away through a drain on the floor. The toilet gets soaked when I turn the tap on, but I step under the warmish water and revel in it splashing over my head and body waking me up. Hmm, now I feel more human.

I've had this dress for years but it only sees the light of day on holidays and hot days at home. It's like a comfort blanket, and I certainly need that now. It doesn't reveal too much either so I won't be drawing unwelcome eyes to myself and as it covers my shoulders I won't get burnt.

4

I brush my wet locks slowly, taking deep breaths at the same time. It's not going to take long to dry naturally.

Everyone at home will know by now and they'll either be worried or angry. My beloved sister Beth, and Hannah, will be bitching away about me and old Uncle Denis will be shocked. If he knew where I was he'd come after me. Ha, he's always after me. I've no idea what Mum and Dad will say if they even speak to each other.

Rob, poor Rob – he'll be lost. I hadn't anticipated this guilt.

The thought makes me retrieve my phone and switch it on to see if I have any signal. A load of alerts come through and I can see several messages from Dad, one from Mum, and about seven from Rob. I left notes for all three of them, so they know I haven't been kidnapped. Besides, I've come here to get away from them all, so I switch it off and make a mental note not to look at it anymore. With any luck there won't be any signal up in the mountains.

I fling the phone on the bed, and cover it with a pillow, grab my money belt and ease out into the corridor. Someone's left a plate of food on a cupboard and it's covered in cockroaches. One of them flies right towards me, nearly hitting me. No-one told me that cockroaches could fly.

Back down in the restaurant I order a Coke, something I never drink at home, but often in hot countries. The other guests are all westerners and my sort of age. Two people on their own - a girl and a tall guy. It's funny how all I wanted was to be on my own, but now there's a nagging little feeling in my stomach and throat pulling me down and I suspect it's loneliness. Why am I so contrary?

After downing the Coke, I fasten the money belt round my waist and go to reception.

'I want to buy a train ticket to Shimla. Can you tell me where the station is?'

'You do know it's hard work buying tickets here, do you?' the girl twangs with an American accent.

'No, why?'

5

'Trying to go anywhere or do anything in India is a bureaucratic nightmare. They have papers for everything, and they inherited all this red tape from you Brits, but you could have a go online. Well, I could try online for you.'

'Yes that would be good.'

She taps a few keys.

'Sorry. The website's down. This is India I'm afraid. Do you want to read what it says?'

'I believe you.'

'No, it's funny. Do read it.'

I move round the desk and read the screen.

"Just like people, our system sometimes has a bad day and gets grumpy. We're sorry for the inconvenience, please bear with us while we get it to behave."

'That's quite nice, but it doesn't really help. Don't worry.' I smile at her. 'I need to get out. I'll stroll round. Which way should I set off?'

'Take a map and walk up to Connaught Place. And then it's about a mile or more from there'

'Here,' she indicates on the map. 'We're here, that's Connaught Place and you need to take this road up there. Hold on to your bag and don't be taken in by the beggars.'

'OK, thanks.'

Outside the heat is crushing. I hold up my wrist - 11 o'clock and getting hotter all the time. 'Mad dogs and Englishmen.'

There are people milling around on the pavements and roads, dodging the rickshaws and a red bus goes by with young guys hanging off the back. I can't help staring.

A large red and white ornate building appears which must be Delhi Old Railway Station. Seething masses and long queues in the middle of the concourse. Some people are standing patiently, some are having picnics on the ground, and others are even flat out sleeping. Have they died from waiting? This has to be seen to be believed.

I wish I had a good book with me to sit this one out. I shuffle from foot to foot, watching all the people around me, just taking in what they do and how they gesture in such a lively way whether they're angry or happy. And the noise, the endless noise of humans jabbering, phones buzzing, ringing, singing and blaring loud Indian music, and announcements on the speakers, and the chugging of trains arriving and leaving. I'm just getting to the end of the long line, the clock strikes 1, and the office closes.

'What the bloody hell?' I say louder than I meant to.

'This is India,' offers up a tall lanky guy I saw at the hotel. 'They do everything their own way.'

'How long is it going to be, I'm starving?'

'Tell you what I'll keep your place and you can go and get some food, and then I'll go. They open again at 1.40.'

'That's a funny time.'

'This is India,' he repeats, looking rather pleased with himself.

'I hope you've filled in your form for your ticket.'

'What form?' I enquire.

'You have to put all your details including what school you went to and your mother's maiden name, your next door neighbour's dog's name, etcetera, etcetera.' He seems amused by himself again.

'You're kidding,' I scoff.

'I'm not. This is India.'

I wish he wouldn't keep saying that.

'The forms are available over there – see at the desk where you can buy a local ticket.'

'OK, thank you. I'll just go and get something to eat, and then I can keep your place while you go.'

I wander off, through the mêlée of people and pick up a form. I take a peek at the station restaurant, but everywhere around it there

7

are kids begging. Some of them are barely dressed, or they're in rags. I don't know what to do about them. Shouldn't I buy their lunch?

I fight my desire to help them and purchase a couple of vegetable samosas and a bottle of water at the restaurant, and saunter back to the queue, still focused on the hordes of children.

The tall lanky guy smiles at me and leers at my food. His hair is unkempt and not very clean and simply from his checked short-sleeved shirt and khaki shorts I'd have guessed he was American.

'Thanks a lot,' I say. 'Why are there so many kids everywhere?'

'Don't you know?' he says as if I'm an idiot. 'They are orphans. It's a complete scandal. 80,000 kids go missing every year.'

Not for the first time my mouth drops open of its own accord.

'What?'

'Yes there's a lot to know about India. It seems quite safe, but a hell of a lot goes on in the underground world. Anyway, I'm off to get something to eat.'

'Yeah, you go. I'll keep your place now.'

The samosas are a bit dry but a swig of water washes them down. Children are standing right by me, watching me eat with their pleading eyes, making mouth gestures. I find this impossible, and feel so guilty, something I'm very used to, but not normally in this context.

The lanky guy returns with some pakoras.

'Don't give them food or they'll never leave you alone. You're staying at the Cumberland aren't you?'

I nod assent.

'Are you on your own?'

I nod again casually, wondering if I want him to know this.

'So am I. Perhaps I'll see you later?'

I try to sound vague.

'Ah yeah well. Sorry, I don't know what I'm doing later.'

He is about to say something back to me when the man in the office pings a bell on his desk. Saved by the bell. I might feel like a sad, lonely traveller but I don't feel enticed to spend time with him. Anyway, I prod myself, I'm at the beginning of an amazing adventure, I hope.

Lanky guy moves forward to the desk and I get my pen out. There is a heck of a lot of detail in this form. I lean on my backpack and fill in details of my life's history. The US guy turns round, smiles and holds his hand up to me. I inch forward to the glass, behind which the man is fiddling with papers refusing to look at me. I pointedly look at my watch which has absolutely no effect as he's not looking. I'm flapping my hand up and down in front of my face. I can honestly say I have never been so hot.

I hand him the form and he takes forever to scrutinise it. However could it take so long to get a ticket? I'm hot and tired and I'm fed up with standing here.

'Is this correct? Let me see your passport.'

'I only want to catch a train, that's all,' I venture to suggest.

He mumbles and doesn't look impressed, so I get my passport out of my rucksack and hand it to him. Getting ratty with him doesn't solve anything.

Finally, after what seems like an age, he hands me my ticket, which I examine quickly to make sure I don't have to go through this palaver again because of a mistake. It looks all right – tomorrow to Shimla, via Kalka at 7.40 from this station in the morning.

I carefully tuck the ticket into my bag, zip it up and wander outside. It's much hotter now, as if I've stepped into a sauna. Looking up I see the figures 39 and realise that's the temperature. In minutes sweat runs down my neck and back and my face is soaking wet too.

Chapter 2

It's so hot, I keep panting and wanting yet another shower. A tepid shower cools me down but I want to stay under it forever.

I almost run down the stairs feeling somewhat invigorated and very clean. I ease into a table near a blonde girl whose lipstick is bright red. I notice her red, green and purple necklace and something about the vividness encourages me. We exchange smiles.

'Hi, where are you from?' she asks.

'The UK. How about you?'

'I'm Swedish. Eva. Are you on your own?'

'Pretty much,' I admit. 'I'm Jo.'

'Why don't we go out to town together? You know, safety in numbers as you English say.'

'Yes I'll just finish my tea. Do you have any plans – or any idea where to go?'

'I want to go to the market – maybe I mean the bazaar. It's supposed to be fantastic.'

Rickshaws, cars hooting, hundreds of scooters, stalls selling food and drink all along the pavement, and the heaving masses of people everywhere. Buses saunter past with loads of boys and young men hanging off the back.

'Look, Eva. You'd never ever see that at home. It's so dangerous. Presumably they avoid the fare if they hang on the back?'

'They do the same on the trains, on the top, out the windows. It looks so dangerous, but they think it's normal.'

'We'd better watch we don't get run over.'

I'm fanning myself with the map the reception girl gave me.

'Yes true. It's a hot one today,' Eva laughs. 'They say it just gets hotter and hotter in Delhi.'

10

Running alongside us are numerous boys shouting, 'Baksheesh, baksheesh.'

'What do they mean?'

'It's not us they're after,' Eva explains. 'It's our dollars.'

'I don't like it though.'

A young boy with big brown eyes stands in our path, his head wobbling from side to side.

'Rupees, rupees, please, please.'

I can't resist so I open my purse and take out some coins, and hold them out to the boy. I turn to Eva,

'It's so worthless to us. I can give them some rupees and it's less than one pence back home.'

Another boy comes over and points to a man with no legs, so I delve into my purse again. I know everyone advises you not to but I'm too soft.

'I'll have nothing left soon, even if it isn't worth much.'

'There is an American guy, Josh, staying at the hotel, you know?' Eva asks. 'He said to say no – it's a principle. We'll have to.'

'I think I met him at the station and he said the same to me. It seems so mean. Maybe I need to be more assertive. It doesn't come easily.'

The crowd around us is getting huge, all boys, no girls. Eva turns to them all.

'No money, no baksheesh. No.'

We amble along to Connaught Place and the crowd swells.

'You want shoes shined? Shoes. Shoes,' a man points at our feet.

'Even wearing these – how do you polish flip flops?' I giggle. 'And you're wearing them too!'

Suddenly, Eva grabs my arm and guides me quickly past the restaurants, shops and travel offices dodging people along the way.

11

I'm waving them away now, or pretending I can't see them. Perhaps I'm getting the hang of it.

Eva stops and holds up her camera.

'I have never seen anything like this, she says. 'It's great.'

I nod but I wonder if I'd call it great. It's different, it's shocking, it's distressing and it's a huge culture shock after home.

People lie on the pavement intermingled with the street traders and tourists. No-one takes any notice of them, and even tread on them. There are far too many men without legs pushing themselves along the ground on their bottoms.

'I wonder what they have wrong with them that so many of them lose their legs,' I muse to Eva.

'I was told that some of them have their legs cut off so they can get more money.'

'That can't be true. Surely they must have been diseased?'

'I change money. You come with me,' a young man wearing a little white sun hat says.

Eva grabs my arm and whisks me off in another direction. Thank goodness I came out with her. The Main Bazaar is packed with stalls and open air shops. Young men, some smaller than us, are wandering among the tourists.

'Come in, we have anything you want.'

As if by magic group of young boys appear in front of us again.

'What you want? We have everything.'

A man nearby doles out green liquid from a street stall.

'What is this?' Eva asks him.

He picks up a plastic cup and pours out some greeny stuff for her.

'Lovely, lovely sugar cane juice, the best in India.'

'Here, I'll treat you Jo.'

'No, don't.' I reach into my money belt.

'Yes. I insist,' Eva says in her perfect English.

The man hands the green liquid to me, and I sip with pursed lips.

'Yuk. It's horrible,' I say, taking care not to let the vendor hear me. Holding it in my mouth I move away and spit it out.

'Sorry to be so rude, Eva, but I can't drink it. It's so sickly and sweet.'

'Yes, it's foul.'

We get out of his sight and tip the sugary sweet juice down a drain.

'Can't be too careful here,' Eva says. 'You can easily get bad stomach from drink or food.'

'The dreaded dysentery. I've heard a lot about it. I know someone who lost a stone in a month in India!'

'Where are you coming from?' a shopkeeper asks.

'The hotel nearby,' I said.

'No, where you are coming from?'

'I think they mean which country,' Eva says. 'I'm from Sweden and she from England.'

'England. You must know my aunt. She lives in London.'

'It's a big place you know,' I mumble, trying not to laugh.

'No not big, not like India.'

'I've never been anywhere like this in my life,' I tell Eva. 'I keep feeling as if I am in a film. It's a weird feeling as if this isn't really real. It's so unlike life in England that it doesn't seem real to me – do you know what I mean? Everyone should come here to see how people really live.'

'I feel as if I've been away for weeks,' Eva lets out a sigh.

'Are you homesick?'

'I miss home, but I'm enjoying this too much. How about you?'

13

'Far from it, mind you I've only just arrived,' I claim with a bit of bravado. 'There was plenty I wanted to get away from. Although I'm really tired and it's hard to take all this in.'

We wander back to the hotel and have yet another drink in the restaurant. Eva's really easy to chat to and it's comfy under the cool fans. A lively group of young guys saunters in and sits down at the table next to us. They're a lively looking bunch and I keep looking at them, but they're throwing a few looks our way too.

'Hey, where are you two from?' one of the guys asks us in a heavy Antipodean accent.

'I'm from Sweden and Jo is from England.'

'Do you mind if we come and sit with you? I'm Pete.'

Pete is tall and has a permanent smile on his face. Immediately I like him.

'I guess you're from Australia then?' I ask him.

'He won't like that,' pipes up another one with an Aussie drawl.

'He's a Kiwi. You know we can't stand them and they can't stand us. I'm Tim.'

Tim puts out his hand to Eva and then me and then sits down next to me. He's got lovely warm brown eyes.

'I can never tell the difference,' Eva says, but maybe that's because I'm not a native speaker.

'It's blindingly obvious,' Pete guffaws. 'We speak much better than this lot.'

Pete is a big burly guy with all the physical attributes of a rugby player. He has tousled messy hair and a stripey rugby shirt with Christchurch emblazoned on it.

'I'm Wayne,' says a somewhat quieter third guy also putting out his hand.

'What are youse girls doing tonight? We could all do with some company or we'll be talking about footie all night long.'

14

'Haven't discussed this evening, have we?' I look at Eva.

'How long have you two known each other?'

Eva's face breaks into a smile. 'Two, three hours.'

'Fancy coming for a meal?' brown eyed Tim asks, looking directly at me. My stomach lurches a bit. I look at Eva, although in truth I don't need her permission.

'Why not?'

'Sure. I haven't got anything else planned,' Eva adds.

'Well, how's about 6.30 down here?'

Tim's eyes linger on me and that twinge of excitement comes back. God, I've only just arrived and I'm finding attractive men already while Rob's probably in mourning.

I nod,

'Fine, why not?'

I might be tired but the adrenaline is giving me an extra burst of energy. I put on a pair of white cut offs and a green top, flick back my long dark hair with a brush, and more carefully than usual I apply fresh eye shadow and mascara. There's a well-worn old mirror in the room and I look in it about three times before going downstairs.

Eva's there already and the guys are all smartened up.

Tim walks beside me.

'It's mighty hot isn't it? It even shocks us.'

'Where do you come from in Aus?'

'Sydney, the most beautiful city in the world. Apart from London, of course.'

'Well, I'm not from London, so you don't have to say that.'

Pete seems to be in charge of where we're going so we follow along, avoiding beggars and bikes and rickshaws along the way. We are just standing in Connaught Place for the third time today and suddenly everything around me starts moving and becomes darker.

15

'I'm really sorry,' I mumble, 'But I'm going to have to sit down.'

Indians crowd round and Tim kneels down beside me.

'What can I get you?'

'Just water, water will do.' I put my head in my hands.

Pete comes over. 'This guy has just told me that you have to wrap up warm on a day like this.'

'You're joking mate,' Tim says.

He screws off the top from a bottle of water and holds it close to my mouth.

'How are you feeling?' he says to me. Even in this state I can pick up the concern in his voice.

'A bit better. Sorry everyone.'

'No worries, sweetheart,' Tim says. 'You had me worried there. Can you get up?'

I manage a nod of assent and he holds out his hand and pulls me up. Then he puts his hand on my back, which makes me almost feel like fainting all over again.

'This is the effect he has on women,' Pete teases. 'They all swoon.'

Tim looks quite coy and I manage to smile at them. I couldn't have planned it if I tried, as now he is really attentive and stays by my side all the way along the road. We stop at the front of a restaurant with dark windows and ornate carvings inside.

'Looks a bit pricey,' Tim says. 'I've got to last on a budget you know, mate.'

'It's not,' Pete said. 'They're all like this here, cheap and cheerful, but this one comes highly recommended in my guide book. Come on guys.'

I appreciate the air-conditioning as we walk in. And Tim sits right next to me. Trust me to meet a nice guy who I'm never going to see again. Pete's on the other side of Tim and Eva is squashed

16

between Wayne and Greg who started out travelling together. Pete and Tim met in Mumbai.

'How long have you been here?' I ask Tim.

'Only two weeks.'

'And you?'

'Yesterday, no it's today. Sorry I've lost all sense of time. I arrived in the early hours this morning. That's maybe what accounts for what happened earlier. I'm jet-lagged and tired.'

'Where are you off to all alone then?'

'I am going to a place called Jasanghari. It's a retreat up in the Himalayas not far from Shimla. I wanted to get away, and it seems just the right sort of place. There's yoga, massage, and you can learn languages or new skills if you want to.'

'How did you hear about it?'

'It was in an article about foreign retreats and it's not like these really upmarket places, it was affordable and I wanted to go away, so it kind of fitted into place.'

As I'm speaking he's looking into my eyes so that I almost forget what I am talking about.

'Why did you want to get away? You don't have to tell me.'

'No I don't.'

I smile back at him and return the eye contact.

'No it wasn't one thing. Just family and other things were getting me down. There's no big story or anything. How about you?'

'I guess I wanted to get away too, and I've always wanted to travel so I thought I would. It might only be for a couple of months, but I decided it was the right time. It obviously was.'

'Watch these Aussies. You know what they're like with women,' Pete interrupts.

Tim looks away and I smile at Pete. Exquisite guilt but there is no need for that anymore. I can do what the hell I like, and with whomever I choose.

17

The waiter comes to the table balancing lots of dishes. Dhal, chicken curry, okra, Bombay potato and potatoes with spinach – *sag aloo* - mutton pasanda, rice and vegetables covered in batter.

The volume of Pete's voice increases in line with the consumption of Tiger beers.

'Sorry about him,' Tim says to me so that Pete can hear. 'You know what these Kiwis are like. Not as refined as the Aussies.'

The whole evening makes me forget about home, about being lonely, about taking a big risk. Everyone has to get up early the next day, so we're on the way back to the hotel at 9 ish. All the time Tim stays by my side speaking softly to me. Despite still feeling a bit wobbly, I'm loving every moment of it, my only regret being that tomorrow we go our separate ways.

'Are you feeling all right? You had me quite worried earlier on.'

'I feel fine now it's not so hot. I just felt odd. Everything was going black, nothing else.'

Pete comes up on the inside of them,

'Yeah, they all say that,' he ripostes.

'Where are you going from here Tim?'

I've wanted to ask this all evening. I wish he was coming to Jasanghari, but it's probably not his scene.

'Pete and I have a flight to Nepal in the morning and then we're going trekking outside Kathmandu. Not sure where after that.'

We spend the next hour or so drinking tea in the hotel restaurant but at 10.30 it shuts up shop and I'm struggling to stay awake. We say our goodnights and I almost skip up the stairs to my room feeling the thrill of such an unexpected encounter.

I so much need sleep and all I can think about is the evening. I run over and over it in my mind and what was said, and just wish it could have continued. Now I'll never see him again, but wasn't I sure I didn't want another relationship? And really I need to get a grip. I've known the guy for less than a day and I feel as if I'm in love. He's probably not nearly as nice as he seems.

18

It's 5 a.m. when I wake up so I figure I must have slept. Quick shower, get dressed and pack my things. I put on a T-shirt and a pair of shorts and look at myself in the mirror. My skin looks smooth enough and my hair's gone a bit frizzy with the heat but it lies neatly down over my shoulders. I look passable, but I'd better hurry if I'm going to catch him before I go.

All the guys are eating breakfast. I sit near them and when they get up Tim leans over and gives me a kiss on the cheek which turns my knees to jelly.

'I'll catch up with you later. Why not give me your address in the UK? You never know I might be over some time.'

'I can give you my parents' address although I don't live there but I haven't got a base now. I'm not sure when I'll be back, but of course you're very welcome to come and see sunny Bristol. I'll give you my email address too, but where I'm going I don't suppose I'll have wi-fi.'

I'm gabbling. I tear a piece of paper out of my paper diary and write down Mum and Dad's address, my email address and phone number. Pete is smirking as he waits for Tim.

It gives me just a faint feeling of hope. They leave and I try to act normally with Eva, who's just arrived. We have breakfast and swap email addresses too. I ask for the bill, pay it, and give Eva a quick kiss on the cheek.

'I've enjoyed meeting you. It was great to have someone take me to the bazaar. Have a good time, Eva.'

Outside the city is as alive as ever with just as many people as during the afternoon, all going about their business. The beggars are out, the scooters are dashing everywhere, women are walking with pots on their head, people are tidying up their pavement 'homes', and cars and rickshaws zoom past at a dangerous pace.

My nerves kick in again. Today's a new experience, off to my new home, I have hardly had enough sleep, and I've already had one great evening. Well, it's a completely new set of things to worry about from the ones I had at home. I walk at speed towards the station and into the massive station concourse.

19

Chapter 3

Three months earlier, Christmas Day

Jo still had a key to her parent's house and let herself in. The first thing she heard was her mother shouting.

'Where the bloody hell have you put the wine? I am sure I put one down here and now it's gone.'

'Don't you think it's a bit early to start on that?' her father said sarcastically.

He never spoke to anyone else like that.

'Sod off Mark. You're no bloody help. How am I supposed to cope with such a stressful day?'

Jo walked into the kitchen and they both turned round towards her. Her father looked sheepish. Her mother seemed beyond caring.

'Hello darling,' Mark said. 'Lovely to see you.'

He put his arms around Jo and pulled her close.

'Happy Christmas, darling.'

Her mother mumbled, 'Happy Christmas,' and gave her a quick peck on the cheek. She had made an attempt at Christmas with her newish green jumper and a necklace that she'd had for years. Her grey, dry, frizzy hair was scraped back and her bright red face wore a semi-permanent scowl.

She kept opening cupboards, picking up plates and dishes one by one, and moving them to different places. There seemed to be no real system.

'Your father's hidden my bottle of wine. I've got to cook for 11 people and he thinks I don't need a bit of sustenance to keep me going. I'm, well you know what it's like..,' and her mumbling droned on.

Her Dad provided consistency. Same old checked shirt, grey trousers with a belt, and a Christmas tie. He was given a Christmas tie each year, so he was wearing this year's gem. He had a full head of grey hair and a permanent smile, except when he was talking to her mother.

'I'm here now, Mum. I can help,' Jo said.

'There you are, Maggie. Ever helpful Jo, she never gets flustered by these sort of occasions,' Mark chortled.

'Is that some sort of dig at me?' Maggie snarled. 'Maybe that's because she's never had to do it. Every year I have to do this bloody meal and this is all the thanks….'

The doorbell rang.

'Hello darling,' Mark chirped as he opened the door.

There was a crashing sound.

'Who the hell put that rug there?' Beth shrieked. 'You'll never believe it. I was driving along and this little bastard in a mini came up behind me and started flashing me. I've no idea what he was on about. These blokes, the way they drive, they think they own the roads.'

'Happy Christmas darling. Don't forget that's what you're here for,' Mark chided Beth. She appeared in the kitchen like a whirlwind.

'Sorry. I meant to.'

She peered at her mum.

'For Christ's sake mother what is the matter? You look sooo pissed off.'

'Do you have to use that kind of language darling?' Mark said.

'Jo.'

Beth was surreptitiously beckoning her sister. 'Come here a mo - I need your advice about this present a minute – it's a secret. Come here, here.'

Jo took a deep breath and followed Beth into the lounge. She could see her sister was in a stressed state by the intense look on her face and her body language.

21

'I don't want you to look at a present,' Beth bleated. 'I haven't heard from Jack today. Do you think that's ominous? What do you think? You'd think he'd bloody well ring and say Happy Christmas. I mean, wouldn't you, wouldn't you? I'm not letting my mobile out of earshot in case he does ring. Why do you think he hasn't called me? He's so..'

'Because he's with his family?'

'Piss off Jo. That's not the point. The other night, the other night was just, well you know.'

'He'll be with his family – his children Beth. Forgotten them?'

'God what side of the bed did you get out of this morning? You have no idea about real love. Jack and I are made for each other and it's probably just that he hasn't got any signal, you know he's in the Styx. He's down in Cornwall with bitch features' family.'

'How do you know she's a bitch? She might be a great mother and wife,' Jo said. Two minutes of Beth and she'd had enough already.

'Jo, why are you so? You must be joking. Why do you think he's with me? You know nothing.'

'I'd better get back to the kitchen,' Jo whispered conspiratorially. 'Mum's struggling and I'm going to help her.'

'She's her normal self isn't she? Miserable as sin, even though it's Christmas Day. Every year I think, you know, I wish I could be with, well you know..'

Jo couldn't get out of the room quickly enough.

'You look flustered Mum. Shall I do the potatoes?' Jo said

'Please darling. It's just such a lot for me to do.'

'I'm here now. Don't worry.'

'You are a good girl Jo,' her mum said.

Beth marched back into the kitchen, her cleavage bursting out of the cream blouse she was wearing.

'And I'm not I suppose?' she said.

'No I didn't say that,' Maggie whined. 'You just take everything the wrong way. When I was…'.

'But you bloody meant it,' Beth interrupted.

'Please ladies, it's Christmas,' Mark intervened putting on a smile.

He sidled up to Jo and put his hand on her shoulder.

'C'mon let's open up the champagne.'

'She's had enough already,' Jo mumbled to her Dad.

'What Jo?' her Mum piped up. 'Don't talk about me like that – it's Christmas.'

'I could do with a glass,' Beth asserted. 'Can you drop me off later Jo? I don't want to have to drive.'

'I suppose so.'

'Are you going to leave your car here?' Maggie asked.

'Yes, what's wrong with that?' Beth retorted. 'For God's sake Mum don't make a drama out of a crisis.'

'I haven't said a word,' Maggie almost whispered.

'Yes you have.'

'Beth, why don't you do a job?' Jo suggested. 'Couldn't you whip the cream? You said you wanted that doing didn't you Mum? Mum, did you say the cream needed whipping?'

'Oh yes please, but Beth don't get it all up the walls,' Maggie said.

'I bet you wouldn't say that if I were Jo.'

'How old are you? For goodness sake you sound like a kid,' Jo snapped. She put her head on her hands. If only they'd just shut up, but it seemed like they liked winding each other up.

'Shall I put these potatoes in the tin now and in the oven?' she asked her mother.

'I don't know. There's too much to do,' Maggie replied.

'What else do you want me to do?' Jo asked.

'Just look after everyone.'

Jo went into the hall, glanced at the Christmas tree. She noticed every year, the same old baubles, the same bows, and everything the way as it had been since she was little. It was somewhat comforting, but on the other hand it showed some inability to move on, to take any interest in life. She went up the stairs to the bathroom but she could still hear Beth and her mother.

'You can never listen to anyone, can you?' her mother was saying.

'Not you Mum, you don't say anything much worth listening to,' Beth mumbled to herself. 'You're too sozzled the whole time.'

Jo heard a bang but couldn't face finding out what it was. It sounded like a door slamming. Perhaps her mother had gone out.

She went along the landing and glanced into her old bedroom. It was tired and needed a coat of paint and a new carpet. The blue walls, the oriental cover on the bed, the pictures on the walls, all exactly how it had been when she was a teenager. But now, there were piles and piles of her father's old car magazines on the floor, and a few cases and boxes packed with stuff no-one really wanted.

As she looked out of the window she remembered the many hours she'd spent there gazing out at the lawn and the trees, wishing some boyfriend or other would ring or that something exciting would happen.

She sat on the loo for 10 minutes enjoying the peace. If only she could spend the day there away from them all.

As she came out of the bathroom she heard her father opening the front door and saying,

'Good, now I've got someone to have a drink with.'

She looked down and saw Rob had arrived armed with his own presents for her family. She groaned at the thought of him having more to drink. He was looking very smart in his black shirt and white waistcoat on and he'd obviously shaved and showered.

Last night had been dreadful. She'd sneaked out of the party without him but despite consuming more than a week's worth of units, Rob had spotted her, and turned up in the car beside her before she'd got into gear.

She made him a cup of coffee at her flat. He was lounging on the sofa watching TV, but she turned it off and stood in front of him.

'There's no future in this, Rob. You have to see it. We haven't got on for ages, and we both need a new start.'

'Come here, you don't mean it,' he drawled, reaching out to her. She dodged his hands, but he said, 'You know you need me.'

And to think that she'd been attracted to his sunny face, the way he smiled, the big eyes that seemed to have read her straightaway. Looking at him now, all hunched up and slobby looking, she couldn't find him at all alluring.

He fell asleep on the sofa, so she slipped off to bed alone for a fairly sleepless night. And in the morning he appeared at the door with a huge bag of presents.

'I meant what I said last night, Rob. I'm afraid presents don't make any difference.'

'What did you say last night, darling?'

She should have said it again, but it was Christmas, and she didn't have it in her to ruin it for him.

Jo slipped out of her parents' bathroom quietly and went downstairs and brushed past Rob, but he pulled her over and planted a kiss on her unwelcoming lips.

'Happy Christmas darling.'

He put his hand up to stroke her hair, but she danced out of the way.

'I'm busy helping Mum. Dad will entertain you,' she replied, rushing into the kitchen without a glance back at him.

'Now Mum shall I start washing up?' Jo asked. 'It will make it much easier later on.'

'Please do. There's such an awful lot to do, I'm worried no-one will get to eat.'

Jo threw her head back and looked at the ceiling. It needed painting too.

'It's all fine Mum. How's the turkey doing?'

'Have a look. It seems OK.'

Jo opened the oven and a rush of steam whooshed out into her face. She pulled out the turkey which was browning nicely.

'Fine, it's all fine.'

The doorbell went again and the unmistakeable well-rehearsed sickly sweet sound of Hannah's voice could be heard in the kitchen.

'Where are they all, Mark?'

'In the kitchen, gouging each other's eyes out,' he quipped.

'No change there then.'

Hannah strutted into the kitchen, looking for all the world like someone who expected eyes to focus on her.

'Happy Christmas everyone. That smells good. Oh God what a mess!'

She stood surveying the scene of devastation with a disapproving smirk on her face.

Maggie visibly winced, but turned round and gave Hannah a perfunctory kiss.

'Hi everyone. Wait till you see what I've got,' Stephen called out from the hall.

'Here you are,' Mark sidled up to Hannah, and thrust a glass of champagne into her hands. 'My, don't you look the bees' knees?'

Hannah fluttered her eyelashes and gave him one of her looks. She could flirt for England.

'Where's my son?' Mark asked her, while running his eyes up and down her shapely form.

'Parking and bringing in the presents. He'll be a moment. Don't worry about him.' She waved her hand as if swatting a fly.

'You look awfully hot Maggie,' Hannah said. 'Is it the cooking or the wine?' she sniggered.

Beth pranced in.

'Hi Hannah. Oh you look smart, but you always do.'

'I got it up at Harvey Nicks,' Hannah replied, running her hands down her thighs which almost made Mark choke on his champagne. She kept turning her head from side to side as if she were practising for the catwalk.

' Pretty reasonable you know,' Hannah continued. 'I must say you look nice too.'

'Well don't sound so surprised,' groaned Beth.

'I like that shirt. Where did you find that little number?' Hannah asked.

'Some cheap shop,' Beth responded.

'Suits your ginger hair,' Hannah said.

'It's not ginger.'

'Oh semantics, darling.'

Beth was eyeing Hannah up and down desperate to find something wrong, but everything was as perfect as ever. Her suit was a bright fuchsia colour, neatly tailored and the skirt was so short it was like a showcase for her long slim legs. Her blonde hair was swept back in waves and there was no doubt about it, her expertise at make-up accentuated both her big eyes and her perfect cheekbones.

Stephen and Charlotte burst into the room and Jo joined them in a scrum.

'Come here my darling grandson.' Maggie's face lit up.

Stephen moved to Maggie's side.

'I just love Christmas,' Charlotte said. 'I get so excited.'

'What did Father Christmas bring?' Mark asked.

'Oh come on Grandad I'm not that young. But I got some t'riffic things. I've brought most of them with me so you can have a

27

look. Jo, I want to show you this new make-up thingy I've got. It's really cool.'

'OK Stephen, two ticks. Charlotte you look great,' Jo smiled at her niece. 'Since when did you get this new haircut? You look like Rachel from Friends.'

'Thanks Auntie Jo, but that's so last century.'

'Not so much of the auntie though. Just Jo will do.'

Michael pushed open the front door, laden with parcels.

'Where are you all?' he called. 'Ah, in the kitchen. What a mess.'

'Don't Michael – we are trying our best,' Jo said and gave him an air kiss. He could wind her up in seconds, but her mother didn't seem at all put out.

'Hello darling,' Maggie said, and put down what she was doing. She walked up to Michael and hugged him. He backed away quickly.

'Right, brother you can get working as well,' said Beth as she licked cream off the whisk.

'Women's work in the kitchen,' Michael responded. 'Ask Hannah, she's always….' Hannah's face turned to thunder.

'Daddy you're such a chauvinist,' Charlotte complained.

He raised an eyebrow and smiled at his daughter.

'Charlotte, what a thing to say to me.'

He ruffled her hair.

She slapped his hand and touched her head.

'Dad, you idiot. My hair – you'll ruin it. Get offff.'

'Sorry, I didn't think.'

Charlotte took her fist back and did a mock punch.

'You never think Dad. That's your problem.'

He squeezed her shoulders.

'Why don't we all adjourn to the lounge? Lunch is ready when, Jo?' Mark asked.

'You'd better ask Mum,' Jo said.

'Oh I don't know,' Maggie said. 'It will probably all get ruined.'

'Shall we have presents afterwards then?' Mark persisted.

'I can't possibly stop now,' Maggie groaned.

'OK, keep calm and carry on.' Mark said. 'Keep your hat on, keep your hat on.'

'Where do you get these expressions Grandad?' Charlotte asked. 'They're so last century.'

'Well my darling, I am last century aren't I? Come on Hannah. Bring your champagne and….'

Mark slipped his arm through Hannah's and guided her into the lounge. There was something obscene about the way they flirted, not for the first time.

'Michael bring all those presents in here,' Hannah commanded.

'Look, Rob's in here,' Mark said. 'I see Stephen's got you involved already Rob.'

There were bits of black plastic all over the floor.

'Yes I'm showing Rob this new thing, a bit like Scalextric, Grandad but much cooler. Let's set it up over there. OK? Links up with my tablet – amazing.'

When lunch finally arrived Mark served more wine and Jo and Beth brought in the food. Charlotte was keen to help too and carried in various dishes, smiling all the time. She loved being around Jo and Beth and imagined being like them when she was older.

Maggie's face was so red that it looked as if it might explode. Her apron was covered with gravy stains, and her tired grey hair looked as if it had been in the oven as well. Her make-up was smudged and she was bulging out of the top of her trousers. Jo had never realised how good her mother used to look until she saw her like this. What had become of her?

29

Back in the kitchen looking for the pepper Jo found a bottle of Prozac in the cupboard with *Mrs M. Greaves* on it. It was dated two weeks earlier. How could her father keep filling up her mother's glass of wine when she was probably mixing it with anti-depressants?

She sighed. All over the country people would be having dinners with their families. Loads of them would be as dysfunctional as hers, but some of them might genuinely enjoy each other, instead of pretending and acting out a farce.

You could cut the atmosphere with a knife as they ate dinner. Beth was on the other side of Rob and the more she drank the more she flirted with him. Every time she touched his arm or murmured things to him, Jo was watching. But Rob would think she was jealous if she wasn't careful, yet she'd be pleased to give him up.

Hannah was in full flow.

'These friends, you know the Carpenters, we've told you about them. They've got a villa in Barbados. They're just loaded. Well Jen has asked me if we'd like to go there next summer. You bet, what a great idea.

'The kids will love it so I can laze by the pool all day and float on the Lilo, and soak up the Caribbean sun.'

Michael was completely ignoring what she was saying.

Maggie was picking at her food, and moving it around the plate barely eating. She kept drinking her wine and refilling the glass.

'Come on everyone, let's do the crackers,' Charlotte said. 'You can do one with me Auntie Jo.'

'Oh listen everyone, have you heard about the man with a spade on his head? He's called Doug – do you get it? Come on Mum. Put on your hat.'

'I'm not mucking up my hair,' Hannah mumbled.

'Now,' said Mark, 'Tell me what you got for Christmas, Stephen.'

'I told you earlier Grandad. Don't you remember? I got these games for the play station that Mum and Dad got me and I got this really cool thing for my room.'

Mark grabbed the red wine bottle to fill up Rob's glass, his eyes darting around the glasses on the table, seeing whose to fill up.

'It's not cool,' Charlotte said. 'It's just childish, and boyish.'

'It's not. It's better than those stupid make-up things you got,' Stephen retorted.

'You're so immature Stephen.'

'You are spoilt cos you get so many presents,' he snarled at his sister.

'Will you two spoilt brats just shut up?' Hannah shouted, her pretty face distorting.

'Next year you'll get nothing.'

'Hannah,' Michael admonished. 'Leave them alone. You're the one who spoils them.'

'Oh thanks very much,' she scoffed, glaring at him. Pure vitriol, Jo thought.

She leapt up from the table, nearly knocking over her glass and took a large dish out to the kitchen. Charlotte followed with another one, with Beth and then her mother behind.

'I'm not sitting listening to those two going on again,' Beth moaned in the kitchen.

'She's such a bitch that woman, and he's not much better.'

'Beth,' Maggie slurred. 'Mind your manners. And not in front of Charlotte.'

'Oh for God's sake mother. She has to live with them, poor child. What's the matter with you? Is it your precious Michael that you're trying to protect? Everyone in this family's a bloody disaster.'

31

Charlotte was standing close to Jo, staring at the floor. Jo slipped her arm round her and Charlotte looked up into her face. Jo could see the tears in her eyes.

Maggie slumped in the kitchen chair with a glass of red wine in her hand, and her head dropped forward as if she was going to sleep.

'Are you OK, Mum?' Jo asked, leaning towards her mother.

'Not, no, yes.' She mumbled incoherently.

Mark walked in, completely ignored Maggie, and in a hushed voice said,

'Jo can you spare me a minute? I need to show you something.'

He walked over to the door to the garage off the hall, and yanked it opened it for her. He turned on the light, and closed the door. Once inside he looked past Jo as if he couldn't see her, and then shifted from one foot to the other.

'You know Jo. Things aren't so good with your mother and me.'

'Look Dad, I can't help you. You need, you know to talk to someone who knows about these things, not me,' Jo told him.

'No I don't think that would help.'

'You'll be all right Dad,' she said touching his arm tenderly. 'Let's go back inside now. It looks odd being out here.'

None of them knew what she had been through recently but she couldn't blame them for that. Wasn't it astonishing that her close family didn't even notice that she'd lost her enthusiasm and her confidence?

'What's your New Year's resolution going to be this year darling?' Rob wanted to know. 'Is it to make an honest man out of me?'

'You've got to be joking.' She even managed to laugh. 'No I'm not actually.'

If only he knew. She didn't like herself for stringing him along but if she told him the truth he'd stop her from going. No-one could know. There would be no more Christmases like this one.

32

Chapter 4

It's only 6.50 so I'm very early for the Kalka train. Everyone has told me that the trains are always late, but I can't take the risk of missing the Kalka Shatabdi.

The station is packed to the rafters, and people are hanging off every train that comes in and goes out and some are even sitting on the roof. It's funny but terrifying and I wonder how many fall off to their death.

Men in long robes, some white and some multi-coloured with little hats to match, approach me offering food and drink as if they are giving it away but they're not. Some are selling pieces of jewellery, trinkets and maps, all of which are 'the best you can buy'. At least 10 little faces are looking up at me.

'Where are you coming from?'

'You want give me food?'

'You want give me dollars?'

They are so young it's pitiful to see them dressed in rags begging everywhere. I get my money out, but it's true. You give to one and then the other, and then a load more arrive. I put it away in the belt round my waist and cover it up with my jacket.

There are plenty of people lying down sleeping with all their worldly possessions surrounding them. I sit down on my main bag, which serves two purposes – a seat and a safety precaution. I feel so tired, but excited. Just 40 minutes after its departure time the Kalka Shatabdi is ready to depart.

A fellow passenger in a smart grey suit holding a briefcase smiles politely at me.

'Madam, let me carry your bag on.'

'Thank you, so kind.'

The hordes are clamouring for third class and I can see they're piling on top of each other. Those that can't get in are getting hold of anything they can to hang on.

33

The businessman laughs,

'This is best way to travel. Too many people down there.'

'Yes it looks so dangerous. Don't they fall off?'

'Sometimes they do, but you see they are like monkeys. They can hang on for long journeys. It's quite normal here. But,' he wobbles his head around.

'Sometimes they are killed. It isn't a good way to travel.'

There's a distinct drop in temperature as we climb into the air-con chair car. I settle into my window seat, which is just as comfortable as an aeroplane seat. After all that faffing around at the station, at least I've got it right. Plenty of business people wander in and set up their laptops – just like home.

Sitting back in the chair, I close my eyes and allow myself the luxury of thinking about Tim, which I've been savouring until now. Butterflies flutter around in my stomach for so many different reasons now – Tim, the start of my big adventure, the mess I've left behind, the guilt.

Maybe if I had a stronger faith I might have coped better at home, but religion isn't for me any more, if it ever has been. I'd just love to be able to find some kind of strength inside that I could draw on when times get tough. Despite everyone relying on me so much I don't feel that strong, and they all think I am.

That's my own fault because I've never told them how bad I was feeling, even when I came close to cracking. I always shoulder my own upsets and theirs as well, and I'm not sure if they're that interested in what goes on in my life.

The train chugs through the suburbs of Delhi and the built up areas are receding. Children working in the fields wave at us, and as the train slows down I can see them up close, and see that as well as kids are old men and women wizened by the sun and toiling away. What must they think of these tourists zooming past in relative luxury?

It still looks hot outside. No wonder the Brits used to go up to the mountains to get away from the heat. Apparently they used to think the temperature couldn't possibly get any hotter in Delhi, but it always did.

During the Raj, the British and the rich Indians went up to the Himalayas in summer to get away from Delhi. They created hill stations with cricket pitches, summer houses and churches, just like home. This very train line was built to take the government officials up to Shimla, which was like the summer capital.

My eyes become sleepy and Rob appears telling me how selfish I am. I wake up covered in sweat, with my stomach feeling tight and my mind working overtime. Two young inquisitive male faces are peering at me and smiling. I hope I wasn't talking in my sleep, or maybe it's just seeing a girl travelling alone.

The train stops several times, often without explanation, and I doze on and off, read my book and gaze out of the window. The scenery changes north of Chandigarh and becomes green and hilly, but still here and there are ramshackle huts in the hills that suffice as living space for the locals. I stand up to see more clearly.

'Isn't it lovely?' a girl's English voice says.

I turn and see a tall blonde girl addressing herself to me.

'Yes it is. So peaceful and not too hot. Where are you going?'

'I'm going to Jasanghari – it's a retreat.'

I laugh.

'So am I. How funny.'

'What's your name? I'm Gemma.'

'Jo Greaves.'

A white cap almost covers Gemma's eyes and her long blonde hair is tucked behind her ears. If I wore a cap like that I'd look terrible, but somehow Gemma gets away with it. She fixes her grey-blue eyes on me as I talk, leaving me in no doubt that she is listening to everything I say.

The train pulls into Kalka.

'This is where we change on to the Toy Train, isn't it?' I ask Gemma across the aisle.

35

'Yeah. Doesn't it sound great?'

We lug our bags off the train, go up the stairs and cross to the platform for the Toy Train. What a change from Delhi. There's a gentle breeze blowing, but the temperature is warm and pleasant. Gemma walks ahead of me confidently, as we pull our bags on wheels behind us down the platform.

'It does look like a toy train. It's so narrow.' Gemma enthuses.

Along the platform loads of women and men are queuing. Without speaking we both move nearer and realise that they are carrying buckets and waiting their turn to get water out of the local pump.

We climb on board the Toy Train and settle into our seats, which happen to be near each other. Ten minutes later the train lazily pulls out of the station.

'I've read up on this line. It's incredible – the British built it to get up to the hill station at Shimla and apparently it has 103 tunnels and 864 bridges,' Gemma tells me.

'Wow – that's some statistic.'

'And it was opened in 1903 by us – well not us exactly - apparently.'

'Incredible. What do they do when it snows?' I wonder.

'It's quite capable of going through snow.'

'It's a long haul though isn't it – seven hours just to go 96 kilometres. That's worse than the commuter trains back home!'

The train slows down and stops in a station .We both peer outside.

'Barog - haven't we got some time here?' I ask Gemma, but I don't know why I keep asking her things I know the answer to.

'Not that long, but apparently it's great food here. I could certainly do with some.'

A man and a boy neatly dressed in chef's outfits open the door of the train and climb on board carrying trays of food.

'You want vegetable curry?'

'Looks good,' Gemma says.

A young man in a spotless white top hands her a tray with separate sections in it with vegetable curry in one, plus onion bhajis, yoghurt, some lentils and a huge naan bread.

'I'll have the same,' I add. 'It looks great.'

As soon as we finish our meals, the same vendors offer us water, bananas, nuts and little samosas.

'No thanks.' I try, but they just stand there, showing us their food. I give in. I'm a sucker for pressure.

'I'll have a banana thank you.'

Then a young boy appears for the third time and tries to sell us samosas.

'Never say yes, Jo,' Gemma says, wagging her finger.

'The first thing you learn in India.'

'I keep not learning that lesson,' I laugh.

As we sit back down, a guy wearing an Indian shirt and a pair of cut-off jeans walks towards us with a dish of curry in his hands. He's beaming all over his face as if we are long lost friends.

'So, where are you girls off to?'

'Jasanghari,' we pipe up in unison.

'Well you lucky ladies have got me for good then. Hi, my name's David.'

He puts his tray on a seat and holds out his hand to me and then to Gemma. His whole face lights up as he smiles and his eyes are full of warmth.

'Really? That's great. This is Gemma and I'm Jo, but we've only just met.'

'Is this someone's seat?' he says, sitting in it.

'Probably – it's quite full but you can see if they come back.'

'I'll push them off.'

37

We laugh. I like him already.

'I wonder how many others on this train are going there,' Gemma muses.

'You can spot them a mile away,' David says. 'They've got that hippy look.'

'Oh, have I then?' I asked.

'No not you, nor you.'

He looks me up and down and gazes at Gemma appreciatively.

'So tell me everything about you then,' he continues, while tucking into his tray of food.

'What, everything, you must be..?' I giggle.

'Well leave out some bits.' David smirks. He seems to be a laugh a minute type of guy.

'I've come away and I haven't told anyone at home where I've gone,' I say boldly wondering immediately why I've revealed so much.

'Wow,' he says.

'Are you running away from something, or someone?' Gemma asks quizzically.

'Not exactly. It's a long story. Needless to say I'd had enough of them all. But forget me and what's your story – David, Gemma?'

'I guess we're all running away from something in our own ways, aren't we?' David says and a look of sadness sweeps across his face but is gone in a flash.

'How about you?' He looks at Gemma as he speaks.

'I know where you're coming from,' Gemma says. 'I have needs too.'

'Mmm, very interesting,' David says and we all laugh together.

I take a quick look around to see if the other passengers think we're too noisy, but most aren't paying us any attention. One old woman in traditional dress is smiling at us and nodding her head.

38

'Not like that,' Gemma admonishes David.

'Oh disappointing then,' he banters back.

'I think I'll shut up,' she says, but is obviously enjoying the joke.

'You know I could kill for a Mars Bar right now,' I tell them.

'I know what you mean. Something sweet after something savoury,' Gemma agrees.

'And I have just the thing.' I delve deep into my rucksack.

'I brought some tins of condensed milk which make up for the lack of chocolate. In fact they're so rich you have to be careful you don't overdose on them.'

'I used to eat that at school,' Gemma says. 'It's yummy.'

'Not for me thanks,' David screws up his face. 'That's too sweet. What else do you keep in that bag? Have you seen what the Indians carry?

'I was down south on a train from Calcutta to Rameshwarem and the engine broke down,' he continues. 'Great, there we were in the middle of nowhere and the Indians got off the train, made campfires and started cooking. I couldn't believe it. We were starving and they had pots and pans and food, as if they knew the train would stop there. Perhaps they knew something I didn't.'

A tall Indian man comes up and stands in front of David. The man looks embarrassed but doesn't say anything.

'Is it your seat, mate?' David asks.

'Yes, most sorry, I am most sorry.'

'No, it's your seat, take it,' David jumps up and gestures to the man to sit down.

He winks at us and grabs his bag.

'See you both when we arrive. Can't wait.' He waves and marches off down the corridor.

Outside the vista has completely changed. Large expanses of green lush valleys, the sun shining through tall pines and oak trees, backed up by the snow-capped Himalayas in the distance.

The little train snakes higher and higher at snail's pace. We round a corner and alongside the track women and children are walking right beside the track but next to a sheer drop. I can see a flurry of washing hanging up, so close to the track that it narrowly misses touching the train, and papers and packaging are strewn on the line and alongside it.

'This is so beautiful, and quite unlike India. You wouldn't really know where you were now would you? It could be Switzerland, or Canada (not that I've ever been there). We're always in such a hurry at home. If you took such a long journey at home, you'd get really fed up, but this is just wonderful.'

'We have all the time in the world now,' Gemma replies, her eyes fixed on the scenery. She seems so supremely confident.

How quickly things can change. I set off on my own, slightly apprehensive about being alone. Since I arrived I've spent most of my time with people who feel like friends after an incredibly short time. I haven't even thought about Rob and all my guilt since I met Gemma and David.

I hear a loud horn and open my eyes. I must have dropped off. The terrain has changed and through the trees are red buildings, white ones and even some ugly tower blocks which are ringed around the edges by greenery. A large cloud shrouds part of the town in mist and I realise this must be it.

Gemma is looking out of the window too.

'This is it,' she says.

'I know. I must have been asleep as time's passed quite quickly.'

She nods.

'I did too.'

We jump off the train, and we're besieged by vendors and porters wanting to carry our bags, sell us food and all manner of other trinkets, or take us to go to their stores. Suddenly from behind I hear,

'Hi girls. Wasn't it a great journey?'

David takes up his place in between us. I'm pleased to see him again.

'Fantastic,' I tell him. 'Probably the best train journey I've ever been on.'

'Yeah, next to the London to Birmingham,' he says, giggling as he speaks.

'Do you always joke?'

'Mostly. It's when the laughing stops I have to worry.'

A young boy stands in front of David and looks him in the eye. He says in a serious voice,

'You come my shop. We sell everything. What you want?'

'I'll have an elephant.'

'Yes we got, we got,' the boy responds without a hint of a smile.

Gemma and I both cover our mouths and turn away.

'No, we have, we have,' he carries on.

'Another time, mate,' David snorts, winking at us.

'This temperature is such a relief,' I say to the other two.

'I might be able to sleep at night. What would you say it was – temperature wise?'

'It's still quite hot. Around 25 degrees wouldn't you think? It will be cool at night,' David says and winks again.

I don't need to see his mouth to know he is laughing again. His eyes are full of amusement and he looks like the boy he must have been some years earlier.

'We're to meet at Scandal Point. Sounds interesting,' David announces. 'Come on girls.'

He marches off as if he knows the way, but I don't think he does.

Shimla is a typical colonial town with its mix of cultures – a Christian church near the centre and a large mall lined with houses that would look at home in any British city. But some of the newer buildings are a bit garish with bold colours and no real thought given to the architecture. There are people of all shapes and sizes bustling around, and the people have a completely different look from most in Delhi – more Tibetan or Mongolian looking.

There's no traffic in the centre so we walk freely without risk of getting run over, dragging our bags behind us. But there are so many people dashing around with large trays of food and other things they're selling that we have to avoid being mown down by them. Restaurants are everywhere – Indian, American, Chinese, Italian.

'Who'd have thought it – perhaps they're chicken tikka pizzas?' Gemma said. 'Yuk.'

I notice this incredible Tudor-style building and call the others.

'Look at that. I wonder what that was.'

Gemma and David look up to where I'm pointing.

'I know. I read about it,' Gemma says. 'It's, what was it called?'

'I don't know,' David smiles. 'What was it called, Gemma?'

She tuts at him.

'I know, it was the Viceregal Lodge and it has lovely botanical gardens. This is where the British ruled the country from when they came up to Shimla in the summer. You know that they turned this into a hill station.'

'Yes, I read about that,' I let on. I don't want Gemma to think I don't know anything.

We stroll along taking it all in. The Britishness is so obvious from the mock Tudor buildings, but with that Indian element too that's unmistakeable. And people rushing everywhere.

'I think this is The Mall. Scandal Point should be over there,' David gestures.

'Look at that – look over there,' Gemma cries out.

A crowd of monkeys are jumping over a rubbish skip picking up trash. They look like a bunch of vandals, pushing each other out of the way and doggedly grabbing bits of food and eating them.

'Aren't they sweet?' Gemma coos.

'Quite sweet as you say, but watch your bags,' David warns. 'They nick things.'

'No David you're kidding,' I say.

'I'm not. Watch 'em.'

Among the throngs of people I spot a young man in his twenties holding a sign.

'Jasanghari well comes you'.

I tap Gemma on the arm.

'Well come, Gemma.'

Anouk looks like many of the locals I've seen since we got to Shimla. He shakes our hands and smiles showing a fine set of white teeth.

'I am pleased to see you. Where are you coming from?'

'Delhi.'

'No I don't think. Where you coming from?' He pronounces the *from* loudly.

'He means which country,' Gemma explains. 'We're all from the UK, but we're not together – well we didn't come together.'

'Ah British. Very good.'

Five more people turn up and Anouk walks us down the road to an open truck.

'Interesting transport,' Gemma mutters to me.

'Here's the limousine.'

43

David winks at me.

'It is limousine?' Anouk asks him. Everyone laughs.

'He's joking,' Gemma explains. 'He's a silly English boy.'

'Welsh,' David retorts.

Anouk keeps repeating to himself,

'Silly English boy'.

David keeps correcting him,

'Welsh' but Anouk looks blank.

David climbs up in the front with the driver and Gemma and I get in the open back with a few others. They introduce themselves - one is Dutch, one French, another English guy, and two from New Zealand.

I mumble to Gemma,

'I see the seat belt law is strict here!'

We set off on a very bumpy ride, especially in the back and I start to feel a bit queasy but try not to focus on it. Of course, I'm still jet-lagged and exhausted, but the adrenaline keeps me going. I almost forget that it's only two days since I left home.

The hills are dotted with goats and buffalo, no buildings, no hordes of people. Just open space as far as the eye can see. And some parts are still covered in cloud so they aren't visible, but as we rumble along the slow roads we are still bathed in evening sunlight.

David turns round,

'According to our esteemed driver, if I understand him correctly, it is a land of variety with snowy mountains, green hills, rocky terrain and apple orchards. People go biking, hiking, mountaineering, ski-ing and rafting and it's the perfect place for holidays.'

'Anouk knows excellent English then. You sound like a travel agent,' Gemma calls out to David with a mischievous look on her face.

'I'm just great at interpreting his signs but the only problem is that he takes his hands off the wheel to make them, and it's a bit scary,' David tells us.

'Do me a favour, David. Don't ask him anything else then as we wind up these mountain roads,' I suggest.

'Oh and not far away in Dharamsala the Dalai Lama is in residence since he's been exiled from Tibet. Actually I said that bit because I already knew it.'

'I'd love to meet him,' Gemma says to me.

'Have you read his book, *The Art of Happiness*?'

I shake my head.

'But I'd like to, now I've got the time. All the time in the world.'

Patrick, the other English guy, smiles shyly at me.

There are several farm workers on the roadside, and now unlike the other parts of India I've seen there are more places of worship for Buddhists, and few Hindu temples.

'Anouk says that these are Buddhist 'stupas',' David said waving at one of the buildings.

The truck climbs further and further up into the mountains, and all along the route are brightly coloured triangular flags fluttering in the breeze. Some of them have words on them.

I call out.

'David, would you ask Anouk what the words on the flags mean?'

David turns round,

'I asked him already. He said something, but I can't understand.'

'Actually,' Patrick says softly, looking embarrassed,

'It's the Buddhist chant which means something like 'Hail to the flower in the lotus'. It's Om as in 'om' that you chant 'mani padme hum'. They put them at the top of mountain passes so that the

45

winds can carry the prayer to the gods. The lotus flower is really significant in the Buddhist tradition. And the idea of the flags is that they promote peace and compassion.'

'Very interesting, thank you. You can be our guide,' Gemma says to Patrick, smiling sweetly at him.

He goes bright red, but looks pleased.

'I thought you were English,' I tell him, 'But I hear a hint of Irish, is it?'

'Yes, you're right,' Patrick answers. 'I'm from Limerick in the south.'

'That's somewhere I've never been,' I say. 'But I want to one day.'

'Yes, you'd love it. We have wonderful weather,' he says and his face creases into laughter lines.

My ears are popping as we gradually wend our way upwards in the truck. It's a rocky ride in the back with the truck rattling along the narrow roads.

'Look,' Gemma says, pointing to a group of monkeys playing in the trees.

'Look, look, please stop Anouk,' Gemma calls out.

'Not friendly. We beat with stick,' Anouk replies, slowing down.

Gemma's mouth opens wide in shock. Patrick and David laugh.

'I told you they nick things and they're quite vicious. They pinch your sandwiches, if you've got any,' David calls to us from the front.

'Forget your PG Tips chimps, Gemma,' he continues. 'They're wild and aggressive and they're often known to steal things.'

Gemma grimaces.

'Sounds like a tall story to me,' she retorts.

Anouk asked, 'What is PG chips?'

'PG Tips,' David says. 'It was an advertisement for tea – you know what you drink – it was an ad on TV, television. These chimpanzees dressed up as people.'

'What? That's cruel.'

'You're probably right, mate.'

My eyes keep closing, but I jerk awake each time the truck lurches to the right or left. Suddenly I wake up and found myself leaning on Patrick. Talk about giving the wrong impression.

'Sorry.'

'My pleasure,' he says quietly.

He seems like a nice guy, even if a bit straight-laced, but I don't want him to think I'm after him.

The truck turns round a corner and Anouk calls out,

'Up there – that is Jasanghari.'

We all look in awe at a majestic looking palace with mountains and pine forest as a backdrop, like something from a film. No-one speaks as the truck turns into the little track leading up to Jasanghari.

Chapter 5

'I don't blame her,' Maggie said. I think she's got guts. I admire her.'

Mark glanced sideways at Maggie. Was this the mother who had fussed over the children so much? Who was reluctant to let them go out in their teens, and who drove them away from home with her clinging behaviour. How dare she behave as if she didn't give a damn? Was she completely off her rocker?

'Well I'm bothered about it. We don't know if she's in this country, in some foreign land, who she's with or anything. I am really shocked at Jo's behaviour. She ought to know better.'

'She's 32, Mark. She's a grown woman. I expect she's done loads of things we don't know about. I feel more upset about the reasons for her going.'

Maggie was standing in the kitchen holding a mug of tea but she had a different air about her. Mark couldn't put his finger on what it was, but she seemed more upright as if something had changed. She was wearing a half decent skirt and top that looked reasonably smart. She was looking out into the garden as if she was studying something specific.

'What are you looking at?'

'I'm wondering about that tree over there, if it's all right or whether we might need to cut it down.'

'For Christ's sake Maggie. Jo's gone, she's gone, can't you get that into your head? Who cares about the effing tree?'

'There's no need to swear.'

He turned round and stormed out of the house, slamming the door behind him muttering to himself.

'Bloody bonkers, I just don't believe what's going on with her.'

Maggie went out into the garden and inspected the tree more closely. It was a dull morning but everything was becoming much greener and soon the garden would be full of colour.

The phone rang.

'Hello Maggie,' Judy launched into her stride. 'Look Maggie I'm worried about Jo. I wondered if you wanted any help tracking her down.'

'No, no thank you,' Maggie mustered up. What was this woman doing ringing her up to talk about Jo? She wanted to slam the phone down but she couldn't be rude to Judy.

She could imagine her sitting there with her hair all neatly coiffed, wearing a tight dress that was too young for her, even though, she conceded reluctantly, Judy's figure was pretty good for a woman in her 50s. She always had every hair lying precisely in place, so much so that if one strand dared to stand out of place it would cause the others to disown it.

Thick dark lines took the place of what had been Judy's eyebrows and almost overpowered her eyes which were already quite small. She always wore very bright red lipstick almost all the time, and kept applying it at 15 minute interludes. And the scarves. She must have about 100 scarves in her wardrobe and she always wore one draped around her neck, which she swooped back in an ostentatious gesture.

Judy was still droning on about Jo and how the youth of today were so irresponsible. Maggie looked back at the tree in the garden. She really had to get the tree people in to look at it.

'Are you there Maggie? You're not saying much.'

'I really haven't got a lot to say.'

'Well, that's charming. Aren't you bothered about your daughter?'

'She's grown up, Judy. If you want to discuss this why not talk to Mark about it?'

Judy went quiet. Maggie had never confronted Mark or Judy. Years ago she had been devastated but now it seemed like water under the bridge. How strange.

'I don't know what to do about Denis. He's distraught.'

'It's about time though isn't it?' Maggie said.

49

'What – you mean you wanted her to go away?' Judy asked.

'Who?'

'Jo of course, your daughter, Maggie. Why do you think it's about time?'

Maggie had once confronted her brother Denis and told him about the affair. He hadn't believed her, so she'd never mentioned it again. She assumed he'd wiped it out of his memory.

'Judy and I have a terrific marriage,' Denis had said. 'You are delusional Maggie. Stop taking those tablets. You're paranoid.'

'How selfish she is. I can't believe she's done this to you,' Judy said again.

Maggie stamped her foot.

'Jo is a grown woman and she can do what she likes,' she yelled. She had to put a stop to this. 'Perhaps coming from such a totally dysfunctional family like this one she feels the need to get away.

'From what I gather she is going away to have a good time,' Maggie continued. 'I don't think we need to be hunting her down. And if she wants to make something of herself then I fully support it.'

She choked and knew she had to get off the phone.

'I can't believe your attitude. It's a crying shame all of it,' Judy whined.

Who was Judy to talk to her about shame? It made Maggie feel weak and pathetic, just when she'd begun to feel on top of things. Here was a perfect opportunity to air some very long-held grievances but she couldn't.

She never knew what Judy's tongue would do next. Judy probably knew everything about her and she couldn't bear to have all her intimate secrets thrown back at her.

Chapter 6

I step out of the truck and my eyes are captivated by an array of multi-coloured flowers and plants, and tall oaks and pines. A stone palisade runs around the flat roof of the ornate building, and above it a sculpture in stone. At the front of the building are two statues of women, each holding a flaming torch above their heads.

I can hear cooing, howling, tweeting, warbling, howling. Like nothing I've ever heard before. I stand entranced.

'Come on,' David calls from the door and beckons to me.

I pick up my bag and walk towards him.

'Listen, David. It's amazing. I love it already.'

'Come on Mrs Attenborough,' he says laughing at his own joke.

He is holding open a heavy ornate wooden door for me. I step inside and squint as my eyes adjust to the light streaming in through three glass domes in the ceiling. Everything seems to be painted a rather tacky gold colour. At the end of the room there are lots of pictures, flowers and candles, and a huge, almost life-size Buddha. Again I'm motionless looking around for a few minutes, taking it all in.

My eye moves to the pictures along the wall of different yoga postures and I stop in front of one where a slim young guy is bent in two as if he were made of two parts.

A cheerful looking Indian lady in a pink and red sari is smiling from behind a desk, and I wander over to her.

'*Well come* to Jasanghari. You have good journey here?' the woman says to no-one in particular.

'It looks really lovely, what I've seen so far,' I say.

'Yes, we like it. It was palace only 50 years ago owned by Maharajah and then it was left empty for several years. We were very lucky to get. It is special place with vortex in.'

'A vor what – what is that?' asks David, sauntering up to the desk.

The woman wobbles her head and grins at David.

'It's a place where powerful energy meets,' she tells us.

'I see. Wish I hadn't asked,' David whispers to me. I glance up to see if the lady has heard. She's smiling.

'You understand soon, Sir.'

I follow a young Indian girl, dressed in a red and gold sari, along a long narrow corridor and upstairs. She opens a door and I inch inside. Through the window in the distance are meringue-topped mountains as far as the eye can see. One side of the mountains is dark and other side is still in the early evening sun.

'Wow, it's beautiful, isn't it?' I say. The girl nods.

It's a tiny room, but it's nice to have a new haven, somewhere that is mine for the time-being anyway. I plonk my bags down and thank the girl who puts her hands together as if in prayer.

I sit on the bed, feeling a bit edgy. There's so much to find out though so I may as well get on with it. I wander along the corridor and find the stairs. I'm not sure I'll know how to get back to my room again though. Gemma and David are both in the entrance hall looking at the Buddha. I sidle up.

'I looked out of my window and saw paradise.'

David slaps his hand on my shoulder.

'Good one, Jo.'

'It's awesome,' Gemma adds, her eyes moving around fast taking everything in.

Patrick and some of the other guys from the truck are still in the hall. The lady in the pink and red sari claps her hands lightly.

'Everybody, hello, welcome. I am Mira. I show you round now. Come with me.'

We file off after her like schoolchildren. As we turn a corner at the end of a long corridor, light pours in through a row of French windows, which open out onto a courtyard. It sits in the middle of four sides of the building and has an area of lawn and a few well-tended rose beds, just like an English garden.

Catching the last rays of the day's sun are readers and sunbathers as well as some in yoga postures, and one guy standing on his head. I wince.

'My yoga might not be up to scratch.'

'No problem. No worry,' Mira says beaming at me.

'Everyone has own pace.'

I peer into the rooms off the corridor – one with cookers and a lovely spicy aroma, one looks like a library, and another has lots of guitars, sitars and other instruments. We snake our way into a large hall, and my eyes are instantly drawn to a giant picture on the floor, made with mosaic tiles. Coloured light shines into the room through the stained glass window.

Tucked away in the corner is a grand piano.

'I wonder if anyone ever plays that,' I mumble to myself more than anyone else.

Mira opens a connecting door and I gasp. It has large windows and ornate wooden carvings around the windows, and all the walls are clad with oak or similar wood. The floor is covered with two very large Indian carpets, which look a bit tatty around the edges.

'I feel like I'm in some kind of royal palace, but it's got an air of Britishness as well as the Raj.'

'Yes you are right,' Mira says. 'The princes of the Raj, they wanted to be British too, so they took best from your country and combined with best of India.'

I examine the intricacy of the ornate detail of the gold leaves on the ceiling, and my eyes move to the large tapestries and paintings adorning the walls.

David starts doing a mock tango across the room.

'You can just see them can't you? Raj's and rajesses or whatever they are, dancing across here like this.'

He grabs hold of me and I almost fall over.

'David you're a fool,' I giggle.

Mira looks at us and lets out peals of laughter.

'You, funny man.'

Her laughter is so infectious that everyone else starts as well.

'Now I show you main building,' Mira says, wiping her eyes.

'You can look at outside yourselves, to see the rooms for yoga, the gym we have, the gardens, and the meditation rooms. All out on this wing. Enjoy greatly.'

I amble down the corridors with Gemma and David.

'It's like a school, but much better than a normal one,' I remark. 'With subjects you really want to learn, not the old boring ones you have to do when you're young.'

'I know what you mean,' Gemma nods. 'Stay with me though. I think I'll get lost here. I've already forgotten where we came from.'

Outside there are numerous vegetable patches with rows of unfamiliar looking plants, encircled by an old wall, covered in climbing plants. We nose around the old stable blocks and outhouses, now renovated shower blocks or rooms where classes are held.

'Look here's what you can do,' I tell the others, reading from a list on one of the doors, which had a big sign saying, The Peace Room.

'There's tai chi, painting, Indian dancing, yoga, meditation and mindfulness, Ayurvedic cooking, Sanskrit, Japanese and even Indian literature. Look at this room.'

One whole side of the Peace Room is made up of wooden slatted blinds so it can be open to the garden. Bright purple yoga mats and blocks are piled up in the corner and the room has a calming ambience.

'What a perfect place to do yoga in. I'm up for that,' I say to Gemma.

'Me too,' she nods.

'You won't catch me with me feet around me ears,' David says, bending himself in two. 'Come on now girls. Show us how you do it, come on.'

'Not now. Too tired,' I say. 'But we'll give you a demonstration soon. I've never put my feet round my ears though.'

We walk up a set of stone steps that lead to a stone bench where we all sit down. I yawn. The sun is just dipping behind the mountains and dusk is creeping up.

'There's so much snow on the top of the mountains for this time of year,' I say. 'You wouldn't believe it's the same country as Delhi. And the trees. Can you believe there are so many trees and forests? It's not like India at all.'

'Come on guys, I want to go and get my things put away and have an early night, ready for tomorrow,' Gemma says.

'You're so organised,' David answers. 'I'll keep my stuff in cases for about two months.'

'Tut,' Gemma says.

'See you two downstairs for a little drinkie then?' David asks.

'Yes OK, but you know it will only be the tea variety,' I remind him.

'More's the pity.'

I've so little to unpack that it only takes me 15 minutes. Home seems like another world now. When I'm spending all my time with people it gives me a break from all those heavy, horrible feelings inside. What came over me, leaving them with just a brief note, without forewarning? And Rob, I really did dump him, something I've never done before to anyone.

I tidy up and leave the room, tucking my key into my trouser pocket. Descending the nearest stairs I realise I have no idea where I am, so I go back up again and wander further along the corridor and down some different stairs. Again, I don't know where I am, so I try once more and find the main stairs and end up near the entrance hall.

Gemma and David are sitting in the restaurant with the others from the truck, sipping cups of tea.

'I got lost,' I say throwing my hands out in despair.

'How about I issue you with some string and a piece of chalk to mark the way?' David guffaws at his little joke.

'It's serve yourself,' Gemma says. 'The staff have gone.'

A string of people come up to us all.

'Hi, you are all new aren't you? Is there anything you want to know? I've been here for six weeks so I know the ropes. Any of you English?'

'Yup, well British, us three, oh and Patrick – he's Irish,' David leans forward and points at Patrick who towers above us all.

'What a change from home. It's so friendly here,' David says.

'But I think a centre like this at home would be just the same,' Gemma says. 'It's not the country so much, but more what people are here for.'

'You're probably right Gem,' David says.

At 9 o'clock we all move to the large wooden-panelled room for an introductory talk by an Asian guy with a gentle voice.

'I'm Rasi. You'll see a lot of me during your stay. And I'd like welcome you all to Jasanghari.

'Who am I? You think I'm Rasi. I am. So what does that mean? I'm Indian, I live here, I used to be planner, but now I do personal development. I have one wife and two children. But who am I? And who are you deep down inside – you find out here?'

'This, very special place. We have vortex here, which we show you – you can't see but you feel. It is where the positive energies meet each other and you feel the power. This palace built by a Maharajah during colonial times - often Indian rich people wanted what they see British have and so they wanted own hill stations too.

'But you understand, we very close to Tibetan border. Dalai Lama lives near here, in Dharamsala near the Kangra Valley. So there is plenty influence from Tibet at centre and strong Buddhist influences.

'This is not a religious retreat, but we take philosophy of Buddhism and some other religions. If you Christian or even atheist it no matter. We not make you do anything here that is against your beliefs.

'There is plenty to do. We want you spend time enjoying to learn other cultures, and follow whatever courses you wish. We do plenty meditation and yoga here because they are our lives and our culture. We say that to find peace of mind and wisdom is essential to spend time every day in silence. This not only improves health but it gives you precious seeing inside into who you really are.'

He looks into my eyes, but I see that he does that to everyone, taking in his audience.

'Everyone has opportunity to have personal development sessions with me and many of other staff you see – Anouk, who is over there. He points to a very young smart looking guy who looks like he does yoga workouts all the time as he's so slim.

We also have many peoples from around the world – from Germany now there is Karl, and from Australia there is Jenny, and also Michel from Switzerland who is taking yoga classes and is such expert. You'll all be headstanding soon!'

'Not me,' I mumble, and David elbows me.

'If anyone becomes ill we have Jahib who is Ayurvedic practitioner. If you don't know what is Ayurveda there are classes. It is ancient Indian system of medicine and includes massage, mindfulness and meditation, diet, yoga and herbal remedies, but – and this is most important – also spiritual and emotional parts of life too. Here we are locust's leg away from Tibet, so we have Tibetan medicine too – very natural and very powerful.

'We ask you all see Jahib to have personal talk about your health and find out what type you are. In Ayurvedic medicine you are in three types. It's really interesting, even if you not health freak! So please book appointment with him.

57

'And I forget – not really. Also Deepika, our Ayurveda cook. She teach you to make healthy Ayurvedic food – lovely Indian food with special healthiness.

'Always tell us if you have problem. We have weekly programme and you choose what you do although we want everyone come to early morning meditation. If you not do this before, we do beginners' session each morning until you ready to join main group. If you like sleep late in morning, it no good! The benefits of early meditation before breakfast too good to sleep.'

'I hate getting up early,' I whisper. 'How will I manage?'

'You'll manage,' David reassures me. 'We'll come and prod you won't we Gemma?'

David is just the type of guy I get on with, although there is something about him that reminds me of Rob – one of the sides to Rob's character that I did like. Don't forget, I don't want to get involved. I'm not here for a man, except perhaps. I think of Tim, lovely Tim. I might have had to forget my principles if he'd been here.

Annoyingly I can't sleep when I get into bed as my mind is racing away. I am over-tired and getting images of home in my head. I keep worrying about what they'll all be saying to each other.

I must have fallen asleep after a couple of hours with the bed clothes pulled up to my neck. There's no need to get up and shower in the night to cool down. That is just as well as the bathrooms are way down the corridor. But what is that scrabbling sound, rats or cockroaches?

Chapter 7

Rob is begging.

'Please come back. How can you do this to me?' He moves towards me with arms wide open but a really menacing look on his face.

'Leave me alone,' I scream but my voice is all muffled, as if I've got a sock in my mouth.

He lunges at me, and I try to run but my legs can't move and suddenly he turns into a horse, flicks his mane and canters off, leaving me watching him disappear into the distance.

I sit up in bed startled. Thank goodness it's only a dream, or a nightmare. But the feelings of fear, of guilt and shame, they are very real.

For a fleeting moment I think I'm back in my flat at home, but I look around my new little room and take in the surroundings. The curtains aren't fully across, and the sun is pouring in the part of the window which isn't covered, reflecting off the white walls. A hand-painted picture on the wall shows a man leading a herd of what look like cows with horns and snow-covered mountains in the background. I wonder who painted that – an earlier guest who lived in this little room maybe.

It's a very sparse room with a tiny old-fashioned dresser which I've just managed to squeeze my clothes in. It may be bare but it is a safe haven, and no-one even knows where I am.

It's only six when I wander down to breakfast before meditation. I walk into the restaurant and find Gemma and David sitting with Nicola, Toni and Hans, who was on the truck.

'Hey, you guys. I didn't think you'd all make it,' I say.

'All very keen here, you know. You're late Jo,' David says.

The floor to ceiling windows along one wall make the restaurant area so bright and sunny, and the huge French windows in between them lead out on to a terrace. A little ripple of excitement runs through my body. I love this place already.

Up at the breakfast bar there's a selection of local fruits, yoghurt, boiled eggs, flat bread and chapatis. What a feast.

'I can't believe that they've got apple pies and lemon meringue tarts here,' I comment to the others when I sit down.

'I thought that when I went to Kathmandu,' David says. 'But they are a sort of speciality there too. It's funny isn't it – a bit like mother's home cooking!'

Hans laughs and laughs. He hardly ever says anything but he seems to appreciate everything that David says.

'You guys, now the sun's up why don't we go out onto the terrace?' Gemma suggests.

Everyone gets up and walks outside. I follow with my tray of food, but I'm so overwhelmed by the view that I stop in my tracks. The floor is wooden slatted and tables and chairs are dotted around the terrace. Beyond the terrace the ground falls away to a sea of green lushness backed up by a forest of tall pines, all against the background of imposing mountains.

Gemma is waving at me from the table she's picked.

'Sorry,' I say waking from my reverie. 'It's just breath-taking. I can't think of anywhere I'd like to have breakfast more than this.'

'It's perfect, just perfect,' Gemma agrees.

Ensconced in a wicker chair I examine the statue on my left, which is old and tarnished. The young girl's face is so expressive, as if she has also seen something beautiful for the first time. Just like me.

Although the sun is quite warm the air is pleasantly fresh so unlike the sauna conditions of Delhi. I relax and savour my green tea and fruit.

'So what are you ladies up to today then?' David asks.

'I'm spoilt for choice really,' I tell him. 'I'm thinking of going to environmental studies because it interests me, provided it's not

60

too scientific. And then I'd like to do yoga, tai chi, learn a language, go to the water colours class, or Ayurvedic cooking, and so on and so on.'

'Not much then.' David muses. 'You Hans. You going for Ayurvedic cooking?'

'No, I thought I'd try mountain biking. Want to join me?'

'Blimey,' David blurts out. 'I suppose my thighs could do with a bit of exercise. What do you reckon Jo?'

Hans puts his hand in front of his mouth and tries not to laugh.

'Don't ask me. I don't know anything about your thighs.'

'Give me time, give me time.'

Hans bangs his legs with his fist and everyone starts laughing. They all buzz around David like bees round a honeypot.

Patrick even pipes up,

'Are you going mountain biking then? I'll come with you.'

'Right that's it then,' David said. 'The men are off doing physical stuff while you ladies are in the kitchen cooking.'

'I'll tell you something,' Gemma says wagging her finger at him. 'Don't forget that I'm going to *Taekwondo* so I won't put up with any more nonsense from you.'

She gives him such a firm look it's hard to know if she's joking or not.

'Come on everyone. It's time for meditation.'

Hans jumps up, stands by the entrance and waves them back into the building.

'You know you're not really supposed to eat first,' he tells David who groans.

'Is it really me? I'm not sure I'm the type for all this hippie stuff,' David comments.

'Become the type – anyone can do it. Don't worry,' Gemma says.

'Not worried, just thinking of my reputation.'

'You and your reputation,' I say, prodding him gently.

We wander along the corridors looking around for the ballroom as none of us has a clue where it is now. I open a door and it's the right one. Loads of people are sitting on the floor, so David grabs a chair and sits at the back.

'Me knees won't take sitting down there.'

'Morning everyone. Bonjour. Guten morgen,' a voice says from the front.

I grab a big cushion and sit on the floor.

A tall willowy young man is speaking, He has a narrow angular face with prominent cheekbones, and fluffy hair dropping on to his collar.

'I speak English not well, but more well than other languages. If you don't understand please say. I write on this board here some words that you can choose a mantra from. The mantra is just a couple of words that don't mean anything to you – they are Sanskrit words. You choose words you like and they become your own mantra to keep forever.

'Please choose one. If you don't like it later you can change. I am going to guide you into stillness now so that you can meditate for the next 20 minutes. Repeat your mantra to yourself with the first word on the in breath and the second on the out breath.

'Close your eyes and be still. Start repeating your mantra slowly to yourself and keep eyes closed. If you get other thoughts in mind just push them away and go back to mantra. Very simple. After 20 minutes you hear gong.'

He bangs the gong and we all laugh – no idea why.

'When I do theees you come back. Don't worry if you do not well, you get better each time.'

I close my eyes but my mind is jogging around at a fast pace, from home to Rob, what he's doing now, how he'd feel if he could see me, how David is getting on, what a good group of friends I'm making, what class I'll go to this afternoon, what will happen when I go back home, if I ever want to. This is hopeless. I'm supposed to be calm.

After 20 minutes I open my eyes and see Gemma yawning and stretching.

'That was amazing. I was off in a dream somewhere but I feel really refreshed. How did you get on Jo?'

'Don't ask. My mind was all over the place.'

We catch up with David at the back of the room.

'How was it for you?' I ask him slightly smirking.

'It was OK. I've never been one for quietness so I didn't find it that easy. You?'

'I'm hopeless. I can't concentrate so I'm not doing it properly. All the time I start thinking about home, what I'm going to do next, whether I should write to them, what I'm going to make in my Indian cookery class, so it goes on.'

I miss out what's really bothering me, but they don't know anything about Rob or why I came away.

'Don't worry. Everyone has that happen,' Gemma tells me. 'You can't do it wrong – it's not like that. It's for you and you only, so don't give yourself a hard time about how you do it. I was doing it for years before I could relax. This great master I met once told us that it's the human condition to have thoughts flying into your head endlessly. It means you're human, Jo.'

'Nice to know.'

I like Gemma but she always seems to know everything and appears to be good at all of it. She is going to be quite hard to match up to and in some ways she makes me feel a bit hopeless. If she is so adept at meditation I wonder why she came to the beginners' class but it would sound a bit bitchy if I ask her.

'I'm definitely doing Ayurvedic cooking and nutrition,' Gemma tells me. 'Are you coming too?'

'Yes, why not? I like the idea of being able to cook healthy meals, particularly spicy ones. And tai chi, or maybe I'll do the

63

Taekwondo so I can defend myself. Always seems like a useful skill.'

'Pretty useful in the UK these days,' she agrees. 'You might take up something and decide to change. The world's your oyster.'

'Shall we go and find out what we're doing next?' I suggest.

'I need to go to my room,' David says. 'Can you wait for me here? Won't be a minute.'

'Yes, sure,' I tell him. Everyone has gone and just Gemma and I are left on our own in the ballroom.

'I think this room is incredible,' I say. 'You can imagine all sorts of things happening here when it was full of Indian princes and their entourages.'

'Mmm, yes. Is yoga on today, Jo?'

'I hope so. I love doing yoga. I find it makes me feel a lot less stressed and it keeps me tight and supple.'

I push my chest out and run my hands down to my waist, just as David walks back in.

'Don't let me stop you.'

I can feel my face flushing.

'I was only showing Gemma what yoga does for my shape.'

'As I said, don't let me stop you,' he adds. 'I'm very interested.'

He winks at me and beams at Gemma.

'Did I hear you say you were going to self-defence, Jo?' he asks. 'I'd better come with you, I don't want you women chucking me over your shoulder if you don't like what I say.'

'Better behave yourself then,' Gemma admonishes. 'We'd better go and plan our day. Come on.'

She walks towards the door and when she turns her back David puts his hand to his head in a salute

Chapter 8

One month later

Gemma, David and I are in our favourite spot in the garden lying on the sun loungers. I can't see David's eyes behind his glasses but he appears to be gazing at both of us.

'Jo, when you came you said you'd run off without telling anyone? Was there a husband too?' Gemma asks me.

My hand immediately flies to the chain around my neck and I twirl it around in my fingers.

'No, but I had this really possessive boyfriend and things were getting on top of me, so I decided to get away from it all. I guess I just needed some space. It sounds a bit silly, and part of me wonders what the hell was the matter with me, but I couldn't take any more of them all.'

'I never settle anywhere for long,' Gemma says. She's still lying down with her eyes closed.

'I don't know if it's because I haven't really got roots as my family kept moving when I was young,' she continues. 'But I don't know where home is. I don't particularly mind, as it makes it easier to go away.'

'And you David? Why are you here, or is it a secret?'

'Well, it's a long story, or maybe it's not,' he says in the most serious tone I've heard him use so far.

He rubs his hands together and examines them closely as if looking for something.

'I got into a very bad scene in London. I was drinking a lot, and I'd got into some of the other stuff as well.

'I just needed to get my head together. I felt I was ruining myself and I was upsetting other people as well. My girlfriend kicked me out, and now I'm sort of stone cold sober I can see why.

'I wasn't addicted to anything, it was just a lifestyle thing where I couldn't stop. Since I left home I've hardly had a drink, and I can assure you I haven't touched anything else because I've heard about the rotten jails they have here.'

He's close enough for me to touch, so I sit up and put my hand on his arm. He put his hand over mine. I glance at Gemma. She's still lying down with her eyes closed so it feels like a clandestine moment between him and me. I gently extricate my hand and move back on my chair.

There is something about David – he is the star of the show. I'm almost sure he fancies me, but while I'm flattered I am really determined to stay solo for the time being. Rob shoots back into my head – I had yet another dream about him last night.

I'll have to get in touch with the family soon. It's nearly five weeks since I left and Dad's birthday is coming up. They're bound to think I've lost the plot. It's all so out of character. I know I was always the considerate one who was there for everyone, but this feeling of freedom is intoxicating. Perhaps I'm not really the nice person they all thought I was, and so did I. But the way I treated Rob, it was shitty and cowardly.

I take my opportunity when one of the staff tells us at breakfast,

'Anybody who want send messages home, we going to Shimla today to the Internet café. You give me message and I send. It does not cost big money.'

'An Internet café – that's hard to believe. It seems like you've left it all behind when you come somewhere like this,' I say to no-one in particular. I never bother looking at my phone because there's clearly no signal, but maybe I rather like that. I think I will send an email though. I haven't been in touch at all.'

I grimace.

'Do your parents know where you are?' she asks.

'Nope. No-one does. That was the way I wanted it.'

'That's quite exciting isn't it?' David says. 'Mysteriously disappearing. Didn't they ask you?'

66

'They didn't know I was going. Oh God it's a long story. Let's not go there now.'

I smile and look at the ground. I jump as I feel David's arm come round my shoulders.

'I like my women to be mysterious.'

Is that a look of jealousy on Gemma's face? It is as if David has become the special prize but only one of us is going to get it. I don't want anyone, I just want some space. But the other day I saw Gemma and David locked in intimate conversation outside in the garden. When I walked up they appeared to break off and smiled at me politely. I felt a pang inside – a left-out kind of pang.

I deliberate for a while and then write out a brief message for Dad to his office email address.

DEAR DAD,

JUST TO LET YOU KNOW I'M FINE AND WELL AND HAVING A GOOD TIME. I HOPE YOU'RE ALL OK SINCE I WENT AWAY. HAVE A LOVELY BIRTHDAY ON SUNDAY AND GIVE MY LOVE TO EVERYONE. I'M HAVING A GREAT TIME AND DISCOVERING A NEW ME SO DON'T SPEND ANY TIME WORRYING ABOUT ME. YOU CAN REPLY TO THIS ADDRESS BUT IT'S NOT ON SITE. I'LL GET THE MESSAGE MAYBE A WEEK OR SO LATER. I'M AT A WONDERFUL PLACE IN THE HIMALAYAS, LEARNING LOADS OF NEW THINGS, WITH A GOOD GROUP OF FRIENDS. HAVING A BALL! DON'T WORRY ABOUT ME!

LOVE YOU.

JO XX

I write it clearly so that the guy transcribing it will be able to read it well. It may end up in slightly odd English but it salves my conscience so I can relax, even though it might not arrive until after his birthday.

Chapter 9

'Shit. Sorry.'

As I open my mouth I wish I hadn't said it.

'It's just that I've got turmeric on my white T-shirt and you know how it never comes out.'

'Perhaps not the best colour to wear to cookery lessons,' Gemma tells me.

'Yes I know. It was a bit silly, but I haven't got a huge wardrobe of clothes with me. Deepika, is this OK?'

'Let's taste it. Good cook always taste the food. You know that?'

'Yes I suppose so. You taste it. I daren't.' I laugh.

'Is good. But you need plenty coconut, you know the coconut is the most wonderful of things – the healthy fats not held in the liver and adds the delicious taste and makes it not too hot. Although you English, you like hot. The curry places in England have stupid hotnesses.'

'Vindaloo?'

'We don't do that here. We use lots of vegetables, and very subtle lovely tastes. Spices are for relish, you know what I mean?'

Deepika is a small round lady and today she's wearing a vibrant red, orange and gold silk sari around her. She has a smiling face all the time.

She claps her hands.

'Time for one of the first lessons. You understand in Ayurvedic cooking we have six tastes. Not like you sugary English people who eat the curries so hot that you sweat. We have sweet but not sugar – it can be fish or carbohydrates, and we have sour like lemon or limes or yoghurt, which we use a lot of.

'Then there are salts, but not that cheap stuff you get in supermarket, real Himalayan crystal salt, and bitter – you know

68

some green *veggietables* that are bitter like okra. What you call now? Ladies?'

'Ladies' fingers,' Gemma suggests.

'Yes, yes, ladies' fingers – they are bitter. Pungent – that's when you eat garlic or onions or peppers. And astringent - dhal made from these things. How you call?'

'Lentils.'

'Lentils. Yes and soya and green tea. You drink plenty green tea. Good for you.'

'You eat all six of these tastes and you get all the nutrients you need. You healthy girls. You end up look like me.'

She laughs raucously and pats her big thighs.

'Good healthy Asian woman, me. You come to see me later. We discuss your doshas. You know what I'm talking about.'

'Yes,' Gemma answers. 'I know about doshas.'

'OK. You know which ones you are.'

'I have an idea but would like you to tell me.'

'Yes I do. But first I tell you how wonderful Ayurveda is – ancient system of health here for thousands of years. You know it incorporates everything to help with physical and mental wellbe..?'

'Wellbeing,' Gemma suggests.

'Well being, good.'

'And everyone is an individual so you eat for your type - dosha. You understand?'

Gemma, Nicola, Alain and I all nod and smile at her. She's in full flush now, and I've got to go in a minute.

'You look after here.' She pats her big tummy. 'And your indigestion – no your digestion.'

Deepika cackles at her own mistake. We join in too.

'Your digestion it is good and you, your whole body also good. You see, my darlings?'

69

She comes to a stop and I take my opportunity.

'I've got to go. I'm so sorry. I love everything you are telling us, but I've got to go and talk with Rasi at 3,' I say.

I quickly wash my pans and untie the apron.

'Ah yes,' Deepika nodded. 'He very good Rasi. You will talk about everything that you have kept in here forever.'

She points to her chest.

'And he will make it better. He lovely man, not too lovely. He married.'

She wags a finger at me and guffaws. I can feel my face going red. Luckily they're all looking at Deepika and she's too busy laughing so none of them notices.

I dash down the corridor remembering how much trouble we got into with our teachers at school when we ran along corridors.

Chapter 10

'Last Christmas things got really ugly and a plan started to hatch in my mind.'

'What you mean ugly?' Rasi asks.

'Sorry, I mean things were going very badly.'

'In which way?'

'Everything. I had a terrible evening out with Rob on Christmas Eve where he got drunk and made a fool of himself and me, and then he came home with me when I didn't want him to.'

'How?'

I've noticed that his questions are always quite short.

'Yes you may say how,' I sigh.

'I suppose I'm so soft that I let him come home with me because he could get quite nasty when he was drunk and it was easier to do that.'

'Do you think saying what you want?'

'I don't know if you know what people are like when they get drunk. It's just impossible, particularly with him – you can't reason with him or anything, so no, I didn't, because I felt I couldn't. Quite frankly Rasi this is why I ran away, because I can't face people and tell them what I think.'

'Is it easy way to run away?'

'It feels it because it's so hard to talk to people who don't want to listen.'

'But Jo that is you, not these people. Maybe Rob, he want listen but you need be heard so it's you who tell people.'

'How? What can I say?'

'It is no good me tell you what you say, you have to feel for it. I say that you shouldn't let people treat you like this and you say, 'No', but it has to come from here.'

He rested his hand on his heart. That gesture again.

'So why can't I do it?'

'You can do. You find it difficult, but you can do. Why is it difficult? What you afraid of?'

'In what way, Rasi?'

'Why you don't say, "Listen me, I have something to tell you about me and I want you hear me" and then you say what is?'

'Oh God, that sounds so difficult! I'm not sure anyone would listen though.'

I'm sitting directly opposite to him. So neatly turned out, with every black hair in place, and his eyebrows almost look as if they've been shaped. His short sleeved calico shirt is white and pristine and his face is serious. I bet some of the women fall for him. Thank goodness he's not my type. Too organised maybe. Perhaps I'm attracted to chaotic people.

He leans towards me watching me studying his face. Now I feel stupid, but at the same time I appreciate that his big brown eyes hold such depth, such emotion. What a lovely guy.

'Yes. People who think they are important and, you know, confident and that other people must listen to them. If you want, and only if you want we work together to discover together why you think you not important. You change belief so that you speak and make people hear you.'

'How do I do that?'

'Here I will help you. It take time, but you also need to sing.'

'Sing. Rasi – you haven't heard my voice.'

'I don't need that. When you meet Chris – the musician who visits – you will understand that we all can sing well. Yes, even you Jo. We put, what you call crap, on ourselves and not speak about, but when you learn sing you more confident.'

'I am not so sure. I wasn't any good at singing when I was at school. When is this Chris here?'

72

'He's not here now, but he coming few weeks. I tell everyone when he here. You go along and you see what I talk about. I have stopped talking about the subject we started – we, what's the word?'

'Digressed.'

'Maybe that's the word but I don't know it.'

He laughs gently, still watching me.

'We were back at last Christmas,' I say in a hushed voice. 'I'm afraid my story is more of the same where I didn't say anything and just kept putting up with everything that was driving me mad. The Christmas day with the family was awful and Rob came too and everyone was pretending it was all right but it was terrible.

'Everyone was bitching at each other, my mother was in a state - from too much booze, sorry drink - my brother, Michael, and his wife were being a nightmare as usual – they argue with each other always. And Beth, my sister, I haven't told you about her. Think of someone who always likes to be the centre of attention – that's her. And the only saving grace was my nephew and niece, Stephen and Charlotte who are about the only normal people in the family.'

'And you. What were you doing?'

'Trying to keep everyone happy, helping with the dinner, trying not to get involved. Appeasing, appeasing. You know this word?'

'No.'

'Keeping the peace, making everyone happy (big joke).'

'Being nice, helpful, lovely *dotter*.'

'I expect so. None of them knew what I'd been through.'

I stop abruptly. I'm not ready to discuss that. I don't even know how much to trust Rasi yet, but I think I will. For now, I'll stick to the family story.

'My sister, Beth is her name, my sister. She's, well.'

I'm stumbling. How can I describe Beth?

73

'She is forever asking me for advice about her various boyfriends. It's so obvious what she should do and I tell her and then she turns it around and is horrible to me.

'I felt wounded, depressed and as if my life had evaporated and no-one noticed.'

I stop and sigh loudly. Put like that I wonder how I coped for so long. Rasi still watches as if he is thinking about it all.

'It's OK, Jo. Good for you to say.'

'I suppose it has been a build up over the years of being the dependable one, whom they all relied on. I try to please everyone, to keep them happy, to make them happy, but they're not my responsibility so why did I do it? Maybe I'd not seen it before, before...'

'Yes?'

'I had a bad time, because something happened. And when I had a problem I couldn't talk to any of them. I just started to see things differently – that perhaps I was stupid really, that I let people walk over me. Stupid. Do you understand?'

'Yes. You hard on self.'

'Maybe.'

'What happened?'

'I hadn't worked out what I would do but I thought about it over the next few days after this awful Christmas. By New Year's Eve I'd made up my mind. When Rob asked me what resolution I'd made I told him I hadn't decided yet. Do you know about New Year's Resolutions – we make them every year, to give up smoking, give up drinking, lose weight or something?

'That's a good idea. Yes, very popular here too.'

'It was going to take some time to get organised and I didn't know what to do about Rob. I just made myself less available but I also found him easier to put up with once I'd made a decision. When he was sober he could be lovely so I tried to enjoy what I could, knowing there was a way out. It's a fact that I didn't love him any

74

more, if I ever had. He somehow seemed to sense he was losing me but we never discussed it, and I even felt sorry for him.'

'Jo we finish soon. But can you tell me why you didn't finish the relationship with him. Why run away?'

'I'm a coward Rasi. I can't bear hurting people.'

'Don't you think he's hurting now?'

'Oh yes. But I don't have to see it. That makes me an awful person doesn't it?'

'No, not awful. But perhaps it's your own pain you can't see.'

'Maybe. I hadn't thought of it like that. Yes I can see I should have been honest with them, but it's because I'm pathetic. And also, in my defence, I have tried before, but Rob just wouldn't accept it. This way he had to.'

'Jo you say 'stupid, pathetic, awful'. You too nasty to you. Don't criticise you so much. We try to understand. You have to learn to love yourself, much more than you do.'

'By going away I was looking for peace of mind, to gain strength so that I could speak out to them all, especially Rob. It's funny I want you to understand, but I realise I don't even understand myself. Maybe you can, with your experience, understand me more than I can. Does that make sense?'

He nods sympathetically.

'Do you think I will ever be free of all this? It felt so bad telling you all about it and I remembered how depressed I felt. And you know what?'

I look at the floor. What am I doing talking to this man I've hardly known for any time at all?

'None of them could give a ff... you know none of them gives a damn about me.'

I don't want to cry so I put my face in my hands. I'm trying to keep the tears back so I stay like that for a while. Then I peep at him through my fingers to see what he is doing. He is just watching.

75

'You knew that I didn't want you to say, "There, there, it will be all right".'

My voice is quavering and strangled.

'"There there" is an English expression but it's so, it's so patronising. And it won't be all right.'

'It probably will now. Now you let out you can let go.'

'Is it that simple?'

'Yes simple, but take time. You have experience it, feel it again and let it go. No good for you to keep and now you want it be gone. Like someone who has died – it is gone. It has run its field.'

'Course.'

'Course, not field,' he smiles. 'I ask you Jo. What purpose you to keep this inside?'

'No idea.'

'I tell you it's none. It eats at your soul like this,' he makes a gnawing face like a rabbit.

Despite my despair I smile.

'No, you laugh. It make you ill if you keep everything that's negative inside yourself.'

'I'll believe you. Thousands wouldn't.'

'What?'

I smile.

'It's another expression Rasi. We have so many of them in our language. I'll teach you English. You teach me to live.'

Chapter 11

Drinking tea in the conservatory, watching the sun going down over the mountains with David feels relaxed and peaceful. I put my hair back in a ponytail today and my white cotton shirt shows off the tan I've acquired since arriving. David watches my face attentively, listening to every word I say.

Twice in one day – first Rasi listens to my every word and now David. Not something I'm used to at all at home.

'I am doing things here that my family – and my friends – would find really strange. There is a view among lots of people at home that if you get into things like yoga and meditation you are a bit weird – my father would describe it as hippyish and be very derogatory.'

David nods and raises his eyebrows.

'I know exactly what you mean. Some of the people I work with would really scoff. It is odd that people can be so dismissive of something they have never tried. And I was exactly like that too. Down the pub getting blasted out of my mind was always my idea of fun, but maybe it's just a way of escaping. I guess people are so derisory because there's so much fear of the unknown. It's threatening.'

'Yes probably. My Dad always relates anything like that to the Maharashi and in his opinion that's when the Beatles went weird. He thinks that it is all weird cults and doesn't understand it was just experimentation – a new world. Mum told me once that he used to love the Beatles until they went to India, and then he became very critical of them.'

I groan.

'Much as I love him he's so pompous sometimes and he pontificates on things that he disapproves of and knows nothing about.'

'It's interesting,' says David, 'But have you noticed how people tell you that this is the best song or film ever, or the worst? They are so opinionated and don't realise that they are stating their own opinion – not a fact. By the way Jo, I've just remembered I used to do that too!'

We laugh. It's so easy chatting to him.

'You must have been a pain. Talking of music, Dad hated the music we were into in the nineties, and kept on harping back to the "good old days" of the sixties and all that stuff. It was good music then, but it doesn't make anything else that follows it rubbish!'

'Yeah. It's unlike you to be angry with your Dad. From what I've heard so far you've only ever had praise for him, but you seem a bit hard on your Mum.'

'Perhaps I'm finding out how I really feel and letting it out at last. It is probably the only thing I have ever really found annoying about him. But it's funny, although he would consider everything I am doing here completely weird, I have never been happier in my life. I'm enjoying everything I'm doing here, the people I've met.'

David puffs up his chest and pats it Tarzan-like with his hand. He has that smirk on his face that I've become used to and even quite fond of. I carry on.

'And I feel that this way of living is a lot more likely to make me fulfilled than anything my father has ever advocated.

'The whole Eastern approach to life, shunning materialism, it makes so much sense. It's so different from life in Britain and yet it can feel so good. I was just like everyone else and needed money to be happy. Don't get me wrong, it's awful being poor and having to worry about it all the time, but money isn't what life's all about.'

'I couldn't agree more. I had a high-powered job in a top London ad agency. I had more money than I could spend, I ate at all the best restaurants, you know the kind of thing. I even bought myself a Porsche. Shall I go on? And I was as miserable as sin. I'd been heavily into coke – and not the liquid stuff, I drank a phenomenal amount of alcohol and my relationships were in a mess. I'm much happier now.'

He never lifts his eyes from my face. I like this one to one connection, but wonder what else is on his mind. The more I talk to him, the more I might be encouraging him and I'm so determined that I don't want a relationship, with him or anyone, at the moment. And from what he's told me he seems to be bad news as far as relationships are concerned.

'Well, I'm off to get ready. See you later.'

David leaves the restaurant and I just sit back and relax, musing to myself. Living in such close quarters with each other and having new and life-changing experiences together means that friendships are on a deep footing right from the start. I've never been this open before and I feel closer to these new friends than to anyone else I've ever known, which seems crazy.

Home seems so distant to me now and I just wonder if I would miss any of them if I never saw them again. I can't believe I even allowed myself to think that.

I like doing things on my own. I don't feel that I seek company for its own sake here. Now it's as if I'm stripped naked and can see inside my emotions, many of which I didn't even know were there.

By now Rob has probably found solace in someone else's arms. That assuages my guilt a bit. It also gives me a stab of jealousy, why I have no idea. I didn't want him, but don't I want anyone else to have him either?

I pick up my plate and bowl and carry them over to the washing up area. I love my breakfasts here. Every morning I eat fresh mangos, grapes, starfruits, oranges, and bananas with lovely thick yoghurt – made from goat's milk. And the crisp fresh apples which grow in the hills nearby, vegetable curries, lamb, chicken, rice, dhal and interesting dishes I've never had at home.

Today is picnic day. We all gather in the reception area at 11. Most of the Jasanghari residents and some of the staff set off walking from the back of the palace, up a narrow path which winds up the mountainside. Alongside all of us are our animal companions – a few old donkeys who are carrying the food for our picnic.

After we've been trekking for nearly an hour, we come across an open clearing of grass where a group of local boys are playing cricket of sorts. They have just two bats between them and their wickets are sticks. We all wave and greet them. Now in front of me is a cable bridge suspended over a fast moving stream. I'm not sure about this as it's shaking and swaying.

'Yikes, I hope this is all right.'

'Of course it is and if you fall in I'll dive in and save you,' David assures me.

'Very noble, David, but I'm not sure either of us would make it. I just won't fall in.'

Rasi and Mira suggest we have our picnic in an idyllic spot by the side of the stream. They spread out the food on a large cloth and everyone helps themselves to dips and bhaji delicious flatbreads, with loads of local vegetables freshly cooked and made into a salad.

Once we've eaten, I take off my dress a bit self-consciously in case David or Rasi are watching. Rasi is busy clearing up the picnic, but as I expected David is lying on his side and I can see that his eyes are on me. I feel even more embarrassed because he hasn't made one of his little quips and is looking at me get down to my bikini. I need to get in the water quickly so I gingerly pick my way across the stones into the stream.

From behind me I hear the guys get up and run off to join the cricketers. David, as usual is the ring leader and he's got Patrick, and Hans laughing at his every word as they make their way like a group of schoolboys.

Feeling less inhibited now I dip my feet in the water and wince at how cold it is. Gradually I clamber over some rocks to a deeper area, and ease myself into it gasping. I swim round and round in a circle to get myself warmer. When I look up Gemma is standing nearby watching. She's all ready to get in.

'Hey, Gemma, come in. Just fantastic and cooling.'

'Is it deep enough to dive?' she asks.

'I'm out of my depth so come over here.'

Gemma dives in. Ever the expert at everything she does.

'How will we ever want to go home after this?' I ask her as she bobs about treading water.

'I don't know. It's pretty wonderful. I suppose life can't be like this all the time though.'

'More's the pity.'

I swim back to the side and crawl along to the edge, trying to ensure that I don't hurt my feet. Strands of my long hair are clinging to my back and I go back to my towel and sit down on it. It feels cool now, but gradually the sun's rays start to warm me up. Hugging my knees I look at my surroundings.

Flowers everywhere - blues and reds, yellows and pinks - and the terrain is like a painter's blend of green and brown. Dark mountains veer up behind us and cast huge shadows over part of the land. Behind the nearby mountains are even higher ones still capped with snow at the very top.

Even though it's much cooler in the mountains than down in Delhi there are still a lot of bugs around. That's one aspect of Indian life I can't quite get used to and I have often asked David to come and kill cockroaches for me.

'I don't get this David. There were two bodies lying there last night, and now they've disappeared. Do you think they carry away their dead?'

'I always knew you were crazy. Perhaps the house is haunted by the ghost of dead cockroaches. You women.'

A sudden movement in the bushes catches my eye, and moving closer I can see a pair of eyes staring at me. The eyes belong to a kind of monkey, but not like one I've ever seen before.

I turn back to the group and Rasi is on his feet.

'Here, Rasi. Look at this monkey.'

He walks over quietly.

'Ah yes it's snub-nosed monkey. Not so many of them now. If you see face, nose is what you call snub I think.'

I peer in closer and can see its upturned nose and lots of black fur.

'Are they dangerous?'

81

'No, but you not get too close. Their noses are to the sky, up, and when it rain, they go 'achoo' 'achoo'.'

'Sneeze?'

'Yes, sneeze,' he says looking pleased that I understand.

'Because water goes in nose.'

He laughs. Gemma joins us with her camera.

'This is priceless,' she says.

I leave Gemma snapping photos, and nip back to my things where I slip my dress back on. My costume isn't too wet now. I just want to lie down and enjoy the peace and beauty of it all.

'Of course it's not that perfect and peaceful here you know,' Gemma says as she stands above me.

'There's plenty of conflict in these mountains.'

'Yes I know you're right. I like living in fantasy land though.'

David comes back puffing and blowing and throws himself down right next to me on my towel.

'So do I.'

He winks at me.

'How was the cricket?' I ask, trying to inch away from him without him noticing.

'There's some real talent there that will go undiscovered,' he admits, rubbing grass off his legs.

'What, yours Flintoff?' I enquire.

'Yes of course. No I mean the locals, you chump.'

He prods me on my side and puts his hand on me. He sits there looking down at me and I feel uneasy and sit up.

'Talking of chumps, we've just met a snub-nosed monkey.'

'Well, who was that?' David chides.

'No really. Gemma, show him your pictures. Apparently they sneeze when it rains because of their little snub noses.'

'You're having me on. Come on show me where this monkey is. I want to see the real thing.'

Chapter 12

David had always been used to glamourous girls in advertising but this was different, because here he could really talk to them. If he got involved with one, it would surely change his relationship with the other, but he knew he wouldn't stick to his principles if the opportunity arose. After all he hadn't been near a woman for two months and that was a long time for him.

Gemma and Jo were both beautiful in their own ways – Jo with her sleek dark hair and her face characterised by a mole near her mouth which he'd love to kiss. She was lovely and so much fun. He knew that Jo really liked him and they had developed a great friendship. They confided in each other, but she had told him that she didn't want a relationship.

Gemma was more self-assured and could be a bit domineering, but he liked a challenge and she presented one. What was best was that they made him forget about Karen. He was surprised at how quickly he seemed to have got over her, and he'd been sure he was in love with her.

Women were so difficult to fathom out. If they liked him, he couldn't tell if they fancied him or liked him in a non-sexual way. It was such a fine line, but if he liked a girl a lot, he wanted more. He knew Jo was the type to have platonic friendships because she had told him about some of her male friends.

He didn't want to frighten her away. Friendship was better than nothing. Gemma, on the other hand, was stunning. She had silky blond hair and a sleek figure and he hoped that there might be a chance that she felt the same about him.

She was very much her own person, totally capable of being independent and he couldn't be sure what she thought of him. There was something overwhelming about her and he was scared of getting too close, but he wasn't always ruled by his head.

Life usually just happened to David while he was busy making other plans. A couple of his friends had planned when they wanted to get married, what their career would be and by what age they'd have children. But of course, it didn't always go to plan, and so he stuck with his more haphazard way of living.

He fell into everything without knowing where it was going. He had loved Karen but he didn't want to make plans, whereas she did. He'd been devastated when she threw him out, but he couldn't blame her.

The first task was to get completely clean and to be able to live without the booze and drugs, and then maybe he could think about how he wanted his life to pan out. In the meantime Jasanghari seemed to be keeping him somewhat stable. There were times when he really wanted to get away from it all and go back to living dangerously, but fortunately for him it wasn't easy to do while he was in the Himalayas.

Life was so much easier than it had been before he went away. All that concerned him now was would it be Jo or Gemma?

Chapter 13

'It was obvious something was wrong. Mum hadn't spoken for days and looked so drawn and tired. Then I heard them arguing about something. It sounded like it was to do with my Aunt Judy, but I must have got that wrong. It was something to do with the fact that he'd spent a lot of time talking to Judy when they'd been out.'

I'm sitting in a big, comfy armchair opposite Rasi. All the slatted blinds that take up one side of the room are open. It's a warm day and there is a gentle breeze coming into the room. I'm just wearing shorts and a T-shirt and my legs hang down from the chair looking really brown. My feet just touch the floor.

Rasi is sitting in an ornate wooden chair with silk cushions behind him. He is looking relaxed in a white shirt and a pair of loose Indian trousers. He is attentive to every word I say. I just love these sessions.

'It was awful. My mother was saying that he didn't care about her and she was getting hysterical. "You don't care if I leave. I'll leave and you can see how you cope with three young children," she said.

'I can remember it clearly. I wasn't able to sleep and I was sitting at the top of the stairs in pink pyjamas. Then the penny dropped. She didn't love me and she wanted to leave.

'My Dad didn't seem to be saying anything. And then I heard him walk out of the room. "If you spent as much time looking after the family as you spend drinking that stuff we'd all be much happier." Or words to that effect.

'Then there was a smash in the kitchen and Mum came running up the stairs and saw me.

'She just shouted, "Go to bed. Go on. You're supposed to be asleep." She sounded hysterical. I guess I was about seven or eight at the time but I've never forgotten it. I didn't understand it then and I can't say I do now, but it seemed to rock my security.

'Mum was never very affectionate towards me. She preferred Michael. She never seemed to want to know if I was OK. She just assumed I was and sometimes I would see her sitting on Michael's bed hugging him. I couldn't understand it. He was so horrible and she seemed to like him more than me, more than either Beth or me.

'And one day he saw me watching through the door and he gave me a smug look as if to say she loves me, but not you. God, I hated him. He was such a horrible boy. He used to lie all the time and get me into trouble with Mum. Dad wasn't quite so gullible and he and I had an easy relationship, but I suppose you could say I was really, really jealous of my own brother.'

'Are you now?' Rasi looks straight at me.

'I don't like him. What an awful thing to say about your brother but I still see the same snivelling little lying brat that he was. He's not straightforward, and he's so rigid. As if he's got no feelings at all. I just don't identify with him. Even Beth and all her drama queen behaviour is preferable. You can have some kind of contact with her, but with Michael I just can't connect at all.'

'But you jealous of him?'

'Rationally no. Who would be – he's married to a bitchy woman, he's shallow and he doesn't seem very happy? But irrationally, yes. I guess he always got my mother's love and ..' I falter, feeling choked. I didn't, I never have.'

'Do you miss it?'

'I never realised how much until I came here and talked to you. I just felt apathetic about her. I felt we had nothing in common, that she was a washed up, miserable woman. I didn't seem to have much feeling for her. She didn't seem to like us girls much, so what could I do? I didn't like her much either. What a terrible admission.'

'It is honest.'

'Yes, it may be honest. But now I realise how much I needed that special relationship with her, like some mothers and daughters have. To be close, to hug and love each other. That would have been great. If I have a daughter I want to have that.'

'Do you love your mother Jo?'

'Doesn't everyone love their mother?'

'No.'

'Don't they? I've always felt programmed to love her but I never felt love for her. You know like you do for a boyfriend – girlfriend, you know what I mean.'

'It's very different from that kind of loving. What about your father?'

'I love him. I know that. Yes I do love him. That feels solid and good, but her. I just don't know.'

'So you as little girl, who loves you?'

'My Dad. He cared a lot about me. Maybe I like to think I was his special one. He and I were like this.'

I put my middle finger over the one next to it.

'Father's love – it's very different from mother.'

'Yes I missed out on that big time. Perhaps it's what I'm looking for in relationships all the time and can't get. Why would I be able to get my mother's love in a relationship with a man? Do you think I'm weird?'

'No. All people the same. Why your mother not loving, do you think?'

'She couldn't, could she? She couldn't give it to anyone, except Michael maybe. She didn't have a good childhood at all. Much worse than mine. Maybe she was too unhappy to love me.'

I bite my lip, so much not wanting to cry in front of Rasi.

'It's OK to cry Jo, that's what here is for.'

I am successfully holding on to the tears but I can't speak. Crying in front of people seems so difficult, let alone with this lovely man. If I let down that defence there's no telling what will happen next.

Rasi leans forward. I notice again how deeply warm his eyes are and I find I'm losing myself in them.

'Have you thought Jo that your mother loves you very much? When people so unhappy they only can concern themselves. They not think about how they behaving to the people they love. They take them, for, for...

'Granted,' I suggest.

'Yes for granted, and do not express. Then something takes place.'

'Like when your daughter runs away?'

'Yes, but often much more sad. It's that someone dies. Then we know how much we love them.'

I look up at him through the tears. Talking like this makes me feel so close to him and all I want right now is to have him hold me in his arms and make me feel safe. Although I look forward to seeing him so much, I cannot forget that he is married and even if he weren't it wouldn't be professional.

Two months down the line the full realisation of what I have done makes me feel so guilty. Why couldn't I have told them all what I was doing? I know I didn't because I felt I couldn't. Because everyone would have their opinions and not understand why I was doing it, persuaded me not to, not allowed me to. Maybe, deep down I just wanted to teach them a lesson.

At least now my father will know how to contact me if he wants to. He'll probably forgive me, but would anyone else? Rob. Every time I think of him my stomach clamps up. What I did to him was really shitty. There's no way of excusing it. I've tried blaming him but it doesn't work.

My Ayurvedic consultation with Deepika revealed that I am a *pitta* type that I worry a lot about other people. It didn't take long for Deepika to realise, as she had probably summed me up already. She gave me some herbs for the headaches I get, and some others to ease my PMS. I feel better already. And Rasi talks about the baggage, which I've been carrying around for years and never let anyone see. That probably contributed to the headaches, he says.

I can hardly relate to home any more – it seems like another world, another lifetime. I recall with amusement that Rasi believes in reincarnation so there could be many lifetimes.

There are days where I can achieve a meditative state but there are other days when I cannot concentrate to save my life. Sometimes things from the past just pop into my head as if they are asking to be looked at and dealt with.

I have tried hard to repeat my mantra while my eyes are closed. It helps me to focus my mind when other thoughts float in. Sometimes my legs get uncomfortable and numb, so I have to change position, which is distracting.

'I can be like this here Rasi, but what about when I go home? That's quite another thing. When the pressure's on and I have to work and my family are there, won't it all go again? Can I stay forever?'

'You build like this – like house.' He mimes stacking up a pile of bricks.

'When you have built your house it becomes easier. Here you have no stress, but at home you have. But you will be relaxing person. It helps you with the normal life – your family, for you.'

Chapter 14

Rob hadn't been to work for two days and was feeling rough from night after night of smoking and drinking. The flat looked like a tip with dirty ashtrays everywhere and several days' worth of washing up.

He spent most of his time just lying on the sofa with the TV on, but not really watching.

He had a pain in the pit of his stomach so tight that he could barely eat. He had existed on a few tins of soup, baked beans and chips which he happened to have in. When he saw his mother on the weekend she was shocked at how thin he looked.

'It's not worth it Rob. No girl is worth making yourself ill for. I'm worried about you.'

'Don't fuss Mum. I don't care what happens to me now.'

'Rob!'

He just shrugged.

Because of his height Rob was a bit stooped at the best of times. Now his shoulders seemed to be up around his ears and his back was permanently hunched over. His face looked drawn and he had bags under his eyes.

Everything was an effort and he couldn't imagine ever feeling better. He had cried for what seemed like days, and he kept wanting to sleep. His limbs felt heavy and he was tired all the time. He had never experienced anything like it.

He simply could not believe that Jo could do this to him. Whatever ups and downs they had had, in his mind he was going to end up with her. She was the woman for him and his future had been assured. She was going to make him a better man.

He wanted to marry her, to have children with her, find some way that would keep her there forever. He used to ask her to stop taking the pill, so she'd get pregnant and their future would be bound together forever.

Now she had changed all that with one devastating blow. She didn't even have the guts to tell him what she was doing. This hurt more than her going. She had treated him with such disdain. Had they all been laughing behind his back, knowing that she was going to leave him? Didn't he remember them being strange at Christmas?

He languished on the sofa, the light off and the curtains not properly pulled back properly. It was dark and gloomy like him. He kept clenching and unclenching fists until they went white as he imagined punching her new man.

The doorbell rang. His stomach lurched – maybe it was Jo, and it would be all right after all.

He leapt up off the sofa, and ran down the stairs two at a time to the communal hall. He opened the door and saw a smiling face looking directly at him. It was Beth – she might have some news. Her face dropped at the sight of him.

She saw an unshaven dishevelled wreck of a bloke. He looked tired and red-eyed and smelt of cigarettes.

'Rob what do you look like?'

'I don't really care Beth. Why are you here?'

'To see if you're all right. I wondered.'

'Did you know?'

'No.'

'Who knew?'

'No-one. Mum and Dad didn't.'

'Did they get letters?'

'Yes.'

He shut the door, pulled her in and motioned to follow him up to his flat.

'Has she gone off her rocker then? Where's she gone, Beth? I want to go and get her.'

'What's the point Rob? I don't know anyway, so I can't tell you. If she's gone and left you she's ungrateful isn't she? Can't you see how selfish she is?'

'Well this isn't the Jo I know. I used to think she was perfect.'

'Then more fool you. She's not so bloody wonderful or she wouldn't leave you in this mess. Think about that for a minute.'

'I think about it all the time, don't I? I can't believe she would ever treat me like this. It hurts me really badly in here.'

He patted his chest. She looked at him in mock sympathy.

'Honestly Beth I can feel the pain.'

'Oh come on Rob. The best way to get over someone is to realise that they're just a mean bastard. Or in her case, a selfish cow. She never was the person you thought she was. She just wasn't.'

Rob's face crumpled.

'Look. I know what it's like. I'm sorry for you Rob. It's tough. Let me in and make me a cup of coffee.'

She pushed past him and walked into the kitchen, swung her bag off nearly knocking the dirty dishes flying, and dropped it on a chair.

'Oh for heaven's sake. What a mess. You've really gone to pieces haven't you? Why don't you go in the bathroom and have a shave and I'll make a coffee and we'll have a chat, but not about Jo all the time. Go on.'

She surveyed the filthy pans and ashtrays and hunted around for the coffee. She wasn't doing his washing up for him. She put the kettle on and went back into the lounge. Rob was slumped on the sofa with the TV on.

'Do you want a coffee? And are you going to shave?'

'No I'd rather have this.'

He produced a bottle of whisky from the floor beside the sofa.

'You've already had plenty haven't you? It doesn't really help does it?'

She sat next to him.

'You think you're in a bad way. You probably know about Jack. Well I've never ever fancied a bloke like I do him, and I'm sure he's going to leave his wife but it hasn't happened yet. I'm getting pretty peeved about it, but he comes round and it's all back to square one again. I just can't give him up, so I know where you're coming from.'

'Not really Beth. Not really. I can't give Jo up and I've been given no choice. And I thought she was going to be my wife.'

'The other day Jack was coming round and he was three hours late. Can you imagine? I spent the whole bloody evening pacing around, trying to keep dinner on the go and then he turns up and all he's got time for is going to bed.'

'Where's that glass?' Rob asked. 'I thought we'd have children. You know I wanted her to get pregnant and I could see my whole life in front of me. We would move into a house together and we'd have a family and I was going to be happy forever.'

'Is life really like that though? Jack's got all that and look at him. He's…'

'But he obviously doesn't care about his wife. That's why he's shagging you.'

'Rob, don't say that. It's much more than that.'

She walked out of the lounge and back into the kitchen. The kettle had boiled, so she hunted around for some coffee and found a tiny bit at the bottom of a jar. Then she grabbed a smeary glass. He wouldn't notice.

She sat down on the edge of the sofa next to Rob.

'Shove up. Make some room for me. No, honestly Rob there is more to my relationship with Jack than just sex. It isn't like that.'

He took the glass off her and started pouring whisky into it. She watched his unsteady hand, but he didn't spill it.

'Come on Beth. If it's more than that why doesn't he leave? Oh don't answer. Tell me what your Mum said, what your Dad said.

Who else did she write to? Are they worried? Are they going to tell the police?'

'I hardly think so. Well I guess you know what Mum's like. She hasn't said a lot. Always preoccupied with herself and not very likely to say much. She seemed to think Jo could do what she liked. Dad is upset, very upset.'

'And Michael?'

'Nose put out of joint. She didn't write to him. And you can imagine Hannah, what she'll say.'

He managed a half smile.

'I just miss the smell of her, the sound of her voice.'

'Hannah?'

'No you idiot, Jo.'

'That's how I feel about Jack.'

She went into the kitchen and found another glass which she washed, then went back and poured some whisky for herself.

Beth sat down a bit closer this time and resting her hand on his knee she leant over and filled his drink too. When she glanced up at him he looked so pitiful that she felt a surge of sympathy for him. He didn't look so bad after all and the smell of cigarettes had waned since she'd had a couple herself. She lifted her hand and stroked his hair.

He moved her gently back on to the arm of the sofa and pulled her legs up, so she was almost lying down. He knelt back and looked at her.

Beth's slim curvy body was accentuated by very tight jeans and a body hugging black T-shirt. Volumes of auburny red hair were spread out behind her and as Rob looked at her he knew that the complete antidote to Jo was lying here with him.

Despite herself and despite the state of him, Beth liked the way he was looking at her. What if her sister's boyfriend fancied her? Perhaps she was just what he needed, and it wouldn't hurt her either.

Neither of them spoke, but the atmosphere was electric.

He ran his eyes up and down her body while she watched but
didn't complain. He moved closer to her and put one arm around her
waist and the other hand on her shoulder. She was smiling now.

'I can't do this,' Beth thought, but the need for some love and
attention was strong. Her brain and her body were at odds with each
other, and lust was overtaking her senses. They lay together silently
while the TV droned on.

The whisky helped and she stopped caring where it all led. As
he touched her ripples of desire went through her. Never in her
wildest dreams had she thought about Rob like this, but now she
couldn't wait for him.

It struck her that he had lovely hazel and blue eyes. Why hadn't
she noticed before?

To Rob, Beth now looked just like Jo with the same mouth.
When she smiled she was Jo and she felt like her. Her cool grey eyes
seemed to have lost that angry look and were incredibly sexy. The
colours in her irises were almost moving seductively enticing him in.

He ran his fingers through her hair with both hands, gently
lifting it and dropping it. He piled her hair behind her and set about
meticulously moving individual hairs that were escaping until her
face had no hair around it. All he could see was these big eyes
looking at him.

'Beautiful, beautiful hair,' he said still looking at her,
tantalising her, coaxing her to want him.

She forgot all about his unshaven face, his unkempt hair, and
the stench of whisky, hooked her arm around his neck and pulled
him towards her. They kissed like there was no tomorrow.

Much, much later Beth was lying awake in Rob's messy
bedroom wondering what the hell she had done. This was her sister's
boyfriend even if she had run off and left him. Beth had forgotten all
about Jack while she and Rob made love on the sofa, and later in his
bed.

She had been really enjoying herself when Rob suddenly called
out, 'Jo' in a plaintive voice. Then he started weeping – it was

pathetic and killed her passion. Any thoughts Beth had had about her taking her sister's place in his arms were quashed.

She held him in her arms because she felt sorry for him as he wept, but it made her feel like a poor substitute for her sister. She didn't know what to say to him. She knew Jo wouldn't have left him if she wanted to have a relationship with him, and now she was beginning to see why she had got away from him.

She felt tired and restless and wanted to go home to her own bed and pretend it had never happened. She didn't really care about what Jo would think but was more bothered about what Rob would think of her.

Her mouth was dry from drinking whisky. She couldn't imagine why she had because she didn't even like it. She'd had several cigarettes, although she'd given up months ago. She couldn't sleep and her pulse was racing from the whisky and adrenaline. Her mind was endlessly churning over thoughts about Jo, and Jack and what she was doing here, and what if someone found out?

It had all been so easy in a rush of passion, but what had possessed her? Now the passion had gone, it seemed completely crazy. He was a good lover, particularly considering he'd drunk the best part of a bottle of whisky. The second time she had revelled in it, wondering how Jo would feel if she knew her little sister was kissing and cuddling her ex-lover. But what was the point?

Rob was snoring on the other side of the bed and she couldn't make up her mind what to do. She picked her way in the dark over the piles of clothes, magazines and CD cases to the bathroom and went to the loo. She sat there shivering wondering if she should go home while it was dark and he was sleeping. The moon was bright enough for her to see where she was going as she picked her way into the kitchen. She poured herself a glass of water, taking care to be very quiet. The mess around the sink was even worse than when she'd turned up, as the dregs of their evening were added to it.

The gloating had gone now. In the cold semi-light of the kitchen the stark truth that she was not a very nice person hit her. It wasn't the best realisation to have at 3 o'clock in the morning in a freezing cold flat. All she ever seemed to be was a substitute for someone else. Maybe it was time to have her own man.

Surrounded by dirty plates and cups, and full ashtrays she resolved to finish with Jack. She needed someone who wanted to be with her.

Rob wouldn't wake up now - he was dead to the world. She crept about picking up a sock here, her pants there, trousers and T-shirt all thrown off in the heat of the moment. She retrieved her handbag and got dressed in the lounge.

Beth let herself quietly out of the flat door, walked downstairs and out through the front door into the street. The streetlights were still on, but all the houses were dark. It was a quiet residential street with only a few houses split into flats like Rob's. She was so relieved to climb into her car, even though she probably shouldn't be driving. The cold night was sobering, so she hoped for the best and drove home. She'd get at least three or four hours sleep before going to work, hopefully without a hangover, but the sense of shame might take longer to go.

Chapter 15

'I went to see Rasi today and I was really fed up, but when I came out I was high as a kite. I feel crazy – these incredible mood swings. One minute I feel as if the world is wonderful and then I'm completely down about it. And I love it here so why all this gloom?'

'I know what you mean, darling,' David said.

I'm shocked.

'Don't worry darling, I call everyone that.' He laughs, as usual.

There is only one other person out in our favourite spot of the garden, and he appears to be asleep. David looks over at him and continues.

'It's tough. I'll be honest with you. I nearly went off the rails the other week, but because we're stuck up a mountain I couldn't do it. I just felt desperate for some beer, or something and if I could have got down to Shimla that day I'd have had it. Don't tell Gemma.'

'Why?'

He looks away.

'Because she's so good. I don't want her knowing. I can't be as perfect as her. I'm more human. I wanted to go wild. I wanted to go out, get boozed up and have as many women as I could find.'

'In that order?'

'Well maybe have the women first. It tends to be more successful that way round, but it's not normally the way I did it!'

'Are you getting through this David?'

I sit up from my lounger and turn towards him. Without thinking I put my hand on his. Instantly he moves towards me. Why did I do that?

'Come here, Jo,' he whispers. I draw away from him taking back my hand.

'No David. I want to know. Are you getting through it OK? It's serious. If you think you were addicted, it's serious. Particularly if you've been feeling like this.'

'What choice have I got? My life doesn't work when I'm tanked up with booze and dope so what can I do? I can assure you if I was at home now though it wouldn't have lasted. I feel like I'm doing cold turkey. There's so much crap behind me.'

He turns away, towards the mountains.

'What do you mean?'

'My life. Things were very difficult at home. My Dad went off with the neighbour – the neighbour – can you imagine how clichéd that is? Mum was depressed and she didn't have any time for me. I was just left to my own devices.'

'And your brother?'

'He was too.'

'You had each other.'

'We didn't really have each other. Kids don't communicate like that. We just fought. I expect we just wanted our mother to take notice of us, but she couldn't. She was so depressed.'

'How is she now?'

'Ill. She's got multiple sclerosis. Her life has been a complete misery and I feel so bad about it.'

'That's tough,' I admit.

'What did I do for her? I just got into trouble at school all the time and as soon as I could get hold of booze I threw it down my neck and got drunk. I didn't give her any solace.'

David puts a hand up to his eye and wipes it.

'But you were a hurt kid. How could you?'

'If I hadn't been so selfish I could have done.'

'Don't be so hard on yourself, David. Maybe that's what it is. You give yourself such a hard time.'

100

I realise that's what Rasi says to me all the time. I'm taking it on.

'Someone has to. And it affects my relationships with women. I want to be nice to them, the way I wanted to be nice to my mother but I treat them like shit. I don't know why. I love women and they make me feel wonderful, but when they get too close I dump them. I don't even tell them. I just don't turn up. I'm a right bastard. Don't get too close to me.'

I take a long intake of air. Maybe my instinct about David is right.

'I do care about you David and I think you need some help. Would you go and talk to Rasi about this?'

'I might. If he can help. He probably doesn't understand stupid Welsh bastards like me. Coming from this culture, how would you? He's so sensible. I've never been sensible.'

'But that's what he's so good at – understanding other people. Please, do it for me.'

'I might if you do something for me.'

He looks at me like a faithful dog. Whatever is he going to ask me?

'Well, what exactly?'

'Forget it. I didn't mean it. You don't want to get close to me.'

He leaps up from his chair, picks up his clothes and slopes off. That isn't like the David I know. But maybe I don't really know him at all.

Chapter 16

Jasanghari feels like home to me. Sometimes at night I lie in bed revelling in my liberated state. Getting away from Rob was definitely the right thing to do even if the way of doing it wasn't good. He used to want to know my every thought and where I'd been whenever I wasn't with him. Now I can't really understand how I'd put up with his possessiveness for so long. He was so controlling.

Although Rob demanded so much from me he didn't want to truly understand me. And maybe I didn't want him to, so I kept him off the scent by telling him a lot about work.

Rasi seems to me like the perfect man, so caring and understanding. It is Rasi's job, but he wants to know what makes me tick. That is seductive.

'I now know that it was right to leave Rob,' I tell him one hot afternoon. 'I wasn't living my truth being with him. I was with him because I needed to be with someone, because he needed to be with me, because it was too difficult to break up with him, because I was getting older and felt worried that if I was alone I might never find anyone else. But it was wrong.'

'Listen to your body – you call it feelings in the..' He points to his stomach.

'Gut feelings.'

'It will tell you truth. Then you can live in truth. Just listen.'

He is so cool and calm and almost serene. I stretch out my bare legs in front of me, and immediately realise that it might look provocative. He notices, I know, but ultra-professional as he is, he passes it over.

'Of course I know that it's not right when you see your boyfriend picking up your phone and going through the messages.'

'He did?'

'Yes, I saw him several times. It made me want to deceive him and once I….'

Rasi waits for me to finish. I stop myself. I was just about to tell him how I went behind Rob's back and saw Matt briefly again but it feels all a bit too hard, too precious and painful even still. And I am so worried about what Rasi would think of me.

The horror of thinking I was pregnant and wondering if it was Matt and then finding out that I wasn't pregnant. I wasn't sure if I was happy or distraught but I was certainly confused. And then Matt did the dirty on me again, so why did I ever let myself go back to him?

Rob was getting desperately suspicious of me and I thought he was going to find out. He started snooping around even more. I even saw him once parked near my flat watching me. That was too much. I don't want to tell Rasi about this though. I couldn't bear him to think badly of me.

Rasi waves his hand and jolts me out of my reverie.

'When you ready.'

He has really dark eyebrows that meet in the middle making it just one eyebrow. His eyes are dark in true Asian style and he has high cheekbones which give him an elegant, almost ballet dancer type look. He has a perfectly formed mouth and I suddenly find myself wondering what he'd be like to kiss. I look up and his eyes are on me. Can he tell what I'm thinking? My face flushes painfully and I make a big show of looking at my watch, jump up and grab my small bag.

'It's 4. I'd better go. I am meeting the others and we've got lots to do today.'

I dash out of the room. What made me behave like that? As I hurtle down the corridor I crash into David who throws his arms around me.

'Not so fast. What's up with you? You look all hot and bothered.'

He is so obviously enjoying this little encounter.

'Nothing. Sorry I was in a hurry.'

'Reeeeeally? What have you been up to?'

He pulls me so close I think he's going to kiss me.

'Come on, Jo Jo, tell Uncle David.'

My face is even hotter now. I push him away with both hands.

'Nothing, what do you mean? Don't be silly.'

I give David a little punch and we amble down the stairs together. He keeps giving me a wistful look as if he wants more, but I've already decided that it is Gemma he is after.

Even though I don't want him for myself I don't really like the idea of Gemma and he being a couple. I know that I'd feel very left out and that it would change everything. I recognise how selfish it is, but in some ways I just want David to feel interested in me so that he doesn't go off with Gemma. That's not really fair on him though.

David tells me that Gemma is having a siesta in her room. How exactly does he know that? So we wander outside and grab two of the sun loungers and put them next to each other. I've got a very strong suspicion that he wants to get me on my own. And as it happens there's no-one else out in the sunbathing area.

There's always plenty to chat about with David and I close my eyes as the sun warms my body. Then my chair suddenly dips over to one side as David plonks down beside me.

He leans over me.

'Hey, what are you doing? You nearly tipped me over.'

I sit up and he seems awfully close.

'It's just you and me Jo. Can you think of something we could do together?'

He still has sunglasses on so I don't know where his eyes are looking, but I have a good idea. There's no doubting what he has in mind, and it's embarrassing. Maybe it's time for me to say something definite.

'Daaaavid,' I start.

'Yes, my dear.'

'I really like you.'

'Good, move over,' he says pushing me over and easing beside me.

'Careful. What are you doing?'

I sound a bit sharper than I meant.

'Sorry.'

He certainly isn't easily put off though. He slips his hand round the back of me and starts rubbing my back very gently. It feels really nice and I close my eyes. But I don't really want this to be happening. He is so close the next thing is he's going to kiss me if I don't say something, do something.

'Shall we go somewhere more private?' he whispers right in my ear.

I sit up and stand up.

'David this is so awkward for me. You know what I'm like, I don't easily say anything to upset anyone. I just, it's well, I really value our friendship and I care about you, but I don't want a relationship at all at present. I'm so sorry.'

His mouth drops and he looks downwards. His eyes are still not visible behind his sunglasses but his face is now expressionless.

I always seem to be hurting people these days.

'How do you know I want that anyway?'

'I could be completely wrong. I suppose but I just got that feeling. Sorry if I'm wrong.'

My face feels boiling hot now and I can feel the blood pumping through my neck.

'And have you got that feeling now?'

'I guess, yes.'

I'm beginning to wish I hadn't said anything. He is so determined. He takes my hands and pulls me close to him. I feel as if I've started to sweat, and I'm not even sure now if it's sheer embarrassment or desire. He puts his hand on my back moving it

105

slowly and seductively. He is still trying to win me over and now I feel as if he is almost succeeding.

He starts stroking my hair. I'm breathing fast, and he might get the wrong impression. Part of me is terrified that someone's going to find us.

'Of course I like you Jo, what man wouldn't? But how is a man supposed to know? I think we could be good together you and I.'

'But what about Gemma?'

My voice sounds weak and little.

'What about Gemma?'

'I thought you liked her.'

'I do.'

Perhaps he likes me more.

'I don't want to spoil a great friendship with you and make things messy. And you know I'm just getting over one relationship, and I really like you as a friend. It feels good having you as a friend.'

'And does this feel good?'

'Yes, no, well yes. Not now. David. No.'

'When Jo, when? I can't wait much longer.'

'David, don't count on me. Please don't. I don't know if I will ever change. I'm not ready at present, but I can't tell you that I will be ready in three months' time, or anything.'

'Darling, I can't wait three months, honest. In my opinion you are making a big mistake but if you're not going to succumb to my charms what can I do? Thousands of women would give their eye tooth.'

'I bet that's true. I know you're a great person, but I'd like to keep you as a friend.'

'A great person, eh?'

'Well yes. You know what I mean. This is very awkward.'

I stare at the ground and continue. My mouth is dry now.

'I don't know what to say. I am just trying to be my own person at present.'

'Don't worry love. I'm not like that awful boyfriend you left behind. Perhaps he's put you off men.'

'Maybe.'

David turns away from me.

'There's plenty more fish in the sea,' he says. He suddenly seems very interested in the stained glass window on the side of the palace.

'Yes there are. And she'll be a lucky girl! Another time, another place, but not now. I want your friendship, and if anything happened we might lose that.'

'You've made your point. OK. I understand.'

'And you're not offended.'

'Deeply wounded, Jo.'

At least he's smiling now.

'Don't flatter yourself too much,' he says in a slightly nasty way.

I put my hand on his arm. He shakes it off.

'Leave me alone woman. I don't want a relationship. You women, you come on so strong. You just want to have your evil way with me. I'm going in now anyway.'

He walks away quickly. It is hard to know how hurt he is or whether he is just so used to getting his own way with women. I did say no, which is a first for me, but it wasn't easy. Life in paradise is changing.

Chapter 17

It's like a big black cloud over me, and it is horribly familiar. Life seems unbearable. What am I doing here? Nothing is ever going to get better and now I've hurt my family and Rob. Poor Rob. Life is just a mess.

The sinking feeling in the pit of my stomach hurts, like it always does when things are bad. I feel completely empty. All that positive thought has gone now. This is how it really is. Life is miserable and anyone who believes it isn't, is kidding themselves.

It might be because I told David that I wanted to be just friends. Maybe I find it so difficult to speak my truth to people. When you've spent your life trying to please people, changing like this is tough. And, how can I possibly think that all I do is try and please people when I've probably broken Rob's heart? What a hard-faced bitch I am.

I don't want to have a relationship at the moment because quite honestly I don't trust myself. So if I had given in to David yesterday, I know that by tomorrow I'd have changed my mind. I'm not reliable, I can't trust me.

So as luck would have it the first person I see when I go into breakfast is David. I feel really bad about him, and yet I'm not sure what I've even done to feel bad.

I get my favourite breakfast and go and sit with him. It would be too ridiculous to sit somewhere else, as if I were making a big thing out of it.

He seems OK, unlike me.

'You don't seem your normal self,' he says.

I feel like I might burst into tears, which would be dreadful. He'd think it was to do with him and that really I wanted to have something going with him. I don't really feel like talking at all but I've got to make him realise it isn't to do with him. Well at least I don't think it is.

'I'm not, I suppose. It's nothing to do with now. It's to do with the past. Sometimes it's so difficult going over all this old stuff. I feel like I'd like to stop. Shouldn't we just live for now, instead of dredging up the past?'

'I know what you mean. I've had my fair share. I've only just realised what an addictive personality I am but finding out why is even harder. Is it worth it?'

Gemma joins us at the table while he's saying it.

'I think you have to have faith that it will be all right,' she says. 'If you're full of past baggage life grinds you down eventually. I'm sure it gets much worse for people older than us – you know you hear about mid-life crisis when people can't cope any more. Well if you consider they're hanging on to all this stuff from years ago and they've got marriage problems, been made redundant or whatever, how much worse it must be.'

'It's a valid argument,' David says, putting his hand on Gemma's shoulder. I feel a pang of what? Jealousy? Or, discomfort – is he trying to make me jealous?

'But it's effing difficult. I can see why some people just choose to drink themselves into oblivion,' he adds with a wry smile.

'David!' Gemma looks positively fierce.

A brief look of irritation spreads over his face, but quickly he brings back his smile.

'I know I'm being negative. It's so hard though. I hope I'll come through this. I want to enjoy my life, but sometimes it seems easier just to forget it all. Get me a bottle of whisky.'

'It may seem easier. I doubt it ends up easier,' I say. I'm almost pleased the conversation has switched to him as it's taken my thoughts off myself and all my self-pitying.

'I do agree with Gemma. I know deep down that this is good for me, but I don't like it either. You know what they say – no pain, no gain. I'm certainly hoping that it will help me to enjoy life, to find some kind of purpose but I think it's going to take a very long time. When I'm down I'm convinced that this is the real truth and happiness is just an illusion.'

109

'Well it is when you feel like that. It's only perception. If you feel that life is bad, then life is bad,' Gemma tells us. 'If, on the other hand, you feel it's positive and worthwhile then that's how it is. One person won't agree with the next person – it's so subjective isn't it?'

Gemma looks at us as if willing us to agree with her. Sometimes she seems just too perfect. She always has an answer for everything and she seems to be so sorted.

'So do you feel you've got it all together?' David's voice is tinged with sarcasm.

There's that slightly unpleasant side of him again, quickly followed by a smiling face.

'Don't be silly. Of course not. Does anyone? I'm just like you guys.'

Gemma holds her hands out to us.

'I just believe that the route to inner happiness is through yourself. Unless you've got it sorted out inside how can you ever make anyone else happy? Like your kids for one. Who wants to repeat the mistakes of their parents?'

'Kids. Oh no don't go there,' David chortles. 'I can't quite see myself being able to have kids. I'm too much of a kid myself.'

He flashes a genuine smile at each of us in turn. When he looks at me I can see the hurt in his eyes. He is doing a good job of covering over what happened yesterday, but I think I've hurt him.

'I feel the same. I don't know when I'll ever feel responsible enough to have children, although I am beginning to get that broody feeling.'

'You will Jo. You just need time,' Gemma says.

'And the right man,' David says and winks at me at the same time.

Gemma carries on,

'Don't believe that either. There isn't a right man. We are so brought up on all this guff about Prince Charming or Mr Right aren't we? They don't exist. Unless we are happy inside ourselves, who the hell is going to have the power to make us happy? If I can't make me happy, why should anyone else be able to do it?'

'But a good relationship makes you happy doesn't it?'

'Does it, Jo? Surely when you feel good about yourself you find a good relationship. That's more likely. All relationships can go wrong can't they? So even a good relationship needs hard work.'

'Why are you so smart, Gemma?' I ask and I mean it. 'Can I get that smart?'

'It takes years, and you can guarantee I'm not that good in relationships myself.'

Gemma glances at David and he gives her a knowing look. Perhaps I was right. Maybe it's not just me I can't trust.

Chapter 18

I'm deep in thought in the restaurant, sipping my aromatic jasmine tea. The others have gone to prepare for the big day and I'm gazing out of the window at the snow-capped mountains in the distance. It is all so beautiful at Jasanghari, will I ever want to go home again?

'Come on Jo,' David calls from the door. 'The room's filling up.'

I take my dirty plate to the stacking area, and wash my hands at the small basin in the corner of the restaurant. David is still waiting for me.

'I can't quite get what this mindfulness is about. Is it meditation or what is it?' I ask him.

'Well, you're about to find out,' he replies.

We run up the main stairs into a packed ballroom. David sits down on the floor next to Gemma and Toni so I join them.

Dee is today's speaker, and he's from Australia. He stands and talks for one hour without stopping, about what makes people tick and how it's possible to experience life on the highest level if you find out who you really are. It's captivating stuff.

'Think of one word that describes you.'

People put up their hands. 'Shy, miserable, self-effacing, unambitious, hopeless'. It certainly sorts out the confident ones.

Gemma says, 'Creative.'

I don't know what to say so I keep quiet. Dee looks around the room making eye contact with everyone in the way that these experienced speakers always do. I hope he doesn't pick me out.

He looks directly at me.

'How about you? What's your name?'

'Jo,' I mumble.

'Sorry, please speak up.'

'Jo,' I call a bit louder, going very red in the face.

'Hi Jo. How do you describe yourself?'

'Different.'

'And you really feel different don't you?'

Was that the wrong thing to say? I feel rather stupid.

'People have such low opinions of themselves and when they interact with other people, especially in personal relationships, their opinions get amplified. But instead of running themselves down, they pick partners who will do it for them.

'If someone has a problem with unexpressed anger, for example, they choose a partner who brings it out in them – a very angry person. Then they criticise the partner for being angry, because it is something they find difficult to face themselves.

'Blame is the biggest problem in relationships,' Dee explains. 'People always blame other people without looking at themselves. It is so much easier to keep blaming someone else – preferably your partner.

'Young children blame their mothers for everything, and somehow we never grow out of it. Unless people look at their own behaviour and bring everything back to themselves, they never move on. They just project the blame on to other people.

'We all think that we're different, like Jo.'

My heart starts pounding. I thought he'd finished with me. He looks directly at me again and some of the others turn around.

'But actually you know, we're not. We all have the same feelings inside and all we want is love. But, and it's a big but, we must all take responsibility for ourselves, our feelings and our actions.'

Dee looks around the room at everyone individually. We could have heard a pin drop, and I sense his powerful force is almost palpable.

'People always choose the relationship they need at the time, to help them work through the issues they need to deal with. Often their needs change and it is difficult for couples to keep their relationships alive unless they both move with it.'

Maybe I needed Rob at first, to get over the hurt of losing Matt, but I didn't any more. It was right to leave him and it was futile to feel guilty because it wasn't meant to be anyway. It's true though. I had done a lot of blaming. I need to take responsibility for choosing him and putting up with his behaviour. Nothing stopped me leaving – except myself. I can see it now.

'Twenty minutes' meditation is worth seven hours' sleep. Yes it's true. So if you meditate twice a day you're bound to feel energised. It's the word people don't like. Too many connotations of hippies and maharashis,' he laughs.

'But all it is really is relaxation. The benefits are amazing – meditation is known to lower blood pressure, and when a group meditates together it has been found to lower the blood pressure of a passer-by. Sure, it's true.

'Now we also learn mindfulness, and meditation is part of that. Mindfulness is not a complicated learning, it's simply being aware of everything you do and being in the moment. Meditation helps you to become more mindful, and the more you can be in the moment the more you can enjoy your life.

'We spend a lot of our time thinking about the past and worrying about things that have happened. But in addition we worry about the future and what is going to happen to us. By staying in the moment you can see that you'll avoid a lot of this worry which leads to anxiety, depression and behaviour that is not helpful.'

'So now a little exercise, which is to help you with your mindfulness. Please find three people – but not your friends, people you don't know.'

I look around the room and see two girls I've only ever seen around but haven't spoken to. There's a guy I smile at occasionally but we have never spoken and he turns to the three of us so we all sit together.

'Now I want one person at a time to speak for three minutes about yourself. The rest of you watch them without interrupting,

114

touching or even gesturing. The only interference you can make is when the three minutes are up and you indicate that to the speaker. Then the next person speaks, but no talking in between.'

We look around at each other and a Belgian girl, Elise, puts her hand up as she wants to go first. But she says nothing and then bursts into tears instead of talking. Finally she talks for about a minute before the time is up. The Canadian guy starts talking, but keeps hesitating. It's making me a bit nervous. They seem to find it so difficult so I want to be able to do this. I do want to speak.

'I knew I had to get away from home. I have been living a lie and been involved with someone I wanted to leave for a long time. I also wanted to get away from my family because I felt I needed something new, something different. I love it here. I've met some really good people here and at the moment this is where I want to be.'

I seem to waffle on for a while and then wonder if my three minutes is up. I am lost for words suddenly, so I tell them what I love about Jasanghari and the Himalayas. Then the guy taps his watch.

Tears roll down my face and the others smiled at me. I've no idea why I'm crying, but it feels like a relief.

When we've all spoken I sit back down again with David and Toni. Dee speaks.

'If you keep up regular meditation everyday you'll see that your mind becomes clearer, you'll feel happier, the memory improves and you are more peaceful. So if you haven't tried it yet, give it a go. The meditation encourages us to become more aware and mindful so it is an integral part of mindfulness. Now, we'll all do it together.'

I close my eyes, and try to concentrate, but it's not a good day for me. I keep thinking about Rob, my guilt and what I've done. I feel ashamed of myself coming away without telling anyone, and hurting them. They all thought I was such a goody-two-shoes and yet I've behaved like a reckless, thoughtless person.

When I hear a jingle of bells I come round again. I haven't been asleep but I went so far off in a dream that for a couple of seconds I don't even remember where I am. Maybe I am getting the hang of this meditation lark.

Chapter 19

Hannah waited until the children were in bed. She'd found it difficult to hold on so long. Every time Michael spoke to her she snapped at him. He seemed resigned to her moodiness. It wasn't exactly a surprise.

He was sitting at the table sipping a glass of red wine, when Hannah walked up beside him. She stood with both hands on hips. He watched and wondered what she was going to say.

'Why is it you have been seen at the park and in the library in the afternoon, when you said that you were out on site? What's going on?'

Michael looked right through her.

'What is it? Don't look like that. Tell me.'

'I haven't told you because I know how you will react, but I lost my job three weeks ago.'

'You what? So you've been pretending to go to work every day in your suit to sit in the park and the library. Why?'

'Because of you. I know what the money means to you and I didn't want to tell you.'

'Well presumably you've got a good pay off and you can get another job. You can ring up a headhunter can't you? Why have you wasted all this time? Don't you think you should do something about it?'

'I'm not sure if I want another job like that.'

Hannah lifted her right hand off her hips and wagged a finger at him.

'You what?' she shouted. 'You will get another job like that. How are we going to pay the school fees and the mortgage if you don't?'

'I suppose you couldn't think about earning some money could you?' he shouted.

'Maybe, just maybe Hannah you'll have to think again. Most of the population send their children to state schools. And why do we need such a big house? There's only four of us.'

'How can you think of taking them out of their schools? Whatever would people think?'

'I don't give a shit what people think,' he raised his voice. 'If you only send them to these schools to keep up with the Joneses then they can leave now. It's depressing enough being made redundant – and by the way there isn't much of a pay-off because the company lost a large contract and I've taken most of the flack for it.

'So before you think about how you are going to spend it you can think again. It's time that you thought about earning some money yourself.'

Michael stormed out of the kitchen, put on his shoes and went out of the front door. Hannah heard his engine start up. Charlotte appeared on the stairs looking worried.

'What's happening? Where's Dad gone? Why are you shouting at each other?'

'Go to bed. It's none of your business. Go and sleep. Your father's let us all down.'

'Is he all right Mum? Why's he gone out?'

'Ask him.'

Rotten little brat – she didn't need to know anything. Her mother was right about that. Why should children know? They don't understand anyway. It was her problem, not Charlotte's. Her world was shattered now.

She'd fight to keep her home and her children's schools. Michael would just have to be responsible. What did he mean he didn't know if he wanted another job like that? What the hell did he mean? She kicked a cupboard in the kitchen and hurt her foot.

She'd have to badger him. He could ring one of those headhunters tomorrow. He'd have to have a new job by the time the money ran out, or even better. If he got one beforehand they could still have the garden landscaped.

118

Chapter 20

When I sent my Dad the birthday message I wondered who I might hear from next. Part of me is terrified that I might get a furious email from Rob. At least no-one can find out exactly where I am, but when Jamil hands me an envelope I get butterflies in my stomach.

It's a print-out of an email, but I can't believe my eyes when I see it's from my brother Michael – the last person I expected to hear from.

Hi Jo,

I hope everything's fine. We gather you're in India and I don't want to make any great explanation but I wonder if I could come and visit you. I don't want to interfere with anything you're doing but I need to get away on my own. Please reply and give me some indication of whether this is OK and where I can contact you, how to get there, etc. etc. Is there anywhere near you where I could stay?

I'll reveal all when I arrive but I am coming for me, not for you. I don't want to persuade you to do anything. I need to get away badly. All the best, your favourite brother, Michael.

'Jesus.'

I notice Mira looking at me. I don't think she was there before.

'Bad news? You look shocked.'

'Yes. No, not bad news. Just shocking. It's OK.'

I'm breathing fast. What is Michael doing asking to come and see me? It never occurred to me that anyone would follow me out here, let alone him.

We're not at all close and I'm sure that I only know him because we share parents. I keep re-reading the comment about coming for himself and not for me. What a selfish and slightly odd thing to put. If the idea weren't bad enough, that comment makes it even worse.

How would he ever fit in here? The thought of how he'd react is so irritating. He'll be disapproving and unlikely to understand anything I'm doing or why I want to do it. It's like my freedom is going to be snatched away. I'll just say 'no', tell him it's inappropriate, inconvenient, there's no room. I can think of plenty of excuses.

My spirits have sunk. I got away from them but I can't run away forever. My whole family considers themselves first and me last so how can I change it? Rasi says it's because I consider myself last as well.

'As soon as you put yourself first and realise your own importance, they will too.'

With the email print-out in my hand I wander slowly back to my room oblivious of everything else. I've just got half an hour before my creative writing class. I lie on the bed and look out at the mountains, hoping that somehow I'll just know what to do.

I waver between guilt, knowing Michael's need must be great for him to consider coming, and resentment that he should turn to me. Why is it that I am the one everyone in the family turns to? Can't they leave me alone? I try to imagine what has gone so wrong that he wants to talk to me. He's never wanted to talk to me before.

He must have split up with Hannah. That was it. I don't like Hannah and never go out of my way to see them. The only reason to go to their house is to see the children, who, despite their parents, I adore.

So why can't Michael talk to Mum? After all, Michael is her favourite. The more I understand myself, the more I realise how unhappy she was, that she was unable for some reason to give me, maybe us, the attention I craved. Don't all kids want their parents' attention? I feel that it's got something to do with Dad, but I don't really know why or what. I think it is the marriage that has made her so unhappy.

There has always been so little love or affection between Mum and Dad, and it's odd I can get to 32 and I've not really thought about it before. I thought we were a pretty average family where there are disagreements and fall outs but maybe it was all to do with their relationship.

There was so much jealousy between Beth, Michael and me, yet they did nothing to dispel it. We all seem to have massive issues and none of us really feels good about ourselves, or so it seems. It is true what people say about unhappy marriages affecting the children sub-consciously. We are all screwed up.

It's becoming more obvious to me now why Michael married Hannah, why Beth is all over the place with men, and why I just can't or don't want to commit. All this mish mash of a childhood – which on the outside looks so good – is now haunting my dreams and my waking moments as it all churns around inside.

So frequently I have the same dream where I'm shouting at Dad because he is being horrible to me. In reality I've never argued with him at all, apart from the odd occasion when I was younger and wanted to stay out late, and he wouldn't let me. But in my dreams I feel this incredible hatred and when I wake up I feel so angry, hurt and confused.

This self-examination is showing me all the time that nothing is really as it seems. It's like having a good clear-out inside and replacing it all neatly. Here I am just getting to grips with the whole process, and my wonderful brother is going to come along and spoil it all.

I look at my watch. Ten minutes to go. I go down the back stairs to the room where my class will be held. I don't feel like talking to anyone else at present.

I sit down in my usual position and take out my papers and notebook. I may as well get on with my writing project. Anouk walks up to me.

'How's it going Jo? Do you need help?'

'I can't concentrate.'

'Why? Too hot for you?'

121

'No, just had some news.'

'What is it? Nobody die I hope?'

I didn't mean to tell him but he feels safe and neutral.

'No nothing like that. I have a brother who I don't get on with, we don't like each other much. He wants to come here to see me and talk to me. I don't want that.'

'Why you don't want?'

'I'm enjoying myself. I don't want him coming along and spoiling it.'

'You have work to do with this brother. It may be the best thing that you can do. Trust that it is for the best. It is you who needs to be able to handle your brother, not for you to stay away from him forever. It's your karma Jo.'

'I'm not exactly sure what you mean.'

'You come into life with your karma – the things you need to work out that are left over from previous life. You are working towards Nirvana, yes?'

'I suppose so, but I seem to have a long way to go.'

Anouk laughed.

'We all do. Everyone at their speed, Jo. Bring it into your writing.'

I keep thinking about what Anouk said. Perhaps it is meant to happen so I can sort out my relationship with at least one member of my family, and Michael is probably the most difficult of the lot. I'm not going to reply for a while though. I'll reflect on it.

Life at Jasanghari is so good most of the time, but what would Michael think about meditation or yoga? He'll think I've gone mad, and start lecturing me about leaving them all and going back and being responsible. And the likelihood of him joining in anything and actually letting go is slim. Oh God – I stamp my foot. Does he have to come?

Michael is such a stiff upper lip it's unbelievable. He can't express anything at all, so how would he take to the openness that people indulge in at Jasanghari? And wouldn't he shy away from any talk about his problem, whatever it is? When I was heartbroken, for some strange reason I told Michael how I felt about Matt, and he cut me dead.

Maybe, if I'm being generous, he didn't know how to handle it and he was embarrassed. We're not exactly close.

At lunchtime I walk out on to the terrace and find Gemma and David chatting. I sit down next to them and they both look at me, as if they expect me to say something so I do.

'I had a shock the other day.'

'Really? Tell us, do,' David says, all ears.

'My bloody brother – you know Michael.'

They both nod.

'He wants to come and visit me. Can you believe it?'

'Doesn't sound like his scene,' Gemma says. 'Why does he want to come?'

'No idea. Something's happened at home and he wants to come and talk to me. Hell, what a long way to come.'

'Intriguing. Perhaps his beautiful wife has run off with the milkman,' David laughs.

I look at what David's wearing. It's always a strange mix of clothes and today is no exception. He is in a smart short sleeved shirt, a pair of baggy shorts and a smart blue jacket. He actually looks like an overgrown school boy but I guess it's part of his charm and I'm getting used to it.

'If Michael comes he will just have to make an effort too, and not keep criticising. Of course he doesn't know what he's in for, because he has no idea where I am. Perhaps he is meant to come and get to know himself. What a thought!'

'Chill out baby,' David says, beaming all over his face. 'You'll know what the right thing to do is, but give it time.'

'I'd rather have you as a brother than Michael you know.'

'Oh don't turn me into family Jo. I'd much prefer us not to be related if you get my drift.'

I smile at him and check Gemma's face to see how she reacts to David's comment. She doesn't give anything away.

'Must be going. You coming, Gemma?' David says.

I close my eyes and sit back soaking up the sunshine.

My mind goes backwards. When I was involved with Matt the advertising agency we worked in was a really sociable place, with a lot of people, many of whom became good friends. Matt joined the agency after me and I noticed him straightaway. From the first day we met his eyes were on me whenever we were in the same place as each other. He was a great looking guy, he was fun and he was everyone's friend. He was so charismatic that people just wanted to spend time with him – girls and guys.

But there was the problem. He was so popular that all the girls liked him. Whenever I saw a girl leaning over his desk I felt jealous, even though he always noticed that I'd walked into the room.

'And how is Jo today?'

'Good.'

Often, the other girl looked miffed that his attention had moved away so quickly. He had barely been at the agency two weeks and we were dating. Then it became intense and we saw each other all the time. I was completely besotted and thought I'd met my dream man.

People started making comments at work and my boss even told me to be careful. They didn't understand, I thought. I was in seventh heaven.

Every time I saw him I'd get a frisson of excitement wherever we were. I used to think how lucky I was to have a man like him. The trouble was he was attractive to all the other girls in the agency and he was a big flirt. He didn't hide his relationship with me because he was hooked as well. He told me had never felt like this before and that he couldn't think about work all day because of me.

I suppose he was my first experience of falling in love, and I wanted to spend every moment with him. When I think of how I no longer had time for my friends, I feel ashamed. I wanted to be available all the time in case he called and initially I saw him almost all the time.

But now I realise that I didn't really trust him, and not being with him caused me great anxiety. I was unable to make plans in case he wanted to see me, and I even let down my parents one evening because I was expecting to see him.

'It's not right Jo,' Mum had told me. 'You're wasting your life mooning over a bloke.'

'Well what's wrong with that? I love him Mum.'

'But if you love someone shouldn't it be a bit more peaceful? Should you have to keep worrying where he is or who he's with?'

'You just don't understand. I love him and I want to marry him and I'm determined that's what I'm going to do.'

Mum shrugged. At least she tried to help me. Then Beth gave me the benefit of her advice.

'Why aren't you seeing Susie any more? And I saw Dave and Portia the other day and they said they hadn't seen you for ages. Is this is all because of Matt? Jo aren't you taking it a bit far? Is he as committed as you?'

I put this down to jealousy.

Even one or two of the other guys at work complained to me that I was no fun anymore since Romeo had come along.

I became consumed with insecurity which was awful. When he wasn't with me, I was worrying that he was with someone else, and at work I often saw a long-legged girl sitting on his desk far too close for comfort.

Sometimes I'd walk in and see a look of guilt flash across his face. Some of the girls gave me gloating looks, particularly Jane Reynolds.

One day a large group from the office were in the pub. Jane was busy holding court,

'I've got this brilliant new flat and it backs on to the new sports stadium.'

'What *the* new sports stadium?' Matt sounded interested.

Jane threw her head back and said seductively,

'Come round and see for yourself one evening.'

Matt had the grace to look embarrassed, laughed and took a sip of his beer. I didn't know where to look. But it wasn't just Jane. Whenever we went to parties, even my own friends' parties, I always found him talking to a girl on the other side of the room, and sometimes I was sure I saw him putting their numbers into his phone.

I was so in love that I decided to overlook it. The insecurity drove me to more and more passion and when we were on our own I was convinced again that it was all perfect. Matt was very affectionate and told me repeatedly,

'I've never felt like this before. I never want to let you go.'

Marnie, a friend at work, spoke to me one day,

'Do you know what Dan said to me the other day? I can't believe that an intelligent girl like Jo would moon around after someone like Matt. I thought she'd have done better for herself.'

I ignored all their comments and for two years the torrid relationship raged on until Marnie asked me out for a coffee.

'Sorry to be the one to tell you this, but I saw Matt out with a girl the other evening.'

'Maybe his sister.'

'I don't think so,' said Marnie. 'Brothers and sisters don't look at each other like that. I feel awful telling you this, but I'd feel even worse keeping it quiet. You're my friend and I don't want to see you mucked around by an arsehole like him.'

Something died inside me. I confronted Matt the next day. I asked him to go out to lunch from work and said,

'Someone saw you out with a girl. Are you seeing someone else?'

'Don't you trust me? Don't be stupid. I want you.'

'So who was it?'

'It's all too heavy with you. I can't cope.'

The hurt welled up inside and I began to cry in the middle of the restaurant. I knew I was bringing attention to myself but I couldn't help it.

'Please stop it Jo. People are looking. Christ, I bet you're not an angel are you? We're not married. For Christ's sake please. I'll stop seeing her. Believe me. It's you I want.'

And I believed him then and I believed him the next time, and the next time until something snapped. I became more and more sad and miserable, and one day my Dad asked me,

'Could life be worse without this bastard Jo?'

It took me ages to get over Matt and during that time I had a few boyfriends but I was never very enthusiastic about any of them. Rob was the one who saved me when I was still on the rebound.

Perhaps I hadn't really loved Matt. My own inability to commit had made me choose a man to love who was completely unable to be monogamous. All those protestations of love for him and really he was all part of the process of my own evolution.

What am I going to do about Michael?

Chapter 21

Bristol

The idea of going to Hannah and Michael's wasn't very appealing but Beth hadn't got an excuse to get out of it. It was her Dad's birthday and with Jo out of the way she ought to make an effort.

She drove up to Michael and Hannah's house and saw she was the first one there. As she knocked on the door she could hear some shouting in the house. When Hannah opened the door Beth stared at her. The normally immaculate little madam was looking very dishevelled, with bags under her eyes and no make-up on.

'Oh, hello Beth. You're early. Come in – the kids are around.'

She took the hint, not to go in the kitchen. Michael was sitting in the lounge reading the paper.

'Hi,' he said and stood up slowly as if he were an old man. He gave her a perfunctory kiss on the cheek, but he looked awful, as if the world were on his shoulders. Beth wished she wasn't there, or that at least her Mum and Dad would turn up.

'Do you want a drink?' Michael droned as if on auto-pilot.

'No don't worry. I'll find the kids.'

Stephen was upstairs on his Play Station.

He looked up at Beth but carried on playing. She felt insulted. Stephen and she used to have a good rapport.

'What's the game?' she asked him.

'Some new football one. It's cool.'

Charlotte came out of her room,

'Auntie Beth, it's a waste of time talking to him when he's on that thing. He can't hear you.'

'Not Auntie please – that went out years ago.'

'Well, Mummy always insists.'

'I don't. How are you?'

Charlotte seemed to have suddenly grown up. She had make up on, a short skirt and looked curvy.

'You're looking good Charlotte. Like the hair.'

Charlotte beamed. Praise from Beth was worth having.

'Good - do you? I'm fed up though.'

'Why boyfriend trouble?'

Charlotte looked awkward. Beth laughed and wished immediately she hadn't said it. Why couldn't she remember they don't talk about things like that at 12?

'It's them.'

'Who?' asked Beth.

'Mum and Dad of course.'

'Oh I thought something was up.'

'He went out the other night and didn't seem to come back. She's shouting at him all the time and he's being awful to everyone which is unusual. Usually it's Mum going on all the time but now he's doing it. I dropped some knives and forks when I was laying the table earlier and he hit the roof, "That's a really good dinner service. What are you doing? Have more respect".

'You know what I mean. Sick and tired of them being stressy.'

'I don't know what to say.'

Jo would have known what to say.

'Come out with me next weekend. We'll go to the cinema and have a burger or something.'

'Really? Thanks,' said Charlotte. 'What about Stephen?'

'Well I'll have to take him a different day won't I? Tell him that's what I'm doing so he doesn't feel left out. I could take him to the cinema some time.'

The doorbell rang and Charlotte ran downstairs with Beth close behind. Mark was standing on the doorstep looking like a lost sheep. Beth gave her dad a hug.

'Where's Mum?'

'I've no idea, dear,' said Mark. He kissed her on the cheek.

'I don't see her much these days. She gads about all the time and leaves me to my own devices.'

He was putting a brave face on, but Beth could see through it.

'This family,' Beth whinged.

'What?'

'Oh nothing. Oh Jesus, Dad, sorry Happy Birthday. I'll get your present. What did Mum give you?' she asked.

'Nothing. Do you have to swear like that?'

'Like what? Oh not Jesus. Jesus, Dad that's not swearing.'

'It's not very nice though.'

If only Jo were there, Beth found herself thinking again. She'd know what to do. Everyone seemed miserable and she wished she hadn't come.

They had drinks and it was almost one o'clock but Maggie still hadn't turned up.

'This meal will be done to a frazzle soon,' Hannah said storming out of the lounge to the kitchen.

Mark followed her, his arms wide open in a despairing way.

'Hannah, get on with it. I can't apologise for Maggie. I've no idea where she is. I never know where she is these days. Please get on with it.'

She smiled sweetly at him.

Beth called out.

'Can I help, Hannah?'

'Someone'd better,' said Hannah. 'Can you get the vegetables out and take them in?'

Beth got up and went into the kitchen. Jo could have smoothed things out, she thought.

Hannah picked up a pan which was belching out steam.

'Ouch. Oh hell,' she cried.

She put her hands up to her face. Beth had never seen her like this.

'Are you OK?' Beth asked.

'Can't you see I'm not? Of course not. And that sodding brother of yours.'

Charlotte ambled into the kitchen,

'Oh Mum isn't there any Coke?'

'Get out, Charlotte. You're more trouble than you're worth.'

Beth saw the look of hurt shoot across Charlotte's face and she smiled at her to alleviate the pain. What a bitch of a mother.

Back at the table Michael was slurring his words. He held up a spoonful of vegetables towards Beth, and dropped them on the table. Beth scooped them up so Hannah wouldn't notice.

'I seem to have taken Jo's place,' Beth thought.

The doorbell rang and Maggie waltzed in with no present and no birthday greetings. She breezed into the dining room, wearing a startling bright green pair of trousers and a matching jacket.

'Sorry I'm late. Have I missed lunch? Sorry I was in Wales and I was haring back but there was a jam on the motorway. So sorry. You can't imagine. I've had this really great weekend and I was so keen to get back in time. Have I held you up? I'm glad you've started. How is everyone? I've been to this fabulous place.'

Beth opened her mouth, partly shocked, but at the same time felt really grateful to her mother. Her non-stop babble and jollity broke up the ghastly atmosphere. Maggie kissed Stephen, Charlotte, Beth and Michael, left out Mark and sat down. Hannah walked in and glared at Maggie who didn't appear to notice.

'This lunch looks great,' Maggie said. 'It's really good of you Hannah. I'm sorry about being late but I've had a fantastic weekend. I was in this beautiful place in the Brecon Beacons. An old stately

131

home and now it's used for courses and workshops and the food's fantastic – all organic I think.'

Beth looked around the table. Michael was frowning at his mother as if he thought she'd flipped. Her dad was open-mouthed and staring at Maggie, while Hannah looked aggravated by all this cheerfulness as if she didn't trust it. Beth almost giggled. Her mum had woken them all up.

'You go for a walk there and you just feel completely at peace, and at one with nature. And we saw this incredible guy. He plays music and sings, and he gets you singing too. Can you imagine – me singing?'

'Singing?' Charlotte said. 'Is that what you were doing?'

'Well I was and I discovered I've got a beautiful voice.'

'Really Mum?' Beth laughed.

'What is she on?' Michael mumbled.

Hannah glared at Michael.

'Like mother, like son,' she said.

'Sorry Hannah?' Maggie asked pleasantly. 'How are you Charlotte and Stephen? What have you been doing lately Stephen?'

'I've got this new game and it's really cool. And last week I was in the 1st team at school and we won. I'm hoping to be playing at the academy next year.'

He glanced at his mother.

'What position do you play Stephen?' Maggie asked.

Beth couldn't believe it. Her mother never took any interest in football so how come she was asking all these technical questions? She sounded as if she was in love, yet she hadn't even greeted Mark or wished him happy birthday.

'I wish Auntie Jo was here. I really miss her.' Charlotte said.

'Yes well,' Michael said.

'I have to say,' Hannah said between mouthfuls. 'I feel that her behaviour is disgusting. Fancy going off like that without a word to anyone and letting everyone down.'

'I think it's great,' Maggie responded. 'I know we don't know where she is. But I don't have to worry about her. She's 32 and she's very sensible.'

Not like you Beth – that's what she'd say next. Beth prepared herself.

'Well I'm surprised at you Maggie,' Hannah whinged. 'It doesn't sound like you at all to just dismiss it like that. What's your view Mark?'

Hannah smiled at him. She could switch from venomous to sickly sweet in seconds.

'I would like to know where she is,' Mark responded. 'I'm a bit surprised that I haven't heard from her on my birthday. She's always so caring and thoughtful.'

Not now's she's not, Beth thought.

'So you thought,' Hannah said under her breath.

Mark ignored her.

'I think she'll be all right because she's got her head screwed on that girl,' Mark responded. 'I just hope she gets in touch soon. I do miss her.'

He looked down at his dinner. Beth felt sad for him, but angry with Jo again.

'I think it's a great opportunity to go off on your own,' Maggie said.

Mark choked on his dinner, Beth stared at her mum and Michael shook his head. Hannah opened her mouth to speak and thought better of it. Her pretty face was spoilt by the anger boiling inside.

Stephen wobbled his Coke around to make the bubbles fizz up, and in the process he knocked it over. A pool of Coke dispersed across the white tablecloth and dripped on to the floor.

133

'I told you not to drink that stuff,' Hannah roared at him. 'Now look at my lovely carpet. Get out of here.'

Stephen went bright red and ran upstairs. Charlotte went after him and Michael got a cloth and wiped up the Coke.

'Was that really necessary Hannah?' Maggie asked her. 'He's only a kid.'

'Yes it was. We can't afford Coke and they waste it.'

'What?' said Maggie and Beth in unison.

'You ask Michael. Go on tell them what's happened. Don't be a coward,' she almost screamed at him.

'You bitch,' Michael snarled.

Beth and Maggie both gasped.

Mark barked at Michael,

'Michael don't speak to her like that. What is the matter?'

Michael put his head in his hands. Maggie, Mark and Beth looked at him. Hannah was staring at nothing in particular, eyes wide open, but full of tears. Did she have to put up with this all the time? Hannah was bad enough, but Michael seemed to have become an ogre.

'I've lost my job,' Michael mumbled from behind his hands.

'Well that's not the end of the world,' Maggie said. 'Lots of people lose their jobs these days and often they find that it's better for them. They find something they really want to do. I thought you were fed up with what you were doing anyway. Perhaps you'll find something you really like – maybe teaching, darling.'

Mark was scrutinising Maggie. Had she had a brain transplant? She never normally said things like this.

'Teaching – are you seriously suggesting that he becomes a teacher?' Hannah said. 'How do you think that will pay the mortgage, the school fees, and our holidays?'

'Well move, find new schools, don't go to the Caribbean,' Maggie retorted but with no hint of nastiness. 'It's quite simple. Life

134

isn't all about money,' she continued in a calm matter of fact way. 'A lot of people have had to change their lifestyles lately.'

Beth winced, terrified what the response would be. Hannah got up from the table and stomped out of the room. At the door she turned on her heel and glared at Maggie,

'How would you know? You know nothing about life do you? Look at your marriage. What a sham.'

Even for Hannah this was incredibly harsh. Beth wanted a hole to open up in the ground and swallow her up. This was unbearable.

Her mother spoke,

'Hannah could you come and sit down please?' Maggie asked politely. 'I've got something to tell all of you now.'

There was something authoritative about the way she spoke, so much so that Hannah stopped in her tracks and moved tentatively back to her chair. Her face was wrought with anxiety. Mark was frowning as he watched Maggie, and he felt on edge. Whatever was coming next?

'I happen to know a lot about life actually,' Maggie said in a gentle voice. 'And I'm just about to find out some more. I'm going to Africa with VSO to work with families who are suffering from poverty and famine and kids whose parents have died from AIDs or been murdered.

'I don't know if any of you have any idea of the scale of this AIDs problem. In the next 20 years 65 million Africans will die of it, decimating whole countries.'

Mark sank his mouth into his open palm and gazed at the tablecloth. Michael frowned and said,

'What?'

'What about Dad?' Beth asked.

'What about Dad? Good question Beth.' Maggie sounded supremely confident, as if she'd rehearsed this speech and got it spot on.

'I'm sorry to disappoint all of you but I'm not considering Dad. Unfortunately for the past 30 years he hasn't considered me.'

'What do you mean Mum? That's outrageous!' Beth cried.

Her mum was going too far.

'What is going on with you?'

'It is not particularly outrageous. In fact it's time you knew something about your father,' Maggie said. She sounded like a nice, kind nurse who had to impart some bad news.

Mark's eyes were focused on the garden outside the window, as if he wasn't really listening. He was doing a good impression of being oblivious to it all, but Beth could see his leg jiggling up and down. She felt very uneasy.

'He'd never have the gumption to tell you himself, but he's been seeing another woman for 30 years.'

Mark's eyes flickered, he glanced at Maggie quickly and then back to the window. No-one spoke.

Hannah looked from Maggie to Mark and back again and whispered,

'Mark?'

Michael stood up and started clattering plates and cutlery to take out to the kitchen.

'You're joking.' Beth stared at her father her eyes ablaze. 'Is it true? Who is it?'

He looked at her sheepishly.

'Dad. Is it true?' Beth's voice had gone up several pitches.

Mark nodded slowly and he said,

'But I'm not seeing her now.'

'So fucking what? Who is it?' Beth almost screamed.

Michael, who had absented himself from the room with some dishes, walked in at that point and looked daggers at Beth.

'Not in front of the kids.'

'They're not here.'

Beth was staring at her father.

'Your aunt Judy,' Maggie said. She sipped her wine and assumed a laid back air.

Beth looked at her mother. Could this really be happening? Hannah had her hand in front of her mouth and kept looking from one to the other. Michael picked up yet another dish.

'Sit down Michael,' Hannah shot at him.

'I'm clearing up.'

'For God's sake, sit down, sit down. This is important.'

He took the dish into the kitchen. He might have been shocked, but thank goodness this conversation had distracted everyone from his unemployment status.

Beth bit her thumb so hard that it started to hurt. Everyone had gone quiet, and then Maggie said.

'At last it's out. I have lived with this for 30 years and all that time you all thought that I was the miserable one. I have protected your father by not telling you.'

'Why didn't you leave?' asked Hannah. Was that a hint of sympathy in her voice?

'I had three children and I didn't want to ruin their world.'

'But they left home years ago.'

'Quite frankly, Hannah. I didn't have the guts. I was a worn down, stupid woman, lacking confidence and believing that I couldn't live without my man. I'm pleased to say that I'm not like that now and I am so much happier. And I've got Jo to thank - it was her going that brought me to my senses.'

'Is this divorce then?' asked Beth with her thumb still in her mouth. She needed to bite it to keep the tears back.

'No. What's the point? I'm not getting married to anyone else. Unless you are?' she said looking at Mark. His face was white. He stammered,

'No. No. I don't want to.'

Beth got up. This had been the birthday from hell for her father. She had to get out and be alone. She helped Michael clear the table, ran upstairs and called to the children,

'Bye. Charlotte can we make it next weekend then?'

'You won't forget.'

'No of course not. Shall we say next Sunday?'

She called out thanks to Hannah, gave her mother a kiss and left. She ignored her father because she couldn't bring herself to look at him. Her head was buzzing and she wanted to cry, so she ran down the drive, into her car and drove crazily home, tears streaming down her face.

Chapter 22

In my dreams I was back at home. I look around my tiny little room and realise that I've grown to love it because it represents my new life. And, what's more Rob can't find me here, and nor can anyone else. And then it dawns on me – Michael wants to come. What should I do?

I roll over and hurl myself out of bed, pull the curtains and look outside. Another beautiful day in paradise.

The gardens of Jasanghari stretch down towards the tea plantation, and right near my part of the building is an ornate square-shaped Buddhist temple where we go and meditate if we want to, or listen to music and sometimes we even get together and sing in the evening.

I've seen new instruments that I've never heard before, such as the shruti – a sort of Indian accordion - and the sitar, and sometimes they play evocative western music like Jean Michel Jarre, Pink Floyd, Mike Oldfield's Tubular Bells and even Adele.

Tonight, Chris, an Australian musician, is going to show us the power of sound to heal, which I have to say is a completely new idea to me.

As the sun is going down we all gather at the temple and take our places. I feel quite nervous for some reason as I've never been able to sing.

'I used to feel so self-conscious when I sang at school,' I tell Gemma. 'We used to have to audition for the choir and I never felt as if I was up to it. They only put me in it when someone was ill.'

I laugh at the memory. How it can shape your life.

'Hi everybody,' Chris says to us all in an Australian drawl. The temple is packed now with everyone from Jasanghari including all the staff. He is an imposing man, quite large, with a big flowing red cotton shirt on. He smiles warmly to us all.

'First of all can you put up your hands if you think you're not good at singing.'

I shoot my hand up, Gemma didn't but more than half of us do. Chris laughs heartily.

'Everyone is born with a beautiful voice,' Chris tells us. 'Just open up your hearts and sing.'

So he makes us do some sequences, oohing and aahing which is quite amusing really, but then it blends into a song and all of sudden, rather miraculously, we sound like a choir as if we'd been singing together for years.

'Singing is both emotionally and physically healing,' he says. 'Finding your own voice is the most powerful thing you can do.'

I'm singing away without inhibitions and begin to understand what he's getting at. The sound we are generating seems to have a powerful energy and we all dance freely and sing our hearts out.

When we finish, I realise I haven't thought once about the impending prospect of Michael visiting.

In the restaurant afterwards we make some drinks.

'I've got to make a decision about Michael soon,' I say to Gemma and David.

'Or I'll bore you all to tears.'

'You already have,' David chuckles at his own joke.

'Jo it's not as if you've got to deal with him on your own. We can all help. I can have man to man chats with him and try and get him into what we're doing.'

'You don't know my brother. He's so rigid. He doesn't talk about anything on a deeper level and I think he'll be horrified about all this.'

'Then tell him about it here,' said David. 'If you tell him what you are doing and explain what Jasanghari is all about he can decide not to come, can't he? If he decides to come it will be up to him to make the best of it. He's not your responsibility, that's the thing to remember.'

'Thanks, David. That's good advice. You're getting wiser.'

David puts his hand on his chest and looks smugly at us.

'Let's see what we can do with him,' Gemma adds. 'Deep down he must be just like anyone else, and if he's got problems, which he presumably has, what better place to come to? And, don't forget, you can't really sort out your own baggage with your family if you want to leave some of them out of it. He might be part of your healing!'

I grimace at David, and then wonder if I should. After all they may be in a relationship, but Gemma is a bit of a smart-arse.

Back in my room I write out longhand the email for Michael. I tell him about the yoga, the Ayurvedic cookery classes, the singing, and the meditation. That must be enough to put him off. There's nothing in there that he'd even consider doing, so he'll probably change his mind.

And of course, there's always a chance that there might not be any room for him at Jasanghari, which I suppose I'm secretly hoping will be another let out clause for me. There isn't anywhere else to stay nearby, so that would put him off.

It seems that luck is not on my side, as I hear that an American guy has just left, vacating a single room. It seems to be waiting for Michael, so maybe I should try to adopt a more positive approach to him coming. After all, he might be a good test for me if I'm trying to make myself stand up to people in the family more. I could start with him. I feel cheerful for about two seconds and then my spirits sink again at the thought of him being here in my space.

Every day is full with writing, yoga, reading, cooking and water colours. I've wanted to pick up painting for a long time now and this seems like the perfect place with so many beautiful views to choose from. My yoga is coming along nicely and I can feel the difference in my body. I enjoy it more now than I ever did before as I feel that I'm doing it more naturally and not forcing myself.

Despite going to mindfulness classes my mind still seems to have trouble focusing at times, but they say we can't change instantly. The next thing I want to do is learn Sanskrit, in which apparently words not only have meaning, but their own vibration as well. There's so much to learn and I'm lapping it up.

And Rasi, of course, is helping me so much. I've uncovered more about myself than I knew even existed and at times I can feel a sense of peace, which I'm not sure I've ever experienced before.

'Everyone wants and needs to be loved and to love, Jo,' Rasi says to me. Often people forget about this.'

'At home they work and they drink lots of alcohol to make themselves forget.'

'What do they want to forget, Jo?'

'About being unhappy. So many people are unhappy. You know I felt so pressured to be in a relationship, to be married. That's all people ever want to know about you, apart from what you do – workwise. My sister was married for two years when she was 20 and I'm sure family and friends feel that's preferable to poor old me on the shelf.'

'On where?'

'The shelf. It means you're left on a shelf and no-one wants to look at you any more. You're discarded, rejected - you know what I mean?'

'Yes, but never you for sure?'

'I tell you that it was this pressure that kept me with Rob. I would never have married him or had his children, but at least I had somebody. It's hard when you get into your 30s. People are in couples and they expect you to be.

'My parents kept saying the biological clock was ticking. It would soon be too late for me to have babies.'

'I suppose it's true but you find timing,' Rasi says gently.

'The right timing, you mean.'

'Yes, the right timing. Maybe some people do not need children.'

'You try telling my parents, anyone's parents that. They seem to be obsessed by having grandchildren. At least my brother has produced two for them, but that doesn't seem to be enough. My mother is always saying, "People get selfish when they don't have children." I think she's having a dig at me. Sorry, you won't know what I mean. I mean that she's giving me a warning through her words.

'I know quite a few people who seem to get selfish when they do have kids, Rasi. I want children but only when the relationship is right. Maybe I feel that leaving it late is better than making a big mistake. There's always someone who tells you how hard it is to get pregnant after 30. Don't they know, that more and more women are leaving it late? And besides there are so many unwanted children in the world. It's good to be ready, isn't it?'

Rasi nods.

'And you never wanted to marry this Robert?' Rasi asks.

'No, but he wanted to. Rob didn't think it through. He wanted me because he wanted to be settled, so it made him feel better about himself. He wants or wanted me – he might not any more - because of his own insecurity, and that wasn't very appealing at all. I could have been anybody.

'I'd almost been in danger of considering marriage to suit other people. My mother has the knack of making me feel guilty. But I know, don't tell me.'

I wave my hand in the air so he doesn't tell me off about feeling guilty, and continue.

'No-one else has the power to make me feel anything, unless I let them. I know. I had this sort of instinct or intuition that it wouldn't be right. My sub-conscious mind always throws up dreams which kind of conveys messages to me. I remember having a dream about marrying Rob. I was walking down the aisle – you know in the church, wearing a big white meringue. That's what we call those big white dresses that women at home wear when they get married. I wave my arms around to show him the shape of a big dress.

'I was thinking, "I don't want to do this. Why am I doing it?" I woke up sweating – all soaked in sweat. You know, all soaking wet? And I vowed to myself I would never marry him. At least I was being true to myself.'

'You be true to yourself. You are beautiful to look, and beautiful inside.'

My insides melt. I could kiss him, but I can't.

Chapter 23

This is the worst row I've ever had with anyone in my whole life. I'm screaming at the top of my voice and Michael's head disintegrates and he turns into an evil looking Indian man. I start to run away, but fall down a hole.

I wake up with a start. My heart is pounding, so I lie still for a while panting. This series of nightmares is going on and on and now they are all about Michael. I'm not sure I've ever even dreamt about him before.

Today is the day. I suggested he fly to Delhi, stay the night and book into the Marriott. I recommended the early train on Tuesday to Kalka, changing there for Shimla and I'd be at the station to meet him. Now I feel a bit sorry for him because he is going to get such a shock when he gets here. One minute I feel sympathy and then the next I have feelings of dread. If I hear one word of complaint from him I'll be giving him his marching orders.

If something goes wrong with his journey and he isn't going to arrive (wishful thinking), I told Michael he should ring the office in Shimla where emails are sent and leave a message for me.

The drive down to Shimla takes about 40 minutes and I sit up at the front of the truck with Sahib driving.

'I'm not looking forward to this – I don't want my brother to come. He is really different from me.'

'It will be fine. You see,' he says and laughs loudly.

I shake my head and screw up my face.

'No. Sahib, no.'

We park near the office in Shimla to see if there is a message from him. No such luck. We amble round to the station to wait for the train. The platform is buzzing with the usual gaggle of people hoping to sell food and offer newcomers somewhere to stay or wanting to carry their bags.

I'm pacing up and down and Sahib smiles at me, seeing how apprehensive I am.

'It helps to calm me down.'

It's a hot day, but not boiling, not like Delhi. The train appears in the distance and slowly draws into the station. Hordes of people get off the train and I look up and down the platform among them all. I see a man wearing a pair of cream trousers and a smart jacket with an open-necked shirt. I haven't seen anyone dressed like that since I left home. Michael walks up to me, looking stern.

'Hi,' he says and gives me a perfunctory kiss on the cheek.

'Jo, I don't recognise you. What are you wearing?' he sneers.

Instant irritation.

'Oh well,' I say, 'We don't dress up here. You might need to loosen up a bit.' Not just with his clothes.

Michael has had the same little boy's haircut for as long as I can remember. His hair is a sort of sandy light brown colour but it is dead straight and his fringe is always very precisely cut straight across, and covers most of his forehead.

If his hair looks exactly the same his face has changed a lot over the years. He is four years older than me but his eyes have big bags under them and plenty of crows' feet. His fringe can't disguise the frown underneath, and his face is devoid of smiles.

Sahib shakes Michael's hand and takes his case. The three of us walk up the road back to the truck. It feels surreal having him here, as if it's another dream, but I don't think it is. He seems such a misery.

'How was the journey? Did you stay in a good hotel?' I ask.

'Bit of a dive really. I had a look round Delhi last night but boy was it hot.'

'Didn't you stay in the Marriot or somewhere similar?'

'No - decided not to spend the money.'

Tight as usual.

'It's not as hot here as you can tell. In fact it's a perfect temperature. It's a wonderful place.'

'Well, where are we going exactly?' He looks at me with a serious face but a hint of anxiety.

'I am staying at the Jasanghari Centre with another 100 or so people. It's very different and what you would probably describe as alternative. We do a lot of interesting things. I think I mentioned them. I don't know if you'll like it.'

I gasp in some air.

'I wanted to get away. It doesn't matter if I like it. Where will I stay?'

'There's a room for you – it's very reasonable – about £100 a week. Is that OK?'

'A lot cheaper than the UK. Do you get en-suite with that?'

I giggle.

Sahib asks,

'What is on sweet?'

'It means that you have your own bathroom and toilet.'

Sahib and I laugh again. Michael screws up his face and looks put out.

'This is India, Michael. I have a lovely little room but the showers are along the corridor. The toilets are OK but none of the rooms have them in. It's not a hotel and it's basic, but to me it's like home.'

'OK,' he looks narked. He must hate us laughing at him.

'I'll go along with it. I just need a break.'

'Why?' I ask.

'I'll tell you later. Perhaps we can go out to dinner?'

'Nowhere to go. We eat at the centre. The food's great but there are always people around. We can go for a walk after dinner. Are you jet-lagged?'

'I feel pretty tired. It's everything – the flight, the climate and getting away. Things aren't easy at home.'

'I'll give you some aromatherapy oils and you can go and soak in the big bath they've got down by the relaxation room.'

He shakes his head repeatedly. I could hit him.

'Here's the limousine!'

Michael looks at the truck, and around the street and sighs. He opens the door.

'You sit in the middle,' he instructs me.

Sahib puts Michael's bag in the back.

'Thanks Sahib,' I say.

'Oh yes, thank you Sar Heeb,' Michael adds.

Twenty minutes later Michael's head starts lolling all over the place as he falls asleep. Every now and then there is a snort, leaving Sahib and I trying to stifle our giggles.

Michael felt the need to sleep, to get out of the situation. He felt disorientated at finding himself somewhere completely alien. What had he got himself into and why had he come? Jo was being defensive and looked weird – like some hippie, although he had to admit she still looked quite beautiful in a natural kind of way.

Leaving home had been awful. Hannah didn't speak to him and didn't even take him to the airport. The children didn't want him to go but while Charlotte went on about it, little Stephen just looked dejected. Michael knew that it was grim to leave him behind with Hannah because she had no time for young boys.

He promised the children that he would ring regularly, that it was necessary to go away, and that he had to sort out some things to do with work. They were obviously aware of the atmosphere but he didn't want to spell it out. He didn't know himself what would happen.

Already he was missing his children. It was surprising how he took everyone for granted when they were there all the time, but now that he didn't have the familiarity of their voices or of knowing that they would be sleeping in the same house, he felt lost.

Splitting up would be a desperate step but was it doing the children any good having parents in such a loveless marriage? He and Hannah hadn't been getting on well for a long time. All marriages went through difficult times, but many of them ended in divorce. Without his job he was no use to Hannah.

Delhi had been quite a shock. Everything looked so different he couldn't take it all in, and the heat was overwhelming. Exhausted from the journey, but wound up and nervous prevented him getting a decent night's sleep. His stomach was playing up so he didn't eat much. Now all he wanted was a meal, a bath and a good night's sleep.

He couldn't face chatting to Jo in the van, so he shut his eyes. She was talking non-stop to the driver and he didn't want to join in. His decision to come seemed crazy now. What did he and Jo have in common even when she was normal?

At home she was too open and honest for his liking. Now she seemed even worse. He didn't know himself most of the time, so how could he explain to anyone else how he felt? He was scared she'd start probing, so he had to keep her at bay.

When he opened his eyes he saw mountains all around, which was very scenic but cut off from the rest of the world. The driver was indicating left and they turned into a drive. At the end was a large palace.

'Is this it then?' he asks me. His enthusiasm is underwhelming.

'Yes, this is Jasanghari.'

I watch his face. No hint of surprise or pleasure.

'It's different,' he mumbles and I can feel my hackles rising.

Sahib carries Michael's bag and I lead him into the reception hall, but it's empty. I can see the way he's looking around and I must admit that it's gaudy at first sight, but I'm used to it now and I love everything about this place.

149

'I know where your room is. I'll take you. Sahib thanks a lot. I'll take Michael's bag.'

'Do I tip him?' Michael mutters to me.

Again I'm irritated.

'No, it's not like that here. Follow me.'

We walk down a long corridor. It is eerily quiet. I am so relieved that the only room available is on the floor below me. I don't want him near me, prying into my business and knowing what I'm doing. Even if I'm not exactly up to much, it's a matter of principle.

'This is your room. Not exactly luxurious but adequate.'

I open the door and watch his face. Like all the rooms there's a small single bed with a white cover over it, a tiny chest of drawers, a small bedside table and a chair.

'Couldn't swing a cat around in here,' he grumbles.

'Why would anyone want to? And besides the only cats up here are fierce.'

I know I sound sarcastic and ratty, but that's just the way he gets to me.

'Just an expression. Where's the bathroom?'

'It's down here. Not too far.'

He has the cheek to roll his eyes because it's not next door to him. We walk down the corridor and I show him a toilet and next door to it a small shower room. He looks in, and makes faces when he sees the very basic shower coming down from the ceiling.

'Hmm,' he mutters. Of course, his bathroom at home is a tribute to modern technology, but he'll just have to get used to it.

Back in his room, he checks his mobile phone.

'Isn't there a signal here?'

'What do you think? We are halfway up a mountain. No, and there's no wi-fi either. I told you it was remote.'

He tuts and starts taking the clothes out of his case and laying them on the bed. I can see straightaway that what he's brought is completely inappropriate for here. Smart clothes that he will never wear. He pulls open a drawer but it gets stuck so he's tutting away and forces it, nearly breaking it. He then inspects it to see if it it's clean, brushing his fingers and looking at them. I know it will be clean, but everything he does grates on me.

'God knows what Hannah would think of this,' he muses.

'Well, perhaps it's a good thing she's not coming,' I can't resist saying.

'Do you want some time to relax?' I ask in hope.

'Yes, yes I do. What time is dinner?'

'I'll come and get you in about an hour and a half. Just wear something casual, and I mean casual. No jacket or shirt.'

Again I can see this look of disbelief and shock on his face and I feel so annoyed with him that already I'm on the brink of losing my temper with him. And that's me who doesn't really ever get that angry with anyone.

Chapter 24

I can feel resentment building inside me that Michael has come along and is ruining my experience. But even worse than his presence is the fact that he keeps running down Jasanghari and the people I care about.

It is three days since he arrived and he hasn't given any explanation as to why he is here. He keeps sleeping, he won't join in with anything, and he makes sarcastic comments all the time. I feel like screaming at him – like my dream is going to come true. And on top of all that I feel responsible for him – embarrassed about his behaviour in front of everyone and concerned that they must be cringing inside. Why on earth do I have to care?

We go for a walk around the grounds on a bright sunny afternoon. The sky is azure blue with just a couple of clouds and the sun reflects on the snow at the top of the mountains. The perfect place to be, without Michael here ruining everything.

'What the hell are you doing here?' he whines at me. 'This isn't the real world Jo. Are you kidding yourself? Are you becoming some sort of hippie recluse? These people are all a load of morons who don't know what it's like to have responsibilities and live a normal life.'

I'm firing up inside and going red. Everything he says I take personally and all I want to hear from him is that he's had enough and he's leaving. I've got to speak up. I can't keep all this inside like I've been doing for my whole life.

'These people are my friends,' I say firmly, for me.

'If you don't like it you know what you can do. You can make arrangements and go home again. Really, Michael I told you what it was like.'

He looks a bit taken aback. He doesn't expect me to say things like this. When he sits there with my friends, who he then has the gall to criticise, I just think, 'What is he doing here?' We have never mixed socially so I've never ever had to experience him being with my friends. Now, in the most wonderful place I've ever been, I've got to put up with him being here. How dare he interfere in my life?

Later that day we're all sitting at a table on the terrace sipping tea. David and Gemma are discussing relationships in a philosophical way, which is strange in itself because I'm not quite sure whether they have become an item.

Michael pipes up,

'Has Jo told you what a disaster she is in relationships? About that Rob and how useless he is?'

He sniggers, looking pleased with himself for the first time since he's arrived. I can't believe that his first contribution to the group is a dig at me. I can feel my eyes filling with tears.

David glances at me, Gemma studies Michael and no-one speaks or laughs, which I'm grateful for. My face feels hot and I'm staring at Michael with venom.

'If we are talking about relationships,' I jibe back at him, 'I think you're the last one to talk. Your wife is the snobbiest most unreal person I have ever met.'

I can't believe I've said that.

'Hey you two cut it out,' says David. 'It's not the time or place to have a spat like this and you're hurting each other.'

I get up from the table muttering.

'I've had it with him. I was having the time of my life before you arrived, Michael, and now it's completely spoilt.'

I pick up my dirty plate, take it back to the clean-up area, and stomp out. I'm crying. What sort of person is he making me into? Now everyone will think I'm a bitch. I run down the terrace steps into the woods and when I'm completely out of view, I drop myself down on the ground in a clearing surrounded by trees and bushes. What is it about my family? How could they get to me so much? The tears roll down my face and I sob.

153

Michael felt really stupid. This was the second time in two weeks that a woman had walked out on him. He stayed sitting at the table. When there was a lull in the conversation he said,

'Sorry, everyone. I guess it's me. I'm a bit stressy.'

'Why don't you walk into the village with me? We can go and have something exciting like a buttermilk,' David said. 'I don't think we can get much alcohol round here, and besides I've not touched a drop for weeks now and it's doing me some good.'

'I could do with a stiff drink quite frankly,' Michael said in a hushed tone.

He looked at Gemma out of the corner of his eye. She was wearing all white – cut off trousers, a white cap and a white T-shirt. Why couldn't she have suggested taking him for a walk? She seemed to have a way of making him feel good when she spoke to him.

He turned to David,

'When were you thinking of?'

'Well, now is a good time. We can walk there and be back before supper time.'

'OK, let's go,' Michael responded.

They navigated the unmade track moving to the side whenever trucks went by. A bus came hurtling round the corner, making dust fly up into their faces.

Michael shielded his face.

'I wouldn't like to be on that bus on these windy roads. It's a sheer drop over there. It's like the end of the earth here,' he said grumpily.

'It's miles from anywhere, here – that's why I like it,' David responded. 'I was used to the bustle of London and you couldn't imagine anything more peaceful than this.'

'What were you doing in London?'

'I was in advertising. It's a great business to be in if you fancy boozing all the time and socialising. I was always the one who went out meeting people and bringing in new business. Work and play if you know what I mean.'

'Can't say I do really. I've never mixed the two. Nice women, I bet.'

'Hundreds of them mate. They always want the lookers in advertising, kind of sells the idea if you know what I mean.'

'What did you actually do?'

'A bit of everything. I was an account executive, but I've got an arty background too so sometimes I'd be involved with design.'

They turned the corner and Michael could see a few ramshackle houses and a number of people milling around.

'This is it,' David announced. 'Our local village – Kechepur.'

On the left as far as the eye could see were mountains while the village appeared to be formed out of rock. As they walked down the street Michael noticed that the back walls of the shops and eating houses were hewn out of the mountain which sheered up above them.

He read the sign,

'Kechepur, 1,900 metres. That's higher than many of the ski-ing resorts we've been to. Why don't people ski here?'

'They do in winter, but there aren't any ski lifts. Mind you, it's so cheap compared with Europe. Bit basic – the accommodation, but one day it'll be your Val d'Isere.'

They passed a set of gargoyles spouting water.

'Want a drink mate?'

'Is it safe?'

'Of course, it's only water from the mountains. Not that tainted stuff you get back home. The water we get at Jasanghari comes from up here. The traditional thing is to take off your clothes and dart underneath the different gargoyles. Are you game?'

'Hardly think so, thanks.'

155

David looked at him. He was a tough nut to crack and so tightly held in. They cupped their hands and drank the water.

'Mighty cold even though it's summer. It never gets warm because it comes from way up there.'

They walked on up the street past the stalls with smoke burning where they were cooking a variety of meats and local vegetables. David walked into what appeared to be a place you could buy drinks in.

'I'm going for the lassi – it's a kind of yoghurt drink, a bit like a smoothie. What will you have Michael?'

'I just want tea.'

'Chai please,' David ordered. 'I'll get these,' he said reaching into his pocket and taking out a few coins.

'Are you sure?'

'If I tell you that the cost of these drinks is less than we have currency for back home, you'll not ask me if I'm sure.'

'Thanks.'

They sat down on wooden benches at makeshift tables made of stone.

When Michael's drink arrived it was in a kind of earthenware pot. He took a sip and nearly spat it out.

'My God, it's sweet.'

'Perhaps I should have warned you. They make them very syrupy here – you can't tell the difference between coffee and tea.'

The girl in the café was laughing at him. Michael frowned.

'Bloody hell.'

'Lighten up Michael. It's not a big deal. Have something different.'

'Sorry. Don't mind me. I'm a grumpy old man before I even get there. I shouldn't have said that about Jo. I am feeling very bad about relationships at present. And I wasn't sure if you and she were…'

156

David looked wistful.

'Well not yet. She's a lovely girl.'

'I'm afraid I find it difficult to appreciate anyone much apart from my own children. I'm missing them like hell and I'm finding it hard. Jo doesn't have a clue what it's like. She's never had children and who knows if she ever will.'

'I think,' said David, 'That Jo understands quite a lot of things now. We've learnt a lot since we've been here. I was very mixed up when I arrived - I used to drink too much, and then I started dabbling with drugs. I realised I could throw away my life if I wasn't careful. I lost the best woman I ever had through my behaviour and my life seemed completely pointless.'

'Drugs, Christ. I've never known anyone who did anything like that.'

'You probably do but you aren't aware of it. A lot of it goes on these days, particularly in business.'

'Why did you come here?'

'I read about it online and I knew I needed something. This has been amazing for me. I've learnt so much about me – do you know what I mean? Us men aren't too good with feelings and all that stuff. We seem to think we're too macho to have them but we do.'

'So I'm discovering. I only feel strongly about my children, and I don't appreciate them all the time. They get on your nerves when you're round them all the time. But now I'm away from them I just ache for them, and I'm going over and over in my mind what to do about them.'

'What do you mean?'

'Nothing. No sorry I shouldn't be talking like this.'

'It is helpful to talk. That's another thing I used not to do. I couldn't talk about myself at all. I have always been a bit of a joker and I found it easier to keep on telling jokes so that I could ignore what was going on for me deep down. But now I feel OK with talking about myself and how I feel. It takes time though.'

157

Michael didn't say anything. His feelings of longing were so unbearable. He had never felt this bad before, but he didn't want to talk to David about it. He wouldn't understand.

He leant forward leaning on his right hand, shoulders hunched, his left elbow resting on the wall made of rock beside him. David looked at him out of the corner of his eye. He looked such a misery, but he did feel sorry for him.

Close to the café a huge cow-like animal with horns was sitting in the road as if it didn't belong to anyone. People were bustling about and the stalls were busy with customers.

'It is probably the most beautiful place any of us will ever see,' David said. 'So make the most of it mate.'

'Yes it's different,' Michael grudgingly agreed.

Tell me about you – what do you do?'

'It's pretty boring really. I'm an engineering consultant.'

'Yeah, what exactly do you do though?'

'I'm involved with projects like bridge building or tunnels like the Eurotunnel, but that was before my time.'

He said no more. He didn't even have a job now and he couldn't tell David.

'Before I came here I went round India,' David said. 'It opens your eyes you know when you see all these different places. It makes you realise how lucky we are, and we seem to make a mess of it all. Some of these people don't have any money, no social security. They have to manage, just beg and they are exploited and ill-treated all the time. Yet, they are so cheerful. It defies belief.'

Michael nodded as if he wasn't particularly engaged with the conversation.

'So many Indians have got nothing, and I'm sure they're happier than we are. It's all this material stuff that we think we need. It doesn't do us any good.'

'I know what you mean, but it's different at home.'

'I think that everyone should travel to get a better perspective on life. When we're complaining about some incidental thing that really doesn't matter, these people are often trying to put a meal on the table. Us and our first world problems.'

'You're probably right.'

David rambled on about his travels but Michael was miles away. What a failure he was with his marriage in ruins and no job to go back to. He was petrified all of Jo's friends would find out and then they would all know that he was a failure too.

'Shall we go mate?'

Michael wasn't used to be called mate, but it was quite nice.

'Is there anywhere at all that I can phone home? My mobile won't work.'

'There's no signal up here, whichever network you're on. We can ask over there – it's a kind of post office place.'

They knocked on the door of a most unlikely looking shop. It was really like an outside shop and Michael doubted they had a phone.

'Is there any chance you have a telephone – for England?'

'Yes, of course, yes. It take long time but yes.'

'Why don't you go back David? I can find my way back and I'll stay here and wait. It might be a long one.'

'Yes, if you get through at all. I spent about an hour getting through to home one day in another place and got cut off after five minutes.'

'It is worth trying though. See you later.'

Michael didn't want David listening to him while he spoke to Hannah and his children. He didn't know what response he was going to get.

He gave the man a number and twiddled his thumbs for about half an hour, getting more and more anxious. Then a voice called out,

'We have it.'

Charlotte's voice came over the line.

'Hi Dad. What are you doing? Are you having a nice time? I really miss you. It's really crackly isn't it?'

'How's school, Charlie?'

'Boring as ever. But this weekend I'm going to a disco in aid of Laura's birthday. It's going to be incredible and I'm getting some new clothes. I can't wait. Love you Dad. Stephen, Stephen – it's Dad.'

'Hello.' Stephen's voice was much less enthusiastic.

'How's school? Have you played any football?'

'No-one saw me scoring a goal,' he complained. 'You weren't there.'

'I'll be back soon I promise.' Michael got a huge lump in his throat and found it hard to speak.

'I love you very much. Please don't ever forget that.'

'When are you coming back?'

'Very soon. Goodbye.'

Before going back to the truck he walked down the road to recover. He sat on a stone wall and put his head in his hands. The tears came. This was the first time he could remember crying since he was 14. He hoped no-one would notice.

When he looked up again a group of local women were watching him and gossiping about him to each other. One walked over and put her hand on the top of his back.

She closed her eyes and gestured to him to do the same.

She just stood there with her hand on his back. He began to feel all hot around the back of his neck and thought he was going to cry again. He covered his face with his hands. She took away her hand and Michael looked at her. She was moving her head from side to side and staring into his eyes. It was as if she could read him.

Her face was full of concern and sympathy. He put his hands into prayer position like he'd seen other people do and slightly bowed to her. It was the only way he could thank her.

He got up, smiled at her and walked off in the direction of Jasanghari. Perhaps he shouldn't have been so hasty coming out here. To add to all his other problems he was now going through the overwhelming pain of missing the children. And if they split up, would it be like this?

Chapter 25

The idea of yoga was anathema to Michael and he felt uncomfortable about all this talk of meditation and mindfulness. None of it sounded as if it would sit very easily in the Christian faith, if he honestly had one. In truth, he only went to church because Hannah had insisted on the family going and because of her own upbringing. He never dared question his feelings, but he didn't think he'd got it somehow.

He was pleasantly surprised to wake up feeling a bit more cheerful. David had been so kind, and made him feel more accepted. Up until then he felt he was intruding on Jo's domain and that she wasn't very pleased about it. He didn't fit in, but now he had a friend of sorts.

He opened the curtains and for the first time he looked at the view. You could pay a fortune for a view like this and he'd not even noticed it until now. The mountains in the background, the pines, the brightly coloured birds and flowers everywhere. How come he hadn't seen it before?

He got dressed quickly in some casual jeans and a T-shirt and walked into the main hall. He scrutinised the noticeboard. He read that someone known as Sare Burgess was visiting and running a workshop called 'Who are you?'. Good point, he thought. Now he had no job and maybe no wife, who was he?

Michael waited until the last moment, and sneaked into the back of the room. He saw Jo near the front, well away from him. He could hide at the back and she wouldn't even know he was there.

He had never heard anyone speak like Sare before. It was all sensible stuff that she was saying but he felt really emotional and was biting his lip. He mustn't let go.

'Everyone puts up a shield in front of them – it's our defence to hide our feelings, our vulnerability,' Sare said. She had a commanding voice, but it was evident that what she was saying came from the heart.

'Unless we put down our shield we can never deal with the emotions hidden behind it. They will fester there for the rest of our lives, unresolved and making us deeply unhappy.'

He started to sweat and feel dizzy. It was all too much for him. This was too much. He was in the middle of a row and if he tried to get out, he'd bring attention to himself. He was looking all around, wondering what to do.

'Is there something the matter?' a voice said.

He waited for someone to reply. No-one did.

'You I mean you.'

He looked up at the front of the room and saw she was looking in his direction. He turned round to see who it was she was talking to, and slowly realised to his horror that she was looking at him. His armpits felt soggy, his face was boiling hot and he suddenly felt as if he weren't there at all.

He spoke, but it sounded like another person's voice, removed from him.

'Me, I'm fine.'

'You're fine,' she said. 'Are you sure?'

'Yes, no.'

'Would you like to come up and talk about it?'

His stomach turned over – he'd have to leave. He was going to have diarrhoea. Everyone was smiling encouragingly and they made a space for him to get through.

'Come on,' she called.

She was looking at him smiling with a huge array of white teeth surrounded by bright red lips. He was looking at her cheerful face, her long blonde hair flowing down on to her shoulders, and he walked towards her as if in a trance.

'Are you still fine?'

'Yes. Not keen at being up here though,' he said in a whisper.

163

Her eyes were deep blue and so beautiful. He stared mesmerised.

'That's understandable. What's your name?'

'Michael,' he said so only she could hear.

'OK, Michael.'

Was he going to be sick? What would that be like in front of this whole roomful of people including his sister? His sister – how embarrassing. Yet this woman was so entrancing he felt compelled to stay.

'I don't want to make you do anything you're not happy about. If you want to, please sit down,' she said pulling a chair up for him.

'Close your eyes,' she said gently. 'Take a few deep breaths. How are you feeling?'

'OK. Well a bit dizzy.'

'Carry on taking deep breaths, and take your time. There's no hurry.'

He felt so confused about why he was there, but he kept his eyes shut. It helped to blot out all the people watching, watching him. He'd never ever had to go through anything like this.

'How are you now?' she asked.

Michael nodded at her.

'OK, thanks.'

'Why are you here, Michael?'

'My sister's here. I came to see her.'

'Good but why?'

'I felt like it.'

'Why?'

'Look please. I'm fine. I don't need this. In fact I don't need any of this. My life is fine. I don't want to talk about it.'

'I'm sorry Michael. I just got the impression you needed something, someone to talk to.'

'Did you? Why me?' He wondered if it was a bad dream.

Jo was looking at the floor. Why Michael?

'I need to talk,' he mumbled so that only Sare could hear him. 'But I can't.'

'Let's just chat then. Tell me about your life. Are you married?'

'Yep. I've got two children – two lovely children,' he said tailing off and looking really sad.

'And what do you do?'

'Well, I'm a consulting engineer.'

'Do you enjoy it?'

'No.'

'Why not?'

'Well I did, but I've left.'

'OK.'

'It's not OK. Because, well because they sacked me.'

'Did that feel painful?'

'It felt bloody awful. How do you think it felt? My wife married me because of my success and now I've lost my job. I'm a failure. My life was so good at work. I used to feel like a king. When I'm at home I feel like I'm being overwhelmed by my mother.'

'Does your mother live with you?'

'No. I mean my wife, Hannah, she feels like my mother.'

'You might be interested to know that lots of men think that Michael.'

'I can't bear it. I loved being at work where I was somebody and then I come home and she treats me like a nobody. She clearly doesn't love me and she only married me for my money. And what do I have now?'

'Two children?'

'Yes and they are the best part of it, but I'm here and they're there and it's such a bloody mess. Sorry, I can't do this any more. I must go.'

Both Sare and Michael left the room.

'I'd like to talk to you later,' Sare told Michael outside the door. 'I didn't want to humiliate you, but I felt drawn to you. I felt that you needed someone to talk to.'

This woman seemed so understanding that he wanted to hold her and let her comfort him. He felt ashamed of his thoughts and worried that she'd read his mind. He looked at the floor but when he looked up at her she was gazing at him as if he was the most important person in her life. It gave him a tiny stirring inside.

'So is that OK? Do you want to talk to me later?'

'Must go – not feeling too good. See you later.'

Was he insane? One minute this woman is making him look like an idiot in front of everyone, and the next minute all he can think about is how lovely she was and how he'd relish some time alone with her.

He scurried to his room and locked the door.

It didn't take him long to know that he wasn't going to talk to Sare again. She'd dig too deep and he didn't want that. How was he ever going to face all these people again after that, especially Jo? He couldn't remember feeling so ashamed since he got caught smoking at school and the headmaster humiliated him and his friends.

Chapter 26

I'm looking down at the floor, listening intently to every word. It is as if Michael can't stop talking once he's started. Now I can't hear what is being said but both Sare and Michael leave the room. I feel completely churned up inside and the most unusual thing is that I feel sorry for him.

As the session finishes, Sare comes up to me.

'I believe you're Michael's sister. Is he OK? I don't want to push anything with him, but I'm here if he wants to talk.'

'Well, I doubt it somehow. I'll go and see him.'

I dash upstairs and down the corridor to Michael's room. I tap on the door and call out,

'Michael, it's me, Jo.'

He unlocks it. His eyes are red, his face is ultra-pale and he looks completely washed out.

'Are you OK?'

'Not really.'

He sits down and waves towards a chair for me to sit down too. He doesn't face me but hangs his head down.

'Why didn't you tell me?'

'I couldn't – there's a lot more yet. We'll have to talk. I don't know if Hannah wants me back.'

'What? Because you lost your job?'

Sitting on his bed, stooped forward with his hands on his knees, he looks pitiful.

'You know what she's like. She's so self-centred and such a gold-digger. What have I got to offer her? And besides Jo I don't know if I want to be with her.'

My mouth drops open, but fortunately he's still looking at the floor.

'What about Steve and Charlie?'

I mustn't sound critical or judgemental.

'They are the problem. I can't bear to be without them, so I don't know what to do. I don't even care about getting a job because the rest is such a mess. Hannah walked out of a restaurant the other day.'

'Oh – so did I. Sorry. What happened?'

'I wanted us to go out for lunch and she asked me with her usual venom if we could afford it. I was already on full pay – I still am, so it wasn't relevant. Although, of course I am worried about money so I chose a restaurant in Pegginton that did a three course lunch for £15. Not really Hannah's type of thing.

'I just felt sick, having to talk to her about it all. I know that she only wanted me for my money. Why else would someone like her have chosen me?'

I was about to tell him not to be silly, but I realise that he could be right, so I keep quiet.

'I told her I was going away for a few weeks, and she was furious that I was off on holiday. I explained I was coming to see you and I explained that Dad had heard from you and you were in India. She was very sarcastic about you - you know the sort of thing, I'm sure it's no surprise.'

I nod.

'She told me I had to get a job. But I said I wanted to decide what I was going to do and when I said I might change careers she hit the roof. It went from bad to worse. I told her that she wasn't giving me much sympathy – I mean where's the support? I'm supposed to be her husband.

'She moaned about being stuck at home with the kids – as if that was a bad thing. And started going on about how I had to bring in the money, not be irresponsible. I said that our relationship wasn't exactly good. And I asked her if she had any idea what if felt like for me, and was I just a meal ticket for her?'

'She banged down her glass, stood up and walked out, without looking back. Everyone in the restaurant was looking and I didn't know what to do. I tried to eat my meal but wasn't hungry. It was so humiliating.'

'I'm sorry to hear this, Michael. Maybe I haven't been very sympathetic either.'

'You didn't know, did you?' he snaps, then holds up his hands in a gesture of surrender.

'Sorry. That's why I've been so... I couldn't cope with all these people airing their feelings like this. I've never done that. I was brought up in an all male school, where if you talked about feelings you were thumped. Women do that, but I don't.'

'Does Hannah?'

'No she doesn't. She's as hard as nails I'm afraid. She doesn't love anyone but herself.'

'I think you're being rather harsh.'

'I'm not. Let's face it none of you can stand her. I know, you know. I'm not stupid.'

'I have never got on with Hannah, but I cannot believe a woman is so hard that she doesn't care about anyone at all. Looks can be deceiving. Perhaps you've married a woman like Mum who's never satisfied.'

'That's enough Jo. I can't be psychoanalysed by you. It's been a dreadful day. I want to just chill out.'

I can't help it but I laugh.

'I never thought I'd hear you say something like that.'

'What?'

'Chill out.'

A frown shoots across his face, and I bristle. He really is hard work – one step forward, one back. Then he puts a hand on my arm, which I don't think he's ever done before.

Chapter 27

'Michael shall we go into Bamesh? I want to get a couple of things, and it might be a chance for you to, well, to see the area. There's a bus that goes past here once a day. If we catch it at 2 I can fit in my morning sessions.

'It's market day today,' I tell him as we bob up and down on the rickety bus. 'You can buy some presents for the family if you want to.'

The bus shakes its way along the windy paths with the engine roaring at times as if it is about to give up the ghost. Michael looks out of the side window at the mighty mountains looming all around us. The bus slows down as a herd of goats are shepherded across the road. No-one complains, no-one is in a hurry here.

The bus rattles into Bamesh where the street market runs along the main road, parallel to the river that winds its way down the mountain. There are people, cars, goats, yaks, and chickens wandering around everywhere. On each side of the road are local women in long flowing dresses over their trousers sitting on stools or on the ground surrounded by a panoply of dishes overflowing with fruit and vegetables.

There are melons, grapes, tomatoes, carrots, okra, beans, bananas, oranges, lemons, cabbages, cauliflowers, and some indescribable vegetables that I have yet to discover a name for. The air is aromatic from the abundant spices and there is a general hubbub of voices, laughing, shouting and a ticking sound. I look everywhere to see what the ticking sound is. And then I spot a spinning wheel going round and round producing wool.

Past the vegetables, spices and herbs, the stalls exhibit a range of fabrics in vibrant colours and then numerous toys and gadgets. I pick up a bunch of bananas and the vendor smiles sweetly at me as she weighs them on her old-fashioned scales.

'Who buys all this stuff? I just can't imagine how they would sell it all,' Michael whispers to me as we walk up the street.

'Tourists and locals, I suppose. A lot of it is not perishable but I can't imagine what they do about all the fresh produce although I think they go to different markets all week to sell it off.'

I pick out a pair of locally made sandals and tried them on. Michael selects a sarong.

'I'd like to get one for Charlotte - what do you think of the colour?'

What a change, Michael asking my advice..

'I quite like it, but what about that lovely orange coloured one?'

He picks it up.

'Yes, she'll like that. I'll get a T-shirt for Stephen, I think.'

'What about Hannah?'

'I can't bring myself to buy anything for Hannah. I just don't know what's going to happen.'

He looks like a frightened child.

'It might be a good gesture to buy her something,' I suggest. 'Maybe a sarong for her as well. Let's go and have a cup of tea.'

We wander down the street and sit down under a small canopy.

'Is this a restaurant?'

'Well, we can get tea here. Not sure I'd call it a restaurant.'

A young boy appears in a white buttoned cotton top which goes down to his knees and baggy trousers.

I point at the jasmine tea on the menu.

'Do you want to try some too Michael, or have normal tea?'

'I tried that sickly sweet stuff when I came in with David. I'll try the jasmine. Is it vile?'

'No. It's fine. Two jasmine teas please,' I say pointing at the menu. 'They don't speak English and why should they? What do you mean about Hannah and you? You don't know what's going to happen?'

'Well I can't see us staying together.'

171

'What about the kids?'

'That's just it, isn't it? What about the children? I can't bear the thought of leaving them or hurting them. I don't want to be one of those fathers who gets visiting rights on a Sunday. Life wouldn't be worth living.'

'Marriages can be made better can't they? Perhaps you ought to go and talk to someone about it.'

He sighs.

'I don't like talking that much. I've discovered that here. It's difficult to start talking about things you have never mentioned before. The fact is I'm a meal ticket for Hannah, or I was. Now I don't know if she has any need for me.'

'As the father of her children perhaps. I'm sure people marry each other for more than money. There must be something more than that.'

'I'm not sure, Jo.'

'And, besides marriages go through bad patches. You can't blame yourself or Hannah really. We tend to do what our parents did.'

'How do you know? You've never been married.'

'I have two parents and since I've been here I've realised how uncommunicative they were with each other. I'm only just getting to learn how to stop it influencing my life.'

'What have you learnt?'

He sits back stirring his tea and looking at me. I'm not sure if I like the way he's sounding smug, but I choose to overlook it.

'How the atmosphere affected me and how they are my role model for marriage, and it isn't a very good one. I mean I know they had a problem.'

'Do you? What kind of problem?'

Why is he asking all these questions? It's out of character and I don't trust it, or more to the point I don't trust him, even now he's being more open.

'I don't know specifically what kind of problem but .. Why are you asking me like that? Do you know something I don't?'

'I think so.'

He looks away.

'What Michael? Don't go all funny on me.'

'It's pretty bad, Jo but you have to know. Dad has been having an affair for 30 years – we all found out the other week.'

My hand flies to my heart. I feel as if I've been slapped round the face.

'Who with? Shit, don't tell me. Well, you have to tell me now.'

'It gets worse. It's Judy.'

This must be one of my bad dreams. It isn't possible. I lean forward on my elbows and cover my face with my hands. I just want to hide from everyone, especially the bearer of bad news.

I'm hyperventilating and my stomach feels as if it is turning over and over. Just one sentence and my whole life is falling apart. That old familiar feeling of unhappiness overwhelms me.

'Christ. Please say this isn't true. This is awful. All those years and I thought Mum was the awkward one. Did she know?'

'Yes, for some while. She's fine – at least she appears to be, who knows? But Mum has completely changed. In fact she was the one who told us all. We were having a dreadful birthday lunch – for Dad. One you were very lucky to have missed. Hannah was in a bad mood because she'd just found out that I'd lost my job.'

'Did you tell her?'

'No, she found out from some nosey parker woman she knew.'

'Why did this woman know? Why didn't you tell her?'

'Would you? Crikey, Jo, she's a money worshipper. How could I tell her?'

'It might have been better.'

'All right, all right. Don't tell me how I should have behaved. I didn't OK? You're not the only one who's upset. Anyway I can barely remember but Hannah was wafting around at some coffee morning and a woman said she'd seen me sitting in the park nearby, and of course I was supposed to be at work. So Hannah was suspicious and grilled me. I had to tell her then. Then at the so-called birthday lunch she spilled the beans and told everyone I'd lost my job.'

'Oh dear, how embarrassing. I suppose if you'd been able to tell them in your own time when you had plans, it would have been much easier.'

'Well that paled into insignificance when my mother, our mother, said she had something to tell us all. It was something to do with your going away, and how she'd decided that she wasn't going to hang around after Dad for any longer.

'I thought she was being unfair to him. And then she dropped the clanger. She told us he had no right to be bothered because he'd been screwing – sorry – seeing Judy for all these years. Poor Mum. I felt so sorry for her that I forgot about my problems.'

'Yes?'

'But the strange thing is she didn't feel sorry for herself, it seemed. She announced she was going off to Africa to do VSO work. She looked different as if she'd turned into a new person – she looked a bit younger.'

'And is she?'

'Is she what?'

'Going away?'

She's gone.'

'She's gone and you didn't tell me?'

'I had to tell you the whole story. I kept waiting for my moment. Jo. You and I haven't exactly been close. I knew how it would upset you. In fact, she said it was because of you. Yes, because you'd been brave enough to up and leave, it woke her up. That's the impression she gave.'

'It's hard to take it all in. I have looked into my childhood so much and I knew there was something I couldn't pinpoint. But of

174

course I didn't know what it was. I have always idolised Dad and now I don't know what to think. I feel really guilty about Mum. I always saw her as the one who was the aggressor, who made life so difficult and all that time he was… screwing … yes your word, screwing Judy. It's disgusting. I feel as if I hate him.'

'It does take two you know Jo. It can't just be Dad's fault. Perhaps Mum wasn't giving him what he wanted.'

'It's a bit difficult to do that when you've got three small kids isn't it?'

I put my hand over my eyes, so he can't see my tears.

'Yes I know. But I'm a man who could contemplate having an affair. In fact I'd love to have an affair but I can't find anyone to have one with.'

He laughs and I just manage a smile.

'Don't start one here. I don't want to have to answer to Hannah. I've noticed the way you keep looking at Gemma. Lay off Michael.'

'I rang Susie the other week. I just wanted to see her.'

'That's pretty unfair. She was so cut up about you and Hannah that she hasn't seen anyone since.'

'Well she's obviously got over it because she told me she had a boyfriend and she didn't want to see me.'

'Good for her. It's only 14 years! It would have crucified her if you started mucking her around again.'

'Again? I didn't muck her around.'

'OK, but you know what I mean. You must know how much she adored you and you just went off with Hannah and got married. Perhaps you'd have been better off with Susie. Sorry.'

I hold up my hand.

'It's none of my frigging business. Forget I said it.'

'It's OK. Don't you think I haven't thought that a thousand times? Susie wasn't exciting or sexy or beautiful like Hannah but

175

she was steady. I might have had an easier life and she wouldn't have kicked up so much fuss all the time.'

'Hang on Michael. Are you saying she'd just let you do what you wanted and Hannah doesn't? I don't think that would have been very good for Susie.'

'Well I certainly don't get that with Hannah. She does exactly what she wants, doesn't earn a penny and spends all my money. She's obsessed by money – mine of course and spending it as well. But she also loves the status of it all – or should I say, she did? She married me because I was a clever engineer, and now since I've been here I'm an unemployed hippie.'

We both laugh.

'Yes she'd love it here, wouldn't she Michael?'

'Well it's not exactly St Lucia, is it? But it's beautiful though in its own way. Just look over there. The sunlight on the snow on top of those mountains. A view to die for really.'

'I'm glad you've begun to appreciate it.'

'I think I had my eyes closed to be honest. Perhaps that's one good thing. They've opened up since I came here.'

'So what are you going to do about Hannah?'

'I don't know. She can't possibly want me now. But I have to go back to get a job anyway. I know I'm being paid for a while but I don't want to let anyone down.'

'Let's go back,' I suggest. 'We can go and talk in the garden. We'll go to my favourite part where it's shaded but you get a lovely view of the mountains. It's quiet there.'

'OK.'

Michael pulls a few coins out of his pocket and puts it on the plate on our table.

'The amount it costs for these two teas isn't even real money back at home,' he says.

I smile and nod. At least he's waking up to where we are. I get up from the table.

'The bus leaves at 3.30 so it's good timing. There it is now, come on, run.'

The bus stops on the other side of the road and we dodge the goats, yaks and buffalo wandering around in the road and get to the bus just as the driver's closing the door. He opens it again and we climb up the steps and sit down at the front. Neither of us speaks on the way back. Michael is just staring ahead and I slump down into my seat and think about the bombshell he's dropped on me.

The bus stops round the corner from Jasanghari. As we saunter up the drive I remember the first time I saw the palace and realise how much I have grown to love it. With all that Michael has told me I want to stay forever. The dysfunctional family is even worse than I'd ever imagined but maybe now I have the key to where the problems stem from.

Michael goes to his room and changes. When he joins me outside he is wearing shorts for the first time since he arrived. I can't help thinking that I haven't seen his legs since he was a boy, which makes me want to giggle but it's probably pushing things a bit too far to make a joke about him at the moment. I'm still unsure how he'll react to things.

We pick up two yoga mats and I lead him up the garden to my favourite spot. We lay them out on the floor side by side and lie down.

'Michael what was it you always wanted to do when you were younger?'

'Get a good job.'

'Why?'

'Because I wanted to be somebody, to earn lots of money and buy a nice house. Doesn't everyone?'

'No they don't actually. The whole eastern concept of life and the religions here have a much better view about money and materialism. You know they're very critical of the west and the way we worship money. I think I've changed since I've been here. I used to love earning lots when I was at Prospect but now I can see it doesn't always make you happy.'

'It seems to make all the people I know very happy. Who wants to be poor? And besides you can go on about eastern religions but these people are different Jo. They're not like us are they?'

'How do you know? How do you know they're different – deep down inside? What do you know about them? And how do you know the people you say are happy are really? How do you know?'

'Because I see them enjoying life, having parties, going on fantastic holidays and enjoying the good life.'

'But that doesn't mean they're happy does it?'

'I suppose they aren't always in good marriages. That might be a problem.'

'Of course it's a problem. So many people are in unhappy relationships and not getting what they want, what they really want that will make them happy. Whether they're rich or poor, perhaps the problem is that they're worshipping money, thinking that if they had more they'd be happy. It's a crazy notion.'

'But a very popular one.'

'I grant you that. Michael.'

'Good, glad you agree with something I say.'

'Did you like the status of your job?'

'Of course I did. Who wouldn't?'

'Why?'

'Because it made me feel important. I felt more important at work than anywhere else.'

'And was the money important?'

'Come on Jo. Don't ask stupid questions. You know whatever you say that it's great to be well off. Would you want to be poor? Of course I love having lots of money but I might have to put up without it now and it terrifies me.'

'Michael who do you sound like?'

'Don't play games. I don't know.'

He was getting ratty, but I carry on. I'm on a roll and he's been listening so I don't want to stop.

'Your wife. Hannah wants status and money. You want status and money. No wonder you're married to her and not to Susie who would be happy to make do on a simple salary and live in a small flat. You're more alike than you realise.'

'Jo – where did you learn all this stuff? It's crap.'

He sits up, and without a word he folds up his mat and walks back to the house. I watch him plodding along in his shorts just like the young boy he used to be.

'Let it go, just let it go,' I say aloud to myself.

I slip back down onto the mat. I've now got a pain in my stomach, my mouth is dry and my throat feels tight. How am I going to get over what my precious Dad has done? Just as I'm beginning to think how good life is, everything is falling apart.

My poor old mother. If only I could see her now. I feel overcome with missing her and loving her, something I haven't felt for longer than I can possibly remember, if ever. Tears splash down my face and on to the mat as I struggle to get a tissue out of my bag and wipe my face.

Chapter 28

For 40 minutes I have Rasi all to myself and we talk about things that I've never discussed with anyone, even my best friends. I walk into reception to meet him for our Tuesday session. He's talking to Mira, but he turns to me.

'There is a film being shown in our normal room today. We need to use the yoga studio outside. No-one's there.'

We walk up to the back of the building and outside to the large yoga studio. Rasi opens the door. The room is empty.

'No chairs. Let's look in here.'

He goes towards a big cupboard and we both bend down to walk in.

We're all hunched up to avoid hitting our heads on the ceiling. Rasi turns round and is so close to me that I put my hand on his chest and look up at him. He gently moves my hand and holds it. I wonder if he's about to kiss me.

'Jo. We need to discuss this. We can't do.'

My face colours up and I feel mortified with embarrassment. I shoot out of the cupboard quickly, but can't look at him. I don't want him to think I'm offended. I'm so shocked at myself. I knew that it wasn't all right to do it, so why did I? I must be crazy.

Rasi brings out two chairs and puts them down opposite each other. He sits down and motions to me to do the same.

I want to run away and hide, not sit in front of him. When I sit down I can feel my shoulders hunched up to my ears and I'm wishing I could be spirited away. It's like being on stage with lots of people watching. I don't know what I can do to put the clock back five minutes and make a different decision.

'I feel a complete idiot. I'm not like that. I don't come on to men. I know it's wrong. I feel awful. Will you still want me to come to your sessions? I can see someone else. Look I'm so sorry. It's just. I find you the only person I can really communicate with.'

180

I'm warbling on.

'Wait,' he says. 'It's OK. It's normal.'

I'm frantically chewing my thumb, trying to hold back the tears. I feel so lonely and after all these months of seeing him so often I almost feel as if I love him.

'You might be thinking – I'm a married man. I am but that is not only why it's not good. Yes it is, because I not cheat, but that isn't reason.

'When you have therapist it's natural to have feelings. I sit and we talk about parts of your life that are intime.. intimate. Often they say that people want to be with therapist, but it's not real.'

My cheeks are on fire. It seems like he's known all along, but what I feel is real.

'I don't want to, you know, I feel quite stupid really. It's just the intimacy. I've never known a man like you. Having a relationship with someone who understood you would be so powerful, and I respect you and your wife. I don't want to..I don't know why it was just..'

'But you do not know me that way. Maybe my wife say I am not wonderful all the time. She think I'm silly man sometimes, that I am not always pleasing her. She say I don't do some thing that she wants. I have problems like all mans.

'You are young lovely woman Jo. Many man want to be with girl like you. I too if I could be but not me now. I have a different world. Things are different here. I am different and we don't do these things that people do so easily in the west.'

'You are a good man, Rasi. I'm just so sorry.'

'You no be sorry. This is part of you that you need discover maybe.'

'Anyway, you'd get the sack.'

'What?'

'They would ask you to leave?'

'Yes of course. What do you think?'

181

'I can see that. Can we go back to where we were and forget this?'

'Yes and the feelings, they will go.'

All I feel now is shame and embarrassment. Am I ever going to be a normal person with a settled life or am I going to carry on falling in love with inappropriate men?

Chapter 29

The ache inside felt so extreme that Michael felt physically sick. He didn't know that missing someone could feel so painful or that it made you feel sick – homesickness of course. He felt desperate to go home, but on the other hand he was terrified of going back to Hannah, of facing the music.

He stirred his spoon round and round the cup of tea as it helped him to focus. Jo was only trying to help but what was the point of being there? He hadn't really worked out what he was going to do with his life but being here wasn't getting him anywhere.

Michael was sitting in his chair staring at his tea when Rasi came in. He knew who he was as Jo had introduced them, but he'd never talked to him before. So he was somewhat surprised when Rasi asked,

'Can I join you?'

'Yeah. If you really want to.'

Michael started stirring his tea again.

'Have you found what you came here for?'

'I somewhat doubt it as I didn't know what I wanted. I didn't even know where I was coming to. I just wanted to get away. And really I don't even think it was a good idea.'

'Things not good for you?'

'Well you know don't you? Everyone in this ff.. place knows. I lost my job and it's not improved my relationship with my wife.'

'Are you private man Michael?'

'Aren't we all? Well maybe you're not but you're not British.'

'What's different about British man?'

'It's the whole stiff upper lip thing. I was brought up not to say if things were bothering me. And at school if you showed any weakness or feelings you'd get beaten up.'

'Do you think British people enjoy that Michael?'

'I don't know. It's just what they do, but I can't imagine they enjoy it. Virtually everyone I know is getting a divorce. No-one's happy. Women think they know everything and they're just leaving men in droves. Men spend all their time working to provide for women who then they decide they've had enough and go.'

'Why is this?'

'If I knew, I could make a lot of money.'

'Is money important to you?'

'For pity's sake, Rasi, what is this? Are you psycho-analysing me? I'm just pissed off. That's all. Can't you give me a break?'

He looked at Rasi, scowling.

'I am sorry Michael I leave you now. I thought you might like friend.'

Michael put his hand across his brow.

'I didn't mean to be rude. I am very rude. I'm sorry. I know you were trying to help but I've been like this for the past 30 years. I can't change, can I? And it seems in this place everyone wants you to bare your soul. It's not me, I can't stand it.'

'You perhaps are going home?'

'Well I don't know. But I can't change.'

'Everyone can change. What it really takes is to get to understand yourself more and to give yourself more time and respect. If you deny your feelings you can't resolve the unpleasant ones.'

'But how do you do it? And what does it achieve? Just because I start to do this it doesn't make any difference to my marriage or my job situation does it?'

'Yes. It may surprise you and you do have to trust outcome. But when you start to be more positive, then life is more positive for you. You never know you might go home to wife who change and appreciates you.'

184

'Pigs might fly.'

'Sorry?'

'It's an English expression. Pigs might fly – because they don't fly. You get the gist?'

'The gist? I don't know what gist is but I know pigs don't fly. Yes it's funny.'

'Now after the lecture, what do you suggest?'

Michael bashed his hands on the table and sighed.

'Sorry. You must think I'm a prat. I'm not normally like this, rude to people. I'm just a miserable bastard at the moment, well all the time maybe.'

Rasi smiled. Michael looked at him, but he saw that he was a genuine man and he wasn't patronising him. He didn't normally meet people like this who didn't seem to be driven by ego.

'You can do lots different things. You could come to some of our classes. Meditation - you know it's a word you westerners don't like. It makes you think beards and long robes like Maharashi but it is relaxation, spending time alone, allowing you to know who you really are.'

'Sounds difficult.'

'It's not difficult and it has very good effect. But if that's not your bag – is that what you English say?'

Michael laughed,

'Yes it's a good expression.'

'You might like to try creative writing, or art therapy or you might want to come and talk to me every day.'

'I'll give the art a go and I'll pop in for a chat with you. Nothing heavy though. I'm not into psychobabble you know.'

'Yes I get the picture.'

'Your English is very good.'

'Your sister. She teach me.'

185

'Hmm. I can imagine.'

'Michael, have you heard of mindfulness?'

'Yes, it's talked about a lot at home, but I don't really know what it is.'

'Awareness of what you are doing, what you are thinking, very good. OK. Tomorrow at 4 in afternoon? Art therapy's in morning.'

'OK.'

Chapter 30

There's a knock on my door. David or Michael?

'Can I come in, Jo?' Michael asks. He's looking rather sheepish.

'I was talking to Rasi, and after I'd insulted him a few times we started having a proper conversation. You'll approve. I'm going to art tomorrow and to see Rasi in the afternoon.'

'How do you mean you insulted him? Was Rasi upset?'

I frown.

'No, why? Does that matter to you? Do you have something to tell me?'

I turn away to pick up a T-shirt. I don't want him to see my face.

'No. I have a lot of respect for him. Anyway, it's good. There's no point in being here and not bothering. And by the way on Thursday there is an evening of music. Local music, your kind of music – Pink Floyd and stuff like that, singing and playing instruments. Anyone who can play an instrument can join in so if you can find a violin somewhere or maybe you could try the sitar.'

'Sounds good. I'll see you later.'

It's a beautiful evening with a bright moon and a sky full of stars. David and Gemma are huddled together under a blanket. That makes me feel uncomfortable. Something must have happened between them as I have suspected, but if so when? Perhaps I've been too preoccupied with Michael to notice what was going on.

My throat constricts and a familiar feeling rises up inside me. Jealousy. I firmly decided that I didn't want David, but I guess I don't want anyone else to have him, especially Gemma.

I can barely speak to them, but I'm trying to look normal because I don't want them to realise. I don't want David to be involved with Gemma and have them talk about things I don't know about. Simply because it makes me feel left out. After the Rasi episode this is not what I need.

Nicola and Alain have been together almost since they first arrived in Jasanghari, and Michael is sitting back to back with Toni. He seems so laid back I can't believe it. He's paying Toni a lot of attention, and that makes me feel even worse. I must be so switched off; I've never even noticed Michael talking to Toni before, so how did he become so familiar with her so quickly?

And then my eye wanders over to where some of the staff are and I can see Rasi. My stomach lurches when I see him. If only I could be with him tonight, but beside him is a beautiful Tibetan looking woman. She is wearing a bright pink sari and has dark wavy hair tied up at the back of her head. She looks very young but I can tell by the way they are communicating with each other that she is his wife.

It's a cool evening and I shudder with the cold. The music is beautiful and evocative but I feel overwhelmed with sadness and I feel like my emotions are going to burst through a dam and take me over. I don't really know what to do with myself. Because everyone is involved with each other, they won't notice if I disappear.

I sneak out to the toilet, but once in there I decide that I'm not going back. No-one will miss me so I hurry back to my room before I am spotted. Better that I don't have to watch the others cuddling up to each other, while I feel like a lemon. I can still hear the music so I'm not missing that, and they'll think I'm sitting somewhere else, even they think about me at all.

I hope Michael isn't going to do something he'll regret. I go over and over seeing Gemma and David together because it hurts. I suppose it's just that they're both my friends and this changes everything. I lie in bed listening to the music, tears rolling down my face. It would be nice to cuddle up to someone. Maybe it was time again, but who am I going to find here?

Rob is like a distant dream now and I know for certain that I never want to go back to him. Even so, why would he want me back? I treated him very badly.

Chapter 31

Despite his inclination and the temptation, Michael didn't allow anything to proceed with Toni. He thought about his marriage and knew that if he was with another woman, it would be over in his own mind, not just in Hannah's. He had to give it another go for the sake of his children, and falling for someone else would only complicate matters and make it impossible to go back to Hannah and be honest.

He was actually going to miss this place when he went home. He looked out of his little bedroom window at the blue sky with clumps of pure white clouds. It was June now and he wondered if it was summer at home or if it kept raining as it had done before he went away.

Everything here was quiet and still. He was so used to glancing out of the window and seeing the picture postcard view, that he realised he had taken it all for granted before. From now on he was going to savour every moment before the inevitable return to home.

He put on the Indian beige trousers he had bought in the market and a cotton shirt and sandals, and crept outside. It was only six o'clock, but many of the residents got up early. Today there wasn't a soul in sight.

He walked down to Jo's favourite spot near the rose garden. This was the best time of day and the birds were singing loudly. He sat quietly in the garden with his eyes closed.

Michael had been avoiding sitting quietly for years, because he was scared of what his mind might conjure up. He began to drift off and Hannah floated into his mind looking lovely. He felt a lump in his throat. He'd been so enthralled by her when they first met, so much so that he had all but dropped Susie. Jo was right – he had done the dirty on Susie because he just couldn't resist Hannah. He had never believed that he could be with a woman like her.

He didn't want to give her up. Perhaps they could start again and be a happy family for the sake of Steve and Charlie. Maybe they could recapture those initial feelings if she still wanted him. This was make or break time and she might not want to carry on. That was too hard to think of. And if he didn't get a job it would be a financial nightmare.

He felt a pang of hunger and got up and stretched. He wandered back into the dining room and saw David sitting by the large picture window.

'How are you doing mate?' David asked. 'Come and join me. There's fresh figs and mango today.'

Michael helped himself to a bowl of fruit and a pot of jasmine tea. This was a far cry from the cooked breakfast Hannah always made him and the endless cups of coffee he consumed at home, but he felt better for it.

'What are you doing today?' David asked him.

'I've got bio-energetics. I don't know what that will be like.'

He made a face and David smiled.

'I know where you're coming from mate. I used to be just like you. It's not British man, any of this stuff is it? But it's only exercises designed to get you moving some of the emotions which are blocked inside.'

'Christ.'

'It will be all right. No-one's going to know about it and it might help you make decisions.'

'I need to. I don't know whether to go or stay at present. Sometimes I wonder if it was better when I wasn't talking about all this. Keeping things to yourself means you don't have to go over and over them with people.'

'But everyone at home is so good telling everyone they're fine, when they're not,' David said, keeping his voice low. 'People have unhappy marriages, drink too much – like me - they work non-stop – also like me. What sort of a life is it? There's so much more to our lives than that.'

'It's easy to say, David, when you're up in the hills in the most beautiful place on earth. You don't have a wife and kids to support. It's easy to say.'

'Yeah I know but we're all the same inside. And I certainly want to have a wife and kids to support one day. I just feel that if I get this bit right now I might manage that all a bit better when it happens.'

'Unlike me you mean.'

'No I don't. I'm not having a go at you. Don't be so defensive. Unlike anywhere else this place is full of people who really care, and I guess everyone wants you to get it so that you can be happy too.'

Chapter 32

The next morning I feel better. All that crying seems to have left me feeling relieved. I check my face in the small mirror and put on my eye shadow and mascara so that no-one will notice my eyes are a bit puffy. It's time for breakfast.

David and Michael are sitting together at a table in the corner. I grab some breakfast and go and join them, somewhat relieved that Gemma isn't there. They both look at me as if they are mid conversation and I've interrupted.

'What's up guys?'

'David here is telling me that I haven't got it yet,' Michael says.

David looks pleadingly at me. He holds his hands out.

'I didn't,' he croons. 'I was trying to help that's all.'

I throw David a knowing look, but Michael spots it. I can tell he feels that we're mocking him, but I don't feel in the mood for it today. I've got my own issues.

'I did a headstand for the first time yesterday and I feel really pleased with myself,' I say to David and anyone who wants to listen.

'When I started yoga here I was hopeless and it hurt my neck. But I did one and stayed up for ages. It's really good for you, you know if you can relax. I was determined I'd do it soon.

'You should try it, David. Yoga is so encompassing – there's the breathing which is obviously important, as well as the exercise and relaxation – my favourite! Why not give it a go?'

'You might persuade me yet. I'll have a think about it. Seeing you upside down might be an incentive.'

He gives me a leery smile.

Michael clears up his plate and puts it with the dirty crockery. He mumbles to us,

'See you later.'

'Don't mind him,' I say to David. 'He's an awkward bastard some of the time. I've never got on with him, until now. What he's doing now is pretty cool. He's having a hard time at home though.'

'I know. I don't take it personally. I just felt I wanted to help, but you know me, Jo. It's not going to upset my day.'

He laughs and I feel pleased that we're normal with each other. So good I kiss him on the cheek. His eyes light up. I smile.

'Don't forget we're friends. And besides I think you're unavailable now.'

My insides squirm as I say it, but it is better for all our sakes to acknowledge it.

'You do, do you? Are you jealous?'

Michael turned up at his bio-energetics class but he was the only one there.

'Aren't the others coming?'

'It's not others,' Anouk told him. 'It's you. No others.'

He was taken aback, and wondered whether to back out, but Anouk started and it seemed too late to stop. They did some simple exercises and Anouk asked him to do some deep breathing while he guided him. Then he asked him to stand in a particular way, leaning forward and swinging his arms back and forth.

'They ache like mad,' Michael said.

'It's in here,' Anouk pointed to his shoulders. 'Tenseeon.'

'Sorry?'

'Tenseeon,' he repeated.

'Tension. Sorry.'

'No sorry. It's OK.'

All the time Michael was exercising Anouk was moving around his body with his hands a short way away from him but not touching him. Michael was quite enjoying it. He felt the tension oozing out of him, making him feel lighter.

193

'Lie down on back please,' Anouk asked.

'Put legs in air and make feet like this.'

Anouk lay on the floor and put his legs straight up at right angles to his body and even managed to flatten his soles so they were parallel to the ceiling.

'I can't do that.'

'Try.'

Michael lay on the floor, but his legs wouldn't go straight.

'Just try best. OK? It doesn't matter how you do.'

He tried but it hurt and then his legs started to vibrate and they just carried on shaking.

'Is good. Is good. Carry on.' Anouk sounded really pleased.

Michael was feeling very strange. He couldn't stop his legs so he had to carry on. The muscles in his stomach felt as if they were being stretched, and then it felt like they had turned to jelly.

Eventually after what seemed like ages he put his legs down. He felt his breath coming in large panting motions as if he were going to burst into tears. He didn't want to cry in front of Anouk so he suppressed it, pushing it harder and harder down inside, but then he felt completely out of control.

'You OK?' Anouk asked gently putting his hands on Michael's shoulders.

He tensed up. He didn't like a man touching him.

He nodded.

'I need to go and lie down.'

Anouk nodded.

'You go now.'

Michael went to his room and flung himself on the bed just the way he used to do when he was a little boy. Years and years of suppressed sorrow poured out of him and he wept like he hadn't done for 20 or 30 years. He sobbed and sobbed loudly, unable to

194

care whether or not anyone could hear him. He didn't know why he was crying, but he felt a deep sense of loss and despair.

Chapter 33

I'm in classes all morning which takes my mind off things. At lunchtime there's no Michael, which is strange. So I pop up to his room to see if he's there. I hope he's not up there with someone, or I'll catch him out. I'm sure he can't be. I saw Toni at lunchtime, so it's not her.

I tap on his door and he opens it. His eyes are red and he looks all flustered.

'Are you all right?'

'I'm fine Jo,' he says looking the other way. 'I've been asleep. The bio-energetics took it out of me.'

'Michael cut the crap. You're not fine. I can see you're upset. I've never seen you look like that since you lost your football in next door's garden. Please don't tell me you're fine. You don't need to.'

'Funnily enough I am fine now, but I haven't been for the last two hours. It was this exercise. I don't know what it did to me but something snapped and I couldn't stop. It just poured out. I feel stupid telling you this. You'll think I'm a big kid.'

'Everyone's a big kid. So what? It's much better to acknowledge it and find out what's inside.'

'You know what it was. What I kept getting so upset about and I shouldn't really tell you this.'

'If you don't want to, don't.'

'But I do want to. I do. It was Dad and you two girls. He always adored you so much and he never really had as much time for me.'

'That's not true Michael.'

'It is. Please don't tell me it's not true. It's how I feel.'

I nod. He is right.

'Go on. They're your feelings.'

196

'When Beth was born and I was five I saw the look on his face and I was so upset and that's all....'

He can't speak as his lip trembles and he visibly fights away the tears. He obviously cannot let me see him break down.

'He looked at her with adoring... And I can remember that look to this day. I felt that he loved her much more than me. He was always cross with me and I was always annoying him. She was so perfect and the two of you were his pride and joy.'

I open my mouth to speak, and think better of it. He's in full flow.

'No. There's something else.'

I give him my full attention.

'I'm doing it to Stephen. I'm doing the same thing to Stephen.'

He puts his head in his hands and shakes it from side to side. I can't help it now. Tears roll down my face and I sniff.

He looks up, sees my face and whispers to me,

'I'm so sorry. It's my fault Jo. I'm sorry.'

'It's not your fault. And I never ever thought that Dad loved you any the less. You don't remember the day you were born do you?'

I lean towards him and put my hands on his shoulders.

'You were his first child. Don't you think he adored you too? Perhaps because you were a boy he saw himself in you and he was even harder on you.'

'That's it. That's what I do to Stephen. Nothing he does is good enough because he's me. You're right. I can't believe that you can just know it. That's so right.'

He opens his arms and hugs me but still keeping a safe distance. It feels good.

'You've got a chance to get it right now and go back and make a go of all these relationships. Even, well especially, with Hannah.'

197

'I can't stop thinking about her today. I had lost my feelings for her. She is a lovely woman but I had forgotten it, and I think it's me that's turned her into what she's become.

'And you know what,' he continues. 'I'm not going to go home next week. Even though I miss them so much that it hurts. I have got to sort this out and I am going to ring Hannah and tell her what I'm doing. I want to get it right so that I can go home and be a good husband and father and make my family a happy one.'

Chapter 34

My classes are over and it's a beautiful hazy day so I wander out into the garden. Gemma and David are lying together on one mat, and Toni and Nicola are sprawled out on sunbeds. I grab the hammock and climb into it.

Just as I'm opening my book up for a spot of reading, Patrick brings some newcomers to the centre over.

'This is André, he's from France, and Carla's an Aussie.'

As I sit up the hammock swings wildly so I grab the ropes and drop my book. Everyone laughs.

Wobbling around I shake André's hand, and say 'Hi' to Carla, a larger than life girl. We all chat for a while and then Patrick takes them off on his grand tour of Jasanghari.

I am incapable of getting my head around Gemma and David being an item. My relationship with both of them has become restricted because of this unspoken fact – their relationship. Neither of them ever mention it to me, even though I've broached it a few times. They always change the subject, which makes me feel really uncomfortable.

It's better when I'm alone with David, but sometimes I feel jealous of Gemma, which makes it difficult to be normal with her. I attempt to speak about general things because I'm worried that she thinks I want David myself, and that's why she doesn't mention it. Yet I am mixed up about my feelings. It seems that I don't want Gemma to have him, but when I had the opportunity I didn't want him!

Her know-all attitude irks me even more than it did before, and I cannot understand why she has to be so secretive. My friends at home talk quite freely about their boyfriends, but Gemma is aloof. She lets – no, encourages - everyone else talk about themselves but never contributes anything personal.

I think about my friends at home, Susie, Jenny and Michele, and realise that I haven't told them anything. What must they think of me? Perhaps I should send them all an email explaining – explaining what? That I fled the country and left everyone because I couldn't cope? So how open am I after all?

'I could never tire of the beauty of this place,' Nicola said. 'To be surrounded by these majestic hills.'

'I agree,' I say. 'It is very hard to think about going back to the daily grind again. Except that I don't think I will ever go back to the same kind of work. I feel that I have learnt so much here that I want to use it in some way back home or wherever I end up living. I'd like to let other people have the opportunity of doing the same and find the key to happiness, if that's it.'

'Has it made that much impression on you?' asks Patrick. 'I'm not sure that I'm not just happy because I'm away and relaxed. When I get home it will be just as bad as ever.'

David suddenly sits up.

'I know what you're saying but it must have a lasting effect. We must be integrating all the ideas we hear and the way of life, don't you think? That must be the trick, to get home and carry on in this way? We can't expect to spend our lives up mountains living like Tibetan monks. Nor do we want to.'

David laughs and runs his hands through the air in the shape of a woman. A look of irritation flashes across Gemma's face, but she quickly recovers her normal composure.

I turn to Patrick.

'I feel very different since I've been here. I know I haven't faced life's major crises yet because I'm single and my parents are alive and so on, but it hasn't been easy. Far from it. I've had my fair share of life's problems – relationships, my parents, and so on. I understand myself more and want to live for me now, rather than running around looking for the next relationship.'

I notice Gemma's watching me. Does she think I'm having a go at her, or am I getting paranoid about this situation?

'I also feel that I'm only here once and it's not a dress rehearsal.' I laugh. 'Of course, I'm not sure about that now. Maybe this is just one of my many lives.'

Gemma nods vigorously,

'That's certainly possible.'

There she goes again, knowing everything. I don't acknowledge her.

'In this current life I want to really enjoy my time,' I continue. 'I have been given all these opportunities and I want to take them. So what I want to do is work with what I've learnt and impart it to other people so that they can make the most of their lives. Mind you I might need to start with my own family. They could all do with it.'

Just as I say it I see Michael sauntering towards us smiling and looking relaxed, not the man who turned up a few weeks ago.

'Speak of the devil,' David says.

'What are you saying about me now?' Michael asks. He plonks himself down on the ground next to David.

'We are talking about what we want to do with the rest of our lives. Jo was saying that she wants to do something with self-development and everything she's learnt here to pass it on to others. How about you? What do you see yourself doing?'

I settle back into the hammock and close my eyes but I'm dying to hear his answer.

'Quite frankly,' Michael hesitates. 'I have decided that I don't want to do what I was doing before. The energy business is OK but it's very pressurised and while it pays extremely well, I just don't like it any more. That's very irresponsible for someone in my position though. I've got to earn haven't I?'

'What do you want to do?' David asks him.

'I have a background in ecology and environmental science and I just wonder if I couldn't do some good in the world, for the planet. We're in such a huge mess really and if the environment isn't taken seriously soon there's no point in earning big bucks. I've never given it much thought before but it's so obvious.

'Having time to reflect like I have here makes you realise that you want to contribute somehow,' Michael explains. 'Since I've been here I've had a sense that I can do what I like, that I could have a purpose in life, but maybe I'm not being realistic.

'I'm just not interested in earning plenty of money for the sake of it, although I'm not sure Hannah will see it like that. She'll think it's irresponsible.'

David nods his head vigorously.

'I think it's a great idea, but I know what you mean. I used to be in advertising. I was a hotshot ad exec with all that goes with it – loads of booze and fun, but it was ruining my spirit. I was very good at it but the pressure and the stress of the job ran me down. I think I'd like to do something else. Of course I haven't got the family ties, so if I decide to be an aid worker or something I can just go.'

I sit up and see that while David's speaking he's got his hand on Gemma's back and he's gently massaging it, just like he did to me a few weeks ago.

'Like Mum,' I say. 'I suppose she feels she hasn't got a family any more – I'm not being funny. I mean she hasn't got to look after us so she's doing something worthwhile.'

'This could be a family revolution couldn't it?' Michael smiles at me. 'We'll all start do-gooding. Although I don't think Dad would ever give up the law do you?'

'No he couldn't. But seriously are you thinking you might do something with the environment?'

'Don't sound so surprised.'

'Sorry it's just you haven't exactly been in favour of that kind of thing. I can remember what you used to say about the Parkers, who were very green I suppose. But you even laughed at me because I was scrupulous about the recycling bins.'

'Yeah. Leopards can change their spots you know,' he responds. 'One thing I have found here is that I've seen another way of life. And quite honestly when you get away from the frantic life we all lead these days you have to wonder what it's all for.

202

'All I see is people working their socks off and getting ill and having heart attacks,' Michael continues. 'And all for money. That's what people back home seem to live for, don't they?

'I've been reading a lot here too. And I've realised that my skills would be useful in environmental ways. It's how to persuade Hannah that we can live on less which is the major problem.'

'You never know,' I say.

'Hannah may have changed her ideas while you've been away,' David says.

'I'd like to hope for that, but I don't know. Although she sounded warmer on the 'phone. You know what Rasi says?'

'What?'

'He says that you must go for what you want in life. He says that western people are too in love with money and that is the basic difference between us and people out here. We worship it and they have decided it isn't worth worshipping. He believes that they are much happier than we are.'

'He could be right,' says David. 'But how high is the divorce rate in India? And think of the number of billionaires – huge gap between rich and poor. '

'And, how liberated are the women, how equal?' Gemma intervenes.

'Good point,' I say to Gemma. 'They may have little choice. I know what Rasi means - they seem to have their priorities right.'

'I don't doubt that some of them are like that,' she carries on, 'But to be honest, there are a lot of ills in Indian society, particularly for the women. And a humungous amount of crime.'

'He also says,' continues Michael ignoring Gemma's comments, 'That I should choose what I want to do and go for it and let the rest sort itself out. It's easy for him to say, but I am thinking about it hard. I've never enjoyed what I do. Yes I know Jo, it's paid excellent money and kept me - or Hannah should I say - in the style we've become accustomed to, but I felt it was an obligation - not something I wanted to do.'

'I know loads of guys like that,' David says. 'They feel that they've got to earn the bread so they do, but many don't enjoy it. Although in advertising there are creative people who seem to like what they do much more than the so-called business people. They like designing or writing although they don't like the pressure that people like me had to put on them. Anyway I must go and have a sleep before my judo class this evening. That's enough philosophy for one day.'

'I found out about Bhutan the other day. I find it amazing,' I said. 'They don't have GDP – instead of Gross Domestic Product they measure Gross National Happiness. It sounds like a fairy tale, but it's true.'

Everyone nods and smiles. David looks at Gemma and they both get up, pick up their things and stroll down the path hand in hand. They're giggling together and I wonder what's so funny. I cringe.

'Want some tea?' Michael asks me.

'Good idea. But I can't get out of this thing.'

'I'll go. You just lie back and be lazy.'

If he'd spoken to me like that a couple of weeks ago I'd have blown my top. I can't remember him ever making me a cup of tea before.

Ten minutes later he reappears and puts my tea on the ground near the hammock. The others have gone so I manoeuvre myself out of the hammock and sit on a chair next to Michael.

'How long have Gemma and David been together? I thought he liked you.'

'Dunno. Haven't got a clue.'

'Do you mind?'

'Course not. I didn't want him anyway.'

'Yes he told me that, but I think he really liked you.'

'Well maybe he liked Gemma more.'

'Sorry.'

'For what?'

'Bringing it up.'

'Doesn't bother me.'

'I was just thinking – it's odd you know. Your going away seems to have been a catalyst for lots of other things. There's Mum. I don't know why it affected her this way but she suddenly decides to pick up her life and go off and do something. And I've come out here. Although I didn't ask to be made redundant.'

'But let's face it. You wanted to be made redundant in a way. You've just said how you never enjoyed your job.'

'I didn't know that at the time though. With Mum I can't imagine what has spurred her on.'

'No I guess it's more to do with her and Dad. I don't know how I feel about Dad,' I say softly.

'He is a problem. I don't know what to say. I'm not a brilliant husband but to have an affair with someone so close to the family for all those years. What was he thinking of?'

'Himself I guess. I feel horrible. I've been thinking really bad things about him and I never did before. I feel really let down. I think, well I know, that I'm so angry with him I could scream at him, hit him almost. I've never felt like this before.'

I can feel the tears coming and crumple up my face.

Michael puts his hand gently on my shoulder.

'He didn't do it to you, Jo. You know he adores you.'

'Yes I know. But it feels like he did it to me, and then I….'

I falter, biting my top lip.

'I've always been awful to Mum and had such a low opinion of her. I thought she was always moaning about him, and that poor old Dad didn't deserve it. How stupid I was. Do you think they'll split up?'

'I don't know. We can't influence the situation much. Dad's living in the past, where the man does what he wants and gets away with it. It's not very 21st century is it?'

'Nope. I shall have to come to terms with it I suppose. What they do is up to them. Does he want Mum back or not?'

'I've no idea. We haven't discussed it. I'll talk to him when I get back, now I've got some idea of what to say. Jo, Mum could have done something about it. Perhaps she should have stood up to him.'

'Yes I agree. She's been a real victim. No wonder Beth and I aren't any good with men. Beth's even worse than me. Forever going off with the wrong men. I find her incredibly frustrating. She can come round to me and talk for hours about Jack. I give her loads of advice and she takes no notice. One of the things that I've learnt from being here is that if people don't want to listen it's their choice, because it's up to them really. None of my business.

'But it is difficult because Beth rings me at all times of the day or night without any thought that I might be asleep or doing something else for that matter! What I've got to do in future is to tell her I'm happy to talk when it's convenient. If she asks me what to do I'll have to tell her "You know my opinion Beth. I'm not going to repeat it."

'Honestly Michael I think she's just seeking my attention. Anyway her problems are none of my business are they, really?'

'Fair enough. No-one talks to me about their problems. I'm probably too ensconced in my own!'

'I kept saying that if she really wanted a relationship she should give up her married man. She'd agree with me. That was what was so annoying. She agreed with me, said she'd do it and then he came round the next day and they were back to normal.'

'On that note I'm going to have a shower. We've got another music evening tonight and it should be brilliant.'

I stand behind Michael's shoulders and gently massaged them.

'That feels nice.'

206

It is novel to have a relationship with my brother after years of mutual dislike.

Chapter 35

I'm surprised to see Michael handing David a photo of Hannah.

'She's lovely Michael, you lucky bastard,' David says. 'Get back there and sort it out. If I had a woman like that I'd know what to do with her.'

He pats Michael on the back.

'What did she see in an ugly mug like you?'

'No idea.'

Michael's enjoying the banter and looking so relaxed. Who'd have thought that he and David would become friends like this? I sit back and observe.

'Why don't you come on this activity weekend we're doing?' David asks. 'It will be fantastic. It involves trekking, abseiling, ski-ing in the winter, but at this time of year you go rafting. It's all about pushing yourself to overcome fear, and it can be life-changing – so they say. You'll be going home soon so it'd be a great finale.'

'I'd really like to do that. It might be my last fling before I go. Is it expensive?'

'Fairly by Indian standards, but you can find out from Rasi. He takes us.'

'I'm still being paid at home. Are you going to come, Jo?' he asks me.

'Nope. It's not really my scene and quite frankly I love all the things I do here. I've got so much to do. If I could possibly afford it I might ski in the winter.'

'Are you staying that long?' Michael looks shocked.

'I don't know. What have I got to go home to? Of course real life is what brings the money in but by being frugal and not going on trips, I can last another eight months here. Then I might have to think about what to do. I've still got some money tied up at home though, although with low interest rates it's probably not worth much.'

'When did you get so rich?'

'Over the years. I was very well paid at Prospect you know and I didn't have anyone to spend it on. It's different when you're single. I just put loads away in the building society for a rainy day and now it's raining. But, no I'm going to leave you to it this weekend. You go. I'll stick to my yoga.'

'OK. I'll do it, David, and then go home,' Michael says. 'When is it exactly?'

'It starts next Friday,' David tells him. 'We travel up by jeep and it takes about four hours so we go really early – about 5 a.m. It gets quite cool up in the mountains so make sure you've got some suitable clothes, particularly now it's autumn.'

'Now you've got me. I believed I was coming to India and I didn't bring winter woollies!'

'Borrow some. I've got a couple of fleeces so you can have one. But you will need proper boots. You might have to buy those. We come back early on Tuesday.'

'Right that's fixed. Where do I get boots here?'

'You'll have to buy them when we get there. They're the only place with any gear. You've seen the local villages!'

'Yes, OK. Who else goes?' Michael asks.

'Not many of the girls go. It's tough really and you don't get many mod cons when you're up there. I'm not saying the girls can't cope though! I daren't. They just like their comforts!' He laughs.

'Is Gemma going?'

'Huh? Yeah I expect so,' David says, looking the other way. 'She's a bit more game than the others. Right must go. I've got a busy morning.'

It's raining outside. I don't want to go on the weekend because of Gemma and David, and because Rasi is leading it, and he might have his wife with him. I need to get over all this, otherwise I'm running my life around uncomfortable situations. But it's not really my scene anyway.

'You don't mind me going do you, Jo?' Michael asks.

'Of course not. You go. You don't need me, do you?'

'No I guess I don't now. It's my last sort of fling before I go home, so to speak.'

'I hope it's not.'

'Not that sort of fling. Have a good weekend alone. You're not up to something I should know about are you?'

'If I was I wouldn't tell you, would I?' I smirk. 'I wish.'

It's really different without all my crowd at Jasanghari so I spend my time doing cookery and yoga, and catch up with reading. Toni's here but she is quite solitary. I enjoy it at first but then I feel a bit isolated. It surprises me to realise I might actually miss Michael when he goes. How much life can change.

So when it gets to Tuesday morning I'm quite pleased that they're back. The first person I see in the restaurant is Gemma sitting alone at one of the indoor tables. I get my breakfast and wander over. We're not as friendly as we used to be, but it would look very rude not to sit with her.

'Hi how did the weekend go?'

'It was OK. Not really my thing.'

She gets up and walks off with her tray. And I was worried about being rude. What have I done to deserve that?

David then bounds in, followed by Michael. They grab their breakfast and sit down next to me.

'Is Gemma OK?' I ask.

'How should I know?' David answers a bit too quickly, and Michael's watching him.

'How was your weekend?'

'I loved it,' Michael says. 'We did some abseiling up this mountain which was terrific. I never thought I'd dare and then we

210

went kayaking. We were completely kitted out and it was scary but a great experience. Wasn't it David?'

'Huh? What? Sorry, I was miles away.'

His eyes are darting everywhere as if he's really distracted.

'Good, it sounds like you had a great time, and you David?'

'Yes, very good. Great experience. You should have come.'

'Yes maybe. Maybe not really me, though. I enjoyed my weekend here.'

I wonder immediately why I said that, because it's not entirely true.

I don't see Gemma for the rest of the day. I wonder if it's appropriate to go and talk to her, but there's this sticky problem of her and David. If it's something to do with that she won't tell me anyway. She's never even acknowledged that they are an item, but they must realise that everyone knows by now.

I pop up to Michael's room in the afternoon. He's just unpacking so I sit on his little wooden chair.

'Are Gemma and David OK?'

'Yes. What do you mean?'

'She's gone very off today. She almost ignored me and now she's disappeared.'

'Oh now you mention it, they did have a very big row on Sunday. It was quite embarrassing because she was shouting at him, and everyone could hear. It was when we were camped out and there was like a storm going on in their tent.'

'They were in a tent together then? What were they saying?'

'I don't know. I just heard her calling him a bastard. None of my business really.'

'No you're right. Oh well.'

I don't see Gemma all day or evening and when I'm ready for bed there's a knock on my door. I've got nothing on at all so I quickly grab my nightdress and put it on. It is most likely to be Michael.

I open the door slowly and there is David wearing shorts and a T-shirt.

'Can I come in?' he whispers looking around him.

'I suppose so, I'm not that decent.'

'I don't mind.'

He doesn't act in his normal jokey way. He sidles in through the half open door and surveys my nightdress. Now I'm panicking that it's see-through.

I get back into bed and pull the covers up high to protect me. I sit up straight so he doesn't get the idea I'm inviting him in. Despite the fact that there's a chair nearby he sits down on the edge of the bed, so I grab a cushion and put it over my lap as a barrier. He is leaning forward looking at the floor as if he has something serious on his mind.

'Something's the matter?' I suggest.

'Yes.'

'What? I know, you know. We all know about Gemma and you.'

'What do you know?'

He looks at me with such a sad look, but there is something else as well.

'That you've been together for weeks now. That you're having a relationship.'

'Had one, not anymore.'

'I'm sorry.'

'Are you?'

'Yes, of course.'

'That's a pity, I'd hoped you might be pleased.'

My hand moves up to the chain around my neck. Am I that easy to read?

'Sorry. Why would I be pleased?'

'I don't know. I just wanted you to be pleased. It's all to do with you, Jo.'

'What is?'

'It's you I want, not Gemma.'

'What? You've been seeing her, so why, I don't understand?'

'I couldn't get you. You kept saying no and then one thing led to another and I ended up with Gemma. Sure she's a great girl, but she's so cold. She isn't you and I suppose I was consoling myself with her, and I think she guessed.'

'What?'

'Sssh. We don't want her to know do we?'

'Know what? What has she guessed?'

'That to be honest, I fancy you like crazy and it hasn't gone away since I've been with Gemma. And she just knew. She knew and she's pretty cut up about it.'

'No wonder she didn't speak to me in the restaurant. I haven't done anything wrong though.'

'No, but she is very jealous of you.'

'Oh God. Why?'

'She just is, partly because of me, and because I guess she sees you as what you are. Very lovely, very likeable and maybe she feels she doesn't match up to that. And we had this row and she asked me straight out how I felt about you. And I told her.'

'You told her. What did you tell her?'

'That I couldn't get you out of my mind.'

'Oh David. That's crazy.'

'Why is it crazy?'

213

'Because you've upset her, made her hate me I suppose, and we don't even have anything going. And I like you as a friend.'

'Tell me that I have a chance. Please Jo. Tell me.'

He turns to me now with a desperately pleading look, that makes me feel sorry for him and I want to comfort him. He moves around on the bed so that he is up close to me and he wraps his arms round me. I put my head on his shoulder. I've felt so lonely lately. It feels warm and cosy and I wonder maybe if I could start feeling for him too. I yearn for someone to hold me like this.

'You've just finished with Gemma I presume. And you want to start up with me? It's not great timing.'

'I'm sure we can overcome that.'

He's stroking my hair, it could all be so easy.

'You've got beautiful hair, just like all of you. Come on, darling, you know how well we get on together. It would just be perfect.'

We are now so near to each other that I feel concerned that it is all going to get out of hand, right now. I know this isn't right for me. I don't think it's right for us, but it's incredibly tempting. I pull myself back so that I'm flat up against the wall, and he pulls back and just looks at me longingly, as if he really loves me.

'Nothing's perfect David. You've just split up with Gemma. Now you want me, straightaway. And I don't know. I just don't think of you like that. It's messy, and you're my friend, and Gemma is too. Oh God. I don't need a load of hassle.'

He picks up my hand and holds it in both of his.

'I've realised that you are the one I want. You know everyone talks about meeting the right one – you are that right one for me. If you gave me a chance I am sure I can make you happy.'

I'm watching him intently and I can see something deep inside his eyes moving, as if he is really hurt. It would be so easy just to fall into his arms, but I am learning to recognise what I really want. I don't want to fall into relationships any more that my gut feeling tells me are not right.

'Think about it, darling, think about it please. I'm begging you. I've never wanted anyone like this before.'

It's incredibly flattering. I swing my feet round and get up off the bed where I feel that I'm a bit more in control. I turn to the door and pick my silk kimono off the back of the door and wrap it around me, doing up the belt in an obvious way. His eyes are watching my every move.

'We'd have to talk much more about you and Gemma. I don't want to know the ins and outs but I can't just suddenly leap into an affair with you. And David I care about you, I'm just not sure it's what I want, and how would Gemma be? She's going to be hostile towards me and she is a friend too. I don't want to end up hurting my two best friends do I?'

'Jo I'm not looking for an affair with you. I want more than that, something long term. I think we could have a great future together and we're already off to a great start as we're good friends anyway.'

'And what if it goes wrong?'

'It won't. Trust me. I only have your happiness at heart.'

'Not yours?'

'That too.'

He stands up slowly, moves towards me and proceeds to fiddle with the belt of my kimono.

'No, no, please don't David. I don't want to fight you.'

'Don't then.'

'No. No.'

He drops his hands and steps back, looking offended.

'I can assure you I'm not some brutal maniac. If you don't want me I'm not going to force myself on you.'

'Look the answer is no today. Maybe that will change, but I have to think about it all. I feel you need some space after the Gemma relationship. I'm not sure if I want all this, because my life has been nice and calm here.'

'Apart from a relationship with a certain counsellor?' he says quietly but his eyes look angry and hurt.

'What do you mean?'

'You know what I mean. Don't come over all innocent. Why couldn't you go away this weekend? Was it because Rasi's wife was going?'

'No, don't be silly. I have never ever had anything to do with Rasi. I promise. He's not that kind of man.'

'More's the pity as far as you're concerned.'

'I think you'd better go.'

'Just tell me. What has happened with Rasi?'

'Nothing. It's the honest truth. He isn't that kind of man, and yes I'm fond of him because I've told him my life history, but he's married. There's nothing between us.'

'I'll believe you. Thousands wouldn't. Christ Jo, you must know how I've felt about you ever since we arrived. Since I saw you on that train that day with those shorts on, the ones that made your legs look as if they came up to your ears. I knew then that I wanted a relationship with you. I've told you many times, and I've put up with your fobbing off. But this is serious now. I really want you and I don't want Gemma to get in the way.'

'So why did you have a relationship with her then?'

'Were you jealous? I think you were. I could see it in your face, in your eyes.'

'Yes. I mean no, not like that.'

'How then? Go on, explain, I'm all ears.'

'That my two friends were suddenly a couple – I felt excluded. As you recall we all met at the same time and we became good, well even great, friends. And there were three of us and then all of a sudden you and Gemma have something going and it's two plus one. And it made me feel, kind of left out. Do you understand?'

'I think that's because you want me as much as I want you.'

'Wow. You're super-confident about these things.'

'I have met a lot of women in my time.'

'I'm sure you have, but you're not always right. I think of you as a dear friend.'

'But I want more than that. I've always wanted more than that. In fact I want to get in beside you now, and show you how much I care for you. I honestly think I love you Jo.'

'But I should remind you that you chose Gemma.'

'Because she didn't put up such a big resistance, and I thought by being with her I might get over you. And a little part of me, I admit, wanted you to be jealous. Correct that – a big part of me wanted that so much. It's all wrong, the wrong reasons I know. But Gemma isn't exactly an ugly old bag. She's a great girl, but she's not you.'

'Let me think David. Let me think.'

He skims my lips with a kiss and gently strokes the side of my face looking intently at me. I am trying to avert my gaze because deep down I am saying to myself, 'This isn't right. It isn't right.'

'I adore you. I'd never do anything to hurt you. You're coming round to my way of thinking though aren't you? I'll just have to hold on,' he whispers.

David lets go of me and eases out of the door into the corridor and the night.

I hear voices and frown. Somebody has seen him and it is almost midnight. What is anyone going to think if they see him coming out of my room at this time? Hopefully it wasn't Gemma.

Chapter 36

Ironically I am really relieved that Michael is here. It gives me a good excuse to give both David and Gemma a wide berth. I walk into lunch with Michael and we go and choose some rice and salad. Michael walks towards the table where David, Patrick, Toni, Nicola and Alain are sitting. They are making a lot of raucous noise when I get out on to the terrace with my food.

I furtively look around for Gemma as I walk to the table. She's sitting in the far corner with some other residents whom I hardly know. I think they arrived a couple of weeks ago and she may have been with them on the activity weekend. Gemma doesn't look up as I walk onto the terrace.

It all feels so awkward. The place I've loved so much now seems fraught with difficult feelings, none of which are of my own making. Being around David is embarrassing as there is so much tension in the air that I imagine everyone can feel it. No doubt he is waiting for an answer.

'I was just saying that I had never seen anyone as shit scared as Michael when he set off for that abseil,' David says to me, his eyes lingering on my face.

'I was petrified, but I'm so glad I did it,' Michael admits. 'There's this amazing elation afterwards when you realise you're still alive.'

Despite the tension with David, I'm so happy that my brother is speaking like this. He's certainly loosened up.

Michael turns towards me and speaks in a low voice,

'It was like a near death experience. I kept thinking, supposing I die now and I never see my children again, and Hannah. It was then I realised I do really love her and I want to go home and try to make it work. Have you got time after lunch? I'd like to go for a walk with you?'

'Sure.'

I'm relieved – another way to avoid David. When Michael and I have finished eating and had a cup of tea, we get up and walk down the steps from the terrace. I can feel David's eyes boring into my back and turn around to see him watching us with a wistful look on his face.

'I'm going home,' Michael says. I'm arranging the flight later today when I go down to Shimla. It will be in the next few days.'

'Yes. Good. Sorry. I was a bit caught up in my thoughts. It's good for you. I'll miss you.'

'You have given me my life back.'

'I haven't Michael. You have done it yourself.'

'I wouldn't even be here if it weren't for you. You led me here, and I so appreciate it. I just wanted to thank you. And Jo, I want us to try to be friends in future.'

I link arms with him.

'We've gone this far. We won't ever lose it.'

Three days later Patrick, David, Toni and I travel down in the truck to Shimla to see Michael off. David sits in the front with Anouk driving, with the rest of us in the back.

'I've said my goodbyes to Gemma,' Michael tells me. 'I don't know what's gone on with her and David but she wasn't keen to come down, which doesn't matter at all. But it seemed awkward.'

'I can't really discuss it because I don't know all the details, but it's complicated.'

'Are you OK, Jo? You seem a bit preoccupied. Is it because you can't bear to see me go?'

'Yes of course I'm upset you're going. There's a slightly complicated situation going on, but I can't really go into it now. I seem to attract complicated situations.'

'Is it David or that chap who ran the weekend?'

'Who?'

'I think you know. You're always fluttering your eyelashes at him. Rasi, of course.'

I lean forward so that he can't see my burning cheeks.

'Let's leave it for now Michael. I'm not in the mood.'

'I've hit the nail on the head then.'

I blush but at the same time try to look nonchalant as if I'm not really paying attention. He knows that I normally do pay attention so it's quite hard to pull it off.

I pretend to doze a bit after that conversation until the noise around us tells me we are arriving in Shimla. All of us fight our way on to the platform at the station through the throngs of people selling food, clothes and plants. Watching David and Michael hugging each other, I think how much my brother has changed. He wouldn't have touched me a month ago and now he is hugging a man!

My eyes fill up as I put my arms round Michael with my new found sisterly love.

'I hope everything goes well, but I'm sure it will. Email the Shimla office to let me know. I've found myself a new brother.'

As I say it I can feel I'm going to cry and I don't want to, partly because it will be embarrassing to Michael, but also because I don't want David trying to console me.

Michael pushes through the hordes of vendors and gets on the train. His face appears at the window and he waves until he is out of sight. We wander around Shimla as a group, getting supplies for Jasanghari.

David is following me around the shops watching me like a hawk.

'Well? Have you come to a decision? Now that Michael's not here.'

'Not really and anyway he's just left. Not one that you are going to be happy with. I still feel that it's too soon.'

'I've known you for how long now, four months?'

'Too soon for you and Gemma. She never even speaks to me and David, it hurts. I haven't said anything to her, but I feel she's watching to see if we are, you know.'

'So what? She has to accept it. Jo, please, you're crucifying me. I can't sleep for thinking about you. I have to stop myself from coming round at night, leaping in your window and ravishing you.'

I can't help laughing.

'It's not funny.'

'You're laughing too.'

'But it isn't funny. I can't stand it. The thing is, Jo.'

I don't look at him but I start touching rugs in the market, deliberately trying to look as if I am extremely keen on buying one. But I hear every word. Someone sidles up beside me. I assume it's David and turn round to see Patrick.

'Hi Patrick.'

What a relief that he's appeared to relieve me of David.

'Jo, we're going in five minutes.'

'Great, thanks Patrick. Do me a favour,' David says. 'Could you go and tell Sahib we'll be there in ten minutes? We just need to look for something else.'

Patrick nods obligingly and walks off.

'Why did you do that?'

'Because I need ten minutes of your time to get you to agree something with me. Let's put a time limit on it and then we go ahead. I'm not a big-headed bloke but I can feel when someone likes me. I know you have feelings for me – I can feel the electricity. We could be dynamite together, darling.'

I laugh again.

'Please don't keep mocking me.'

'I'm not David. It's your use of language, it's so good.'

'Call me Mr Wordsmith. I got Grade A in my English GCSE. I'm not mucking around, I mean it. Honestly you and I could set the

221

world on fire, because we complement each other well. We get on well and we just need to get going. Can I come and see you tonight?'

'No, no. I thought you said there was a time limit.'

'Well it's a very short one.'

'Not that short. Come on David. We've got to go. I'll just pay for this.'

I hand over some rupees for the blue and white rug.

'It will go nicely in my room.'

'Good. Let's hope I'll be using it.'

'You are funny.'

'I am not funny, darling. I'm deadly serious.'

He takes my hand which I feel is OK, so maybe I am softening. We walk back to the truck. As soon as it's in sight I pretend that the rug's slipping and grab my hand away from David, so no-one will see. I don't want to set tongues wagging, particularly when there is probably nothing to talk about.

Chapter 37

I'm feeling very vulnerable because I'm ready for a relationship again, and I want someone to care about me, and David seems so keen. But it is one thing being friendly with David and quite another having a relationship with him in such an enclosed environment where everyone is in each other's pockets. I do care about my friendship with Gemma, which is looking very fragile and is certainly going to be ruined if David and I get together. Shouldn't I be following my instincts now?

After dinner I go to watch a DVD in the ballroom and afterwards nip back to my room before David can collar me. There is a knock on the door just as I am about to get into bed again. I feel quite irritated this time, and sigh, then grab the kimono.

As I open it slightly I whisper through the crack of the door,

'David, I didn't say it was OK.'

'It's not David,' comes back Gemma's voice.

My heart leaps into my mouth. Shit, shit, shit.

'Oh I'm sorry, Gemma.'

Gemma just stands there.

'Come in.'

'Well, I'm wondering if you are expecting company.'

'No I'm not. I don't want company. I mean you can come in.'

'But you normally expect it?'

'No, please don't get the wrong idea.'

'I haven't got the wrong idea. I know it took you no time at all did it?'

'What, what are you talking about?'

'Jo, both you and I know that I'm not stupid. I saw him coming out of your room late the other night, just after we'd got back from the weekend.'

223

I pull Gemma inside gently and close the door. I don't want everyone else hearing our conversation.

'You don't know what went on though – nothing. You are getting the wrong end of the stick. He wanted to talk about you.'

'Oh yes and what did he want to say?'

'That.' I'm aware that I'm fiddling with the hem of my kimono, and that she will spot my discomfort. 'That he was sorry because you'd had a row.'

'And do you know what the row was about?'

'Not exactly. No.'

I look up at Gemma hoping my face doesn't give away the lie. Gemma's hair is tied back and her eyes look menacing. She's a force to be reckoned with when she's in this mood. She has no make-up on except some lipstick which seems odd, and I find myself preoccupied by her nose. I've never noticed before how pointed it is, but it doesn't detract from her looks.

She's dressed in a navy polo shirt with a white stripe on the collar and a pair of track suit bottoms, but she isn't wearing her customary white cap.

I feel as if I'm sweating because I'm so edgy.

'Can you honestly deny that you haven't been funny with me ever since David and I started up our fling, as it turned out to be?'

'I can explain,' I say sitting down on the bed. I gesture to the chair on the other side for her to sit down.

'It just felt so awkward. We were three and then it was two plus one. I didn't want David. I've never thought of him like that. But neither of you said anything and it put me in a very awkward position. I didn't know whether to say anything to you. He didn't mention anything, nor did you.'

'You could have fooled me. All that intimate chatting with him, touching him and gazing into his eyes.'

'What? He's a friend. A dear friend. Don't you do that with friends?'

224

'Not when you know they've got the hots for you.'

'I didn't know then.'

'But you do now?'

'No, well, no not really.'

'Not really. And I'm not your friend?'

'Yes of course, you were. You are.'

'What's changed Jo?'

'You, you changed it. You say that I became different. You became different. You never told me you had a relationship with David.'

'Oh I'm so sorry. Was I supposed to report back about the intimacies of our relationship?'

'Please Gemma. This isn't like you at all. I mean we were good friends and you never, nor did he, told me that you were an item. I suppose when I realised, I felt awkward, embarrassed.'

'Because you haven't got anyone of your own.'

'No, well yes. In a way, yes.'

'So you thought you'd get him back?'

'No I did not. Hell, Gemma. Can't you see that you're being irrational? I never went after David ever.'

'And he. Is it his imagination then? He cannot get you out of his mind it seems.'

'I never encouraged him. I can't help how he feels.'

She stops for a moment and seems preoccupied with the night sky out of the window.

'And in those little tête-à-têtes that you and David have been having at the dead of night, in the passion of it all, did he tell you about who we met this weekend?'

'There was no passion, and no I don't know who you met.'

'Someone else who seemed very interested in you Jo, but I guess David wasn't going to tell you was he?'

She flicks her long blonde hair back in a gesture of defiance. I'm intrigued now but intimidated by her too. Who would know me?

'Who are you talking about?'

'Six foot tall, quite stocky, dark hair, Australian accent.'

I gasp,

'Tim?'

'Yeah that's his name. He asked us if we knew a girl called Jo who came from Bristol and arrived from Delhi last March. I imagined it was you. David looked well pissed off.'

'Where's he staying?'

'He's at the activity centre. I'm not sure if he's helping to run things or just on holiday. It's about 20 miles away.'

'Very interesting.'

'Look Jo. You can't have two men at the same time.'

'As it happens I don't have one actually. I might never see Tim again, and David is – for the fiftieth time – just a friend.'

All thoughts I'd had of capitulating to David evaporated. How dare he try it on with me before he resolved things with Gemma? But more especially, if there was a chance of meeting Tim again, I'd just love to. But how?

Chapter 38

'Watch it or we're going to have a very wobbly mess all over the floor,' Gemma giggles and almost gets hysterical. I'm trying without much success to get my lemony Ayurvedic dish out of the bowl.

It is good to have Gemma back, but there is a wariness on my part because I never know what is going to happen next. I've been trying to avoid David in the day, but am concerned that he will arrive at night. We haven't had a conversation for four days and I know it's overdue. By now he must have seen Gemma talking to me and realised that we're friends again, which doesn't really work in his favour.

Gemma and I walk to the restaurant together after our cookery class. The usual crowd are out on the terrace.

'Please, come over and join us today,' I plead.

'OK,' she says.

David is in the middle of one of his stories, and I pick up two chairs for myself and Gemma. We sit down and listen. David's watching me out of the corner of his eye while he continues.

'And then there was this guy standing in the street with a bunch of bananas on his head and everyone was laughing. You know you can ask them for anything and they can always supply it, or so they say.'

Gemma gets up and says directly to me,

'I'm going to get a yoghurt. Want one?'

'No I'm fine. I'll get something in a minute.'

David watches and raises an eyebrow at me. He clearly doesn't like it that Gemma and I are friends again. This is like an eternal triangle.

I close my eyes. The sun is really warm on my face and I can avoid looking at David. In the background I hear Gemma's voice saying,

'I'll grab you a chair. She's there.'

I open my eyes, wondering who she's talking about. Standing next to Gemma is a tall guy with very short black hair. Because his hair is so short I'm not sure, but then I realise it's Tim.

His eyes are trained on me and he is smiling. My insides lurch up and I feel excited, nervous, and embarrassed. David's chatting stops dead, and he is watching my every move.

'Hello. What a surprise! Gemma mentioned that they'd seen you.'

My heart is pounding so hard in my chest that I can't think of anything to say. I don't kiss him on the cheek, and I think he's feeling too awkward to kiss me. It's tricky having an audience, particularly when one of them has declared his undying love for me.

'Are you eating? Yes I see you've got some food. What have you been up to? I hear you're running the activity centre. How long have you been doing that?'

I'm really gushing now. I keep asking him questions and not giving him a chance to reply. My palms are sweating. My face feels hot and is probably as red as a beetroot, and if I look like a nervous wreck, perhaps he will be disappointed. I am so pleased to see Tim but not here, right now in front of David. What should I do?

'I've been up at the Olympics place for six weeks and I managed to stay longer by giving lessons in kayaking,' Tim drawls in his lovely accent.

David is listening to every word.

'I didn't know you were an expert.'

'Not really, but I can do it. Look, I decided to move on, and when I saw these guys on that weekend they told me that they were at a place called Jasanghari which rang a bell. Gemma here told me you were still here. Thought I'd call in on my way.'

'Your way where?'

'Jeez, not really sure. Home maybe.'

'Oh that's nice.'

My voice sounds ridiculous, but I'm so aware of David's eyes trained on to me that I feel completely inhibited. I have to get away from the restaurant and hopefully with Tim in tow too.

After 20 minutes of agonising conversation and heart pounding, a couple of people drift off and I suggest to Tim.

'Why don't I show you around?'

'That would be great. Look, I need to organise a room first though.'

'I'll take you through and you can sort that out.'

I take my plate back to the washing up area. When I turn around Tim is behind me. He seems awfully big now and his feet look huge. He is towering above me and has big broad shoulders. His hair is so short I'm not sure it suits him, but he is only here for a few days so it obviously doesn't matter what I think.

We walk into reception and there is a note on the desk.

'Come back at 4 pleese.'

We both laugh.

'Spelling English is not their strong point. If you want to leave your bags here they'll be completely safe, I can take you around the building. What brings you here?' I ask, hoping for the right answer.

'I was intrigued when you told me about it, but I like doing extreme sports. Look, it was only when I saw the guys on that weekend that I put two and two together and remembered that you might be here.'

I feel a bit disappointed that he hadn't thought of me before then. I take him on the tour I was given when I arrived, and which I now know so well. Without David in the background I can chat normally, and we stand in the ballroom for half an hour catching up on what we've been doing.

'And do you have any good friends here, apart from Gemma?'

'Yes several, yes.'

'I met David, was it? On the weekend too? He and Gemma I think are a couple.'

229

'They used to be yes, but not now.'

'And there was another guy – I wondered if he was with you, just something he said.'

'Tall with sandy coloured hair, quite big and very English?'

'Yeah that's the guy. Is he your partner?'

'Hardly. He's my brother.' I laugh.

'I see. Where's he then? I didn't see him today.'

'He's gone now. It's a long story – he had marital problems and he came out for a while and it was terrible at first and then it changed and ended up being really good.'

'I see.'

He smiles and I notice those warm brown eyes that I liked so much last time.

'Well I don't see, but that's your business. What a lovely room this is. It's so ornate and there are all sorts of funny faces carved into the wood. You've probably got used to it.'

We sit down in the window seat and he looks around outside.

'Look, it's a beautiful this area, isn't it? Are you happy here?'

I hesitate because the answer's not obvious to me anymore.

'I have been.'

'You are or you have been?'

'I am, I suppose. I thought it was paradise for the first couple of months, but things happen and it becomes like real life eventually. I still love it, but it's not perfect.'

'Is anything?'

He's looking at me, and all those initial feelings I had that night in Delhi filter back.

'Maybe not.'

'What are youse all doing this evening? Do you go out - is there anywhere to go?'

'There aren't many places. I could take you on a walk before it gets dark but we'll have to eat here. There's nowhere else nearby.'

'It's great. It's a date then.'

He smiles again and wins me over.

'I'll come back down with you to sort out your room.'

We find our way back to the main reception area.

'This is splendid this room, with all those deities in here. Is it a religious place?' he asks.

'No not at all. It's up to you to choose what you want. You can find out about Buddhism, Islam or Hinduism here, but there's no set doctrine.'

Mira hears our voices and comes in from the back office. She is wearing a lovely orange sari and she peers at Tim.

'Who have we here? Young man? Friend of yours, Jo?'

'Yes, yes he is.'

'I keep him to yourself.'

We both give a nervous laugh, but as usual Mira goes off into guffaws of laughter at her own joke.

'I put you in Room 22 – it's along from Jo. She show you. OK. No need to pay now. How long you stay?'

'Look, that depends.'

'I see,' Mira says winking at me, and I try my hardest to look as if I haven't noticed.

'Pay me on Monday, beginning of week. Here's the key. Enjoy your stay. Jo will show you all.'

We saunter up the stairs and along the corridor to Tim's room, with me praying that David doesn't appear. I'll have to say something to him now. I don't want to miss an opportunity with Tim. He may not even stay long, but I want to be free to do as I choose.

Tim opens up his room and we both walk in. I feel very aware of the bed in the room.

'They aren't very big are they?' I say.

'No it's OK though, for a little while. Where's your room?'

'It's just two down there. Number 21.'

I wave my arms around wildly because I'm so conscious of the unspoken thing between us.

'OK. Look, where's the shower? I need to get cleaned up.'

'I'll show you. I warn you. It's basic.'

'Look, I've been in India for months now. I know what to expect. I'll have a shower and maybe a lie down. Can I come and get you later?'

'Yes, about 6.'

I walk down the corridor, grinning all over my face. Life has a funny way of throwing up surprises.

Chapter 39

The evening meal is tortuous with David giving me knowing but really hurt looks, Gemma is also watching on and Tim, who thankfully knows nothing about any of it, just chats away. I'm relieved when it's over and I can get outside and show Tim around.

Why should I feel guilt towards David, when I've never made any commitment to him. But I do? Maybe I led him on by not being clear. No, that's not true, but if Tim hadn't turned up who knows what might have happened, and David must have felt that it was only a matter of time.

We walk through the pine forest down the hill towards the terraced rice plains. Tim stops and turns towards me, smiling.

'Why don't we sit down and take in the beauty? The sun won't be around for long. You know I love the Himalayas. And this place seems perfect, doesn't it?'

'I love it here. There are problems, obviously, because there are lots of people living in close quarters together, and that's human nature. But it's so peaceful. I've really managed to step back from my life at home and see things more clearly.'

'So is life good for you?' he asks.

'Yeah,' I smile at him, thinking how much better it was now.

My body is tingling all over. My first impressions back in Delhi, which seem such a long time ago, were right. If only he'd stay for a while. I'll just have to make him want to.

The sun is setting as we walk back through the forest, and across the long gardens of Jasanghari. I'm seeing it all in a different light today, as the perfect romantic setting. Maybe this is all meant to be.

'I might turn in as I've had quite a long day. See you tomorrow,' Tim says.

Outside my room he kisses me on the cheek and lingers a bit and then appears to think better of it and retreats quickly to his own room. I call out,

'Goodnight. Sleep well. See you tomorrow.'

I nip into my room and drop on to the bed. Tim might have made my life even more complicated but I don't want to miss any opportunity of moving closer to him. As I lie there ruminating I go over every minute of the day. Finally, I get up to go to the loo I realise it's 11ish. It may be a rash thing to do, but I go to the bathroom and then to the back stairs and towards David's room. I mustn't be seen.

I knock quietly on David's door and say quietly,

'David.'

He opens it but doesn't say anything. His chest is bare but he has a pair of white shorts on. He holds the door open for me and gestures for me to come in. I sit on the chair and he gets on the bed. His mouth is turned downwards like a child trying not to cry. The laughing has stopped.

'I need to talk to you,' I say softly.

I don't want to cause a row so I need to handle this delicately.

'I'm waiting Jo. I've been waiting for a long time.'

'I know. I'm sorry, but I can't.'

'Is it because of that Aussie? How do you know him?'

'I met him in Delhi before coming up here.'

'And?' he sneers.

'And what?'

'What goes on between you both?'

'Nothing, David. I just met him for an evening with lots of other people around, so nothing.'

'Why's he come to see you, if it was nothing?'

'I don't know. Maybe he fancied the idea of Jasanghari and when he met you all up in the mountains he thought…'

'That he fancied you, I suspect.'

'I've no idea.'

234

'Jo don't insult me. You do know. You can see the guy follows you around like a puppy. What do you think he's looking for?'

Ironically, I like him saying that.

'I met him in Delhi. We haven't seen each other since. We don't have some rip-roaring affair going on.'

'Yet.'

'No. I don't know what will happen. But David, it isn't because of Tim. It is because of me. I never felt that you and I were right. I want your friendship and for that matter I want Gemma's friendship.'

'You seem to be pretty buddyish again.'

'We had a terrible row where she accused me of taking you away from her deliberately.'

'Chance would be a fine thing.'

He is lying back on the bed propped up on the pillows, arms behind his head. He's staring at me, but this isn't the nice David I have come to know and like.

'All I want is to be friends. I care so much about you and I feel that we have a great thing going as friends and I want that to continue.'

'And you expect me to watch while you and that Aussie Timmy fellow get it together. How do you think that will feel? I may as well leave.'

'Please don't leave because of me. There's so much more here than me. I can still be your friend, Tim or no Tim.'

'But he'll be breathing down your neck, and wherever else he chooses and I'll have to watch. I can't bear it Jo. I really, really wanted you for myself.'

'I know, and I feel very bad about it, but even if Tim had not turned up I was unlikely to change my mind.'

'But I'd have worn you down to the point where you were begging for me.'

'What after all the therapy I've had here? Give me a break.'

I smile.

'Please don't leave. I'm sure it will wear off and we can get along happily like we used to.'

'But then there was always a chance and now there isn't. And do you think I'm so shallow that it will "wear off"?'

'I am truly sorry David, but please don't make any decisions without telling me. I had hoped we would always be in touch after all our experiences here. I'm going to go now.'

I turn towards the door and he gets off the bed and comes over. I just want to get out of here.

'Can friends hug each other?' he asks.

'Of course.'

We hug and he holds his face right up close to mine. I can feel the tears coming, which is stupid. He moves his lips on to mine and I pull away quickly.

'No David. I mean it.'

'You're killing me,' he snarls at me.

'Sometimes friendship is better than anything else because it endures.'

'If you say so, Jo.'

He turns his back as I let myself out. I look around and am relieved no-one sees me. I don't want to ruin my relationship with Tim before it's even started. I tiptoe down the stairs and back to my room.

I can't sleep as it all churns around in my mind. David's upset face and my renewed desire for Tim. Things really have changed.

Chapter 40

I'm tossing and turning and having trouble getting to sleep, but when I do the night is full of torrid dreams with David and Tim both making appearances so that half the time I don't know which one is which. I waver from elation to sadness thinking about them both.

After my few hours of sleep I need a shower so I splash water on my face and head to wake me up and go down to breakfast feeling uneasy. Gemma is already there with Patrick, Nicola and Alain. I get my tray of breakfast and go and join them. David walks in, sees me, and gets his breakfast. He comes over and sits next to me. I wonder when Tim will appear.

He doesn't look at me but by sitting next to me he's sending a message. This is going to be far from easy but I don't want any responsibility for what he does, whether he leaves or not, or even starts drinking again. It's not my fault. Because I care about him it hurts even more. I keep consoling myself with the fact that I could have caused him far more harm by starting up with him and deciding it wasn't what I wanted.

Tim walks through the door, looks round and sees me. I jump up.

'Let me show you what's for breakfast. It's a good spread here - yoghurt, figs, fruit and all sorts, or you can get flatbreads this morning. He helps himself and we walk back to the table. I get an extra chair for Tim and sit with him away from David.

'Hi Tim,' Gemma says. 'Have you any plans for the day?'

'I see there's plenty to do. I might go for some of the sporting activities. Wouldn't mind having a go at Taekwondo. I've done judo before.'

David listens and watches all the time but makes no eye contact with me, thankfully. I have to censor everything I say for his ears as well, so I'm not being myself. For once David isn't chatting away or telling tales.

I can't help wondering if Tim has a girlfriend somewhere else and that I might be misreading the signs. Yet he seems interested in everything I say and asks me all about my family and why I came.

Going for walks becomes routine for us and is the best way to keep away from prying eyes. Tim is keen to explore the area so it works well. I'm now finding out how little chance of privacy there is at Jasanghari and relationships become common knowledge quite quickly.

After a lovely walk through the forest we climb up the steps to the stone bench and sit underneath the bower of climbing plants.

'You'd love Sydney, Jo. We lived in a little suburb called Birchgrove on the harbour. I used to get the ferry across to central Sydney when I was at uni and on a sunny morning – it's always sunny in Aus – the water shimmers. We used to sit in the living room and look out onto Sydney Harbour and the bridge.

'On holidays we go up to Palm Beach and surf. It's so cool. And every weekend we have a barby and then on weekends my friends and I often go off to the Blue Mountains or somewhere like that. It's called that because it looks blue.'

'I'd love to go. It sounds beautiful.'

'I'll take you.'

I shiver.

'Is that a promise?'

He runs a finger down my cheek, and looks into my eyes.

 He says gently,

'Of course.'

'I've only known you for a little while and I'm telling you all about my life,' I say. 'You probably think I'm crazy running away without telling them. Well maybe I was.

'I'd felt trapped and unable to deal with it. I couldn't stand up to them. And I had this guy, a boyfriend, who, well it went on for a few years. It wasn't going anywhere and I didn't feel I could get away from him.

'I've changed so much since I've been here. I've learnt a lot about myself and why I do what I do. I'm clearer about what I want.'

'Pleased to hear it,' he says and puts his hand on my arm. I want him to hold me.

'How come your brother was out here?'

'Long story that. He has been having problems in his marriage, then he lost his job and he wanted to come out here. I can't tell you how much I didn't want him to come. I've never got on with him, and I couldn't think how we could manage it.'

'But you have?'

'Yeah. It's unbelievable really but we've grown quite close. It started off badly. I resented him and hated him for turning up and ruining my new life. But he got through some really big things while he was here, and he's changed. I like him now, and in fact I even love him now.'

He listens intently.

'So was it him who told you about your Dad?'

I nod and blink, looking away from his eyes.

'That was awful. I still hurt when I think about it. You haven't mentioned your father.'

'He died quite a few years ago. I was in my early 20s. Since then my mother has really needed me. She didn't want me to go away. I had to get away to break that link. She's treating me like a substitute husband, but I can't take it any more. Look, it isn't natural.'

'If you were so young how did you handle it? Did you look after yourself as well as your mother?'

'I didn't know what I was supposed to do. I kept thinking that my father would expect me to be the one who looked after her. My sister is five years younger and she couldn't deal with Mum at all.'

'How do you feel leaving them back in Sydney?' I ask.

'Pretty guilty but I have got to live my own life. It's 12 years ago now since he died. I just had to get away.'

'Coincidence that.'

We laugh.

'We both needed to get away from our families.'

'And if we hadn't,' he says looking directly into my eyes, 'We wouldn't be here now. Together.'

He puts his hand on mine. My stomach turns over. I'm scared. He's from the other side of the world. How could it ever work?

'I didn't know whether I should come to this place or not. I met the guys on that weekend, but I thought that Michael was with you. It was the way someone said something to him about you. Look, I was really worried that you'd be with someone, but if you were, I was going to spend one or two nights, make an excuse and go. Thank goodness I came.'

'I'm really glad you did. I wanted you to come here.'

'You did? Could you even remember me?'

'Of course.'

Our hands touch again briefly and I hope the pace is accelerating. Every day we go off and do our own thing – our classes, my yoga. I always try and make sure we're away from where David is, for his sake as well as mine. So I hardly ever take Tim to where we all sit in the garden. I'm almost cool towards Tim whenever David is around. I hope he doesn't notice.

It's now a week after Tim first arrived and he's getting familiar with Jasanghari, enjoying his Taekwondo and getting friendly with some of the others. We spend all our free time together but nothing has happened between us. We seem to be taking it very slowly, but deep down I am sure he is interested in me.

I realise now that it would have been completely wrong for me to start up with David. My gut instinct was right. I started my relationship with Rob for all the wrong reasons because I was feeling vulnerable and I was just about to do it again. Now my feelings are clear and definite about Tim and that's how it should be.

When I think of how David has been so forthright in his protestations of love, Tim is positively passive. I also realise that he

240

hasn't said a lot about his life at home. I'm driving myself mad wondering what to do next, and then remember to try and sit back and accept the slow pace.

After supper he asks me,

'Shall we go for a moonlight walk tonight, Jo?'

'Great idea.'

I grab a cardigan and some citronella oil.

'Here, have some of this so you don't get bitten.'

No-one sees us leaving out and when we get away from the house he takes my hand in his. My stomach is fluttering with a load of butterflies. I'm excited and nervous at the same time.

'Can I ask you something Jo?'

I can only whisper,

'Yes, of course.'

'David, your friend, is or was there something between you? I have felt that he is a bit hostile towards me, but you said he was with Gemma.'

'David is a great friend, but it's purely platonic. He was seeing Gemma but isn't any more. I think why he might have appeared to be a bit possessive of me is, well, I felt like that when they got together. It's a friend's thing – you know. I felt awkward when Gemma and he got together.'

'I got the impression he was a bit jealous of me.'

'Maybe. I don't know.'

'What a relief. I don't want to put anyone's nose out of joint.'

So he does like me.

The night is perfectly still. Soon the monsoon will arrive in full force but now the sky is clear and there are more stars than I have ever seen.

We stop and both look up at the moon. Tim points out the Northern Star and the Great Bear. He puts his arm around my shoulders and I shudder.

'Are you cold?' he whispers.

'Mmm.'

I turn to speak to him and he is very close. We move together and we kiss at first slowly and then passionately.

'I've been wanting to do that since I met you, back in Delhi,' Tim whispers in my ear. 'Back in that hostel where we were staying and at dinner that evening. I couldn't concentrate on what you were saying.'

I make an appreciative sigh, but my mind is in a whirl. We kiss and kiss.

'Shall we go back inside?' he whispers.

'I like being out here, away from everyone. It's not very private back there.'

We stay outside talking and embracing for another hour or two. When we get back the lights are off.

'I've got a key,' I tell him.

I unlock the door and we walk up the stairs hand in hand. He walks me past my door and on further to his own room at the end of the corridor.

I can't believe it. I've waited for what seems like ages, but actually only one week, for this moment and now we are here together. We roll on to the tiny bed, which jolts as if it's going to break and we both laugh.

It all seems to happen in such a rush that in too short a time it's all over. He's kissing me and holding me. After skinny Rob, he's so manly, so strong, so powerful. He leans back and looks at me.

'You are beautiful, Jo. I'm so pleased I came to see you.'

The night is very long but with little sleep. We intermittently make love and chat, and then we fall asleep for a short while. In the early hours I say, stroking the back of his neck,

'I'm so glad you came here. I wondered if you ever would.'

'I'd have come with you straightaway but it seemed so pushy. I haven't stopped thinking about you.'

As the light comes up, I lie there watching him sleep. He looks so peaceful. For once in my life, I managed to do the right thing by not taking on David just before Tim turned up. Tim was worth waiting for.

'I don't want to leave you Jo, but I am starving. Let's go.'

I get dressed and slip back to my room to get some clean clothes. I shower quickly and as the warm water splashes down my body, I relive every moment of the night before. Despite how tired I am, I feel really happy.

Chapter 41

David steers clear of Tim most of the time, but still talks to me when he isn't around. Gemma is absolutely fine with me these days, especially now that I am so obviously with Tim and I've noticed that she and David are at least good friends again, if not lovers.

It has crept up on me but after several weeks of spending all my nights and a large part of my days with Tim I'm falling in love. I don't even care that he comes from Australia and that the future is uncertain. It's too late to go backwards.

I try hard to focus on living in the now. I simply want to soak up the happiness with Tim while we are in the first flush of romance, and not even discuss the future.

David seems to have calmed down, and is quite nice to me when I'm around him, and once or twice he has even spoken to Tim.

'Shall we join the others in the garden this afternoon?' I ask Tim.

'Yeah, why not?'

'I need to go and have a shower. Shall I see you there?'

He nods,

'Yeah, fine with me, my darling.'

I shower and change into my cut offs and a pink T-shirt. Glancing in the mirror I realise I look much better now that I'm so happy. It's true that a love affair makes you blossom. I wander downstairs and outside to find Tim. He's talking to David when I arrive, who is lying on a mat on the ground with Gemma beside him. Her hand is on his back. That's a relief.

Gemma sits up and leans on her knees.

'I'm going to get some tea. Anyone else want one?'

'Yes please,' David says. 'You know how I like it.'

He pats her thigh – for my benefit?

Alain, Toni, Patrick and Nicola also want tea.

I'm still standing, so I say to Gemma,

'I'll come with you to help carry them.'

'Want some tea, Tim?'

We get out of sight of the others and Gemma asks me,

'Are you happy?'

'Yes, I am.'

I look at her with a knowing smile.

'I can see it written all over your face and his. You look besotted with each other. Are you?'

'He's lovely, Gemma. I can't leave him alone.'

'Well don't!'

'It's just blissful. I have never really felt like this without worrying that it was going to collapse any minute. We seem so right for each other, and at the moment he seems just perfect.'

'You don't mean that?'

'I mean that at the moment he seems perfect. I know that we're in honeymoon period and that when you get to know someone better things change and it can't last forever – the honeymoon bit. I hope the relationship does.'

'Will you go to Aus?'

'Who knows? I'd be prepared to. Neither of us has any ties so we can go anywhere. He's so easy going and I can't imagine ever having an argument with him.'

'It's good to have arguments. They help you to clear the air and move on to a different dimension.'

'Are you speaking from experience?'

'Of course, plenty of it.

'With David?'

'Maybe.'

'Is it on again? Are you OK together if you don't mind me asking?'

'Yes, we've got over what happened around you. I think it was partly me being jealous. I probably made too much of it and all the time he was very keen on me, but I wasn't accepting it. You know I was looking for problems perhaps to hide my own fears about commitment.'

'Sounds good.'

I'm not at all sure that David is trustworthy in relationships, but I'm not getting involved.

'We are far closer now than we were before,' Gemma continues. 'Maybe the break made us realise how much we wanted to be together. I really want to avoid dependent relationships though and I think we're both mature enough to get the balance right.'

'Will you stay here?'

'Not forever. Perhaps we'll go and live in northern Europe while we still can. It depends if I get work as an artist and if David knows what he wants to do. Perhaps he can work in advertising again in Europe.'

'Would he want to?'

'I don't know. For the moment we're enjoying just being.'

'That's certainly a good approach and I'm pleased it appears to be working out for all of us. I just hope it stays this way.'

'Have you dropped all your defences then?'

'Probably. I was very wary after Rob, but this is so different. I just know it's OK. I feel I can trust him.'

Gemma gets a tray and puts half the cups on them. I put the others on another tray.

'I haven't felt like this for such a long time, if ever,' I continue. 'I don't feel so frantic and excited but more comfortable and at ease. I guess that might be a good thing. Frantic and excited is fun at first but often leads to feeling manic and out of control.'

'C'mon we'd better get back or they'll think we've gone to pick the tea.'

We carry the drinks back, but outside we see dark clouds rolling over us and a distant sound of thunder.

'That sounds ominous,' Patrick says. 'The rains are coming.'

'Just like home then,' Toni says.

Chapter 42

At breakfast Tim is reading a letter from home, and he's very quiet. For the rest of the day I get the feeling he's avoiding me, and when I do get to see him his mood is sombre.

'You don't seem yourself,' I say as they we are lying in bed that night. He hasn't even been particularly amorous so something has to be wrong.

'I'm fine. Just tired.'

He gives me a quick peck and rolls over and sleeps. I can feel myself welling up. Already I am terrified that something's changed and that he's not sure about me anymore. I mustn't do this, it's too familiar.

After a couple of days like this I am beginning to get a pain in my stomach. Everything has been so perfect, too perfect? I know it can't always be like that, but he seems to be cooling on me. What have I done? I don't understand and every time I ask I draw a blank. Why can't he be more open with me?

It seems to me now that I am making all the arrangements to see him, and I toy with the idea of going to bed alone. Would he come and get me?

'Can we go for a walk this evening Tim?'

'Why not?'

We walk through the gate and take the path through the forest to end up near where we first kissed. The ground is wet and we are both kitted out in jackets and boots. It isn't the kind of evening to sit on the ground. I feel so nervous, but I have to find out.

'Have you had bad news from home? Please tell me, Tim. If you don't want things to continue you have to tell me.'

'Jo, of course I want us to continue. It's not exactly bad news.'

'Please Tim can you tell me? I don't like it when you're like this. You've been different all week. Is it me?'

'No of course not. Why should it be?'

'I don't know, you're different. And I need to know.'

'I need to talk to you Jo about us.'

My body tightens and I forget to breathe.

'I think I should go home, for a little while. I only want to go for three weeks or so and then I can come back. I don't want to leave you Jo but I'm worried that my mother might be ill. Will you wait for me?'

'Yes of course. But then what? Are you going to want to come back if she is ill? Perhaps I could come out there. Why didn't you tell me?'

'Which question do you want me to answer? Well, maybe you could come, but I'll be back soon and then we'll make plans.'

'Yes, OK.'

I'm not sure if I believe him. My stomach feels like someone has punched it.

'How long were you planning on staying here?' he asks me.

'I never really planned anything. Don't forget I ran away. I will need to work some day and to face my family too. I've been so worried about going home, but if you came too maybe I could cope. When are you going back to Aus?'

'Tomorrow.'

'What? And you've only just told me?'

I feel furious, but don't want to row with him. He must have booked the flight without telling me. It must have been the day he got the letter – I think he disappeared and perhaps he went to Shimla to book the flight. I feel that everything I thought we had has been made a mockery of, if he couldn't even tell me about going back to Sydney.

In my room in the evening I'm crying my eyes out when there is a knock on the door. I know it's him so I wipe my face with a tissue. He looks at my face, puts a finger on my cheek and wipes away the tears. Then he takes me in his arms.

249

'Don't be upset, Jo. Please. If this relationship is meant to happen it will. You have to trust me. I am coming back. Just give me a night to remember. Please.'

'What about your old girlfriend?'

'Celia. That's firmly out of the way. She's with someone else. Don't worry.'

We lie down on my bed holding each other and I wish I didn't have to let go.

Tim leaves early in the morning. I'm not going to the station with him as I don't want to say goodbye. I spend the whole day immersed in yoga, art classes and an Ayurvedic cookery class. I mustn't feel sorry for myself.

Chapter 43

The strength I've built up since I've been at Jasanghari has completely left me. I've met someone really special for the first time, and there is no guarantee that he'll come back.

Now he's gone I'm not even convinced he's told me the truth about Celia. I so want to believe him, that he'll be back and that he loves me. Now there isn't anyone I can speak to as I don't want to discuss it with Gemma or David, so I try to act cool when I'm around them.

I spend more time with them now but so much has changed that it doesn't seem to work as well as it used to. I'm much closer to Gemma which helps, but there is still an awkwardness with David and I'm not sure how to behave with him. If I am ultra-friendly I'm worried he might interpret it the wrong way and approach me again. Then I'm worried that Gemma will think that because I haven't got Tim, I am going to be a threat. What a tangled web we weave.

It has been a while since I've talked to Rasi, so I think now is the time to go back. My crush on him is over and forgotten now and I am sure I can talk about Tim.

'All the work I've done here trying to prevent myself being so dependent. And now I'm involved with Tim, I feel it's all gone out the window.'

Rasi looks out of the window which makes me smile. He must be doing me good already.

'It's just an expression, Rasi, I mean it's all gone away, gone to pot, oh you understand don't you?'

'Yes, but I don't believe. The strength inside that you have is still there. You are maybe in love but Jo is strong enough to be alone. You not need Tim to survive.'

'It doesn't feel like that now.'

'Maybe too early.'

'I felt very sure that this relationship was going to work and inside I was sure he'd be back, something I've never felt before. It's a kind of gut feeling – right in here – that it's going to work out and we're meant to be together.

'I was completely sure that I could trust him, and now I'm not so much. He's gone home because he has to, I know. He has commitments and I'm sure it's OK.'

'Yes. He has. And you? Your family? After Michael you want to go home?'

'I don't mind so much. I've got to go soon, maybe in September and maybe with Tim, but I can face them all. I just hope I don't revert to type.'

'Pardon?'

'I hope that I don't behave like I used to do. And I hope they don't either. Mind you, Michael has been here, Dad's on his own, and Mum is away. Not sure if she'll be back. Perhaps they are different too. It would help.'

'Yes. You are not perhaps the only one to make change,' Rasi suggested.

'No. Certainly Michael has, if it lasts.'

'Believe in him, believe in you, believe in Tim.'

'Yes I'll try. I suppose that there are always commitments when you get a bit older, and Tim has..'

'Especially, when you have children.'

'Yes, but that's not relevant.'

'What do you mean?' Rasi looks puzzled.

'It's not relevant to Tim,' I insist.

'Well his daughter. He has to see her.'

I look at Rasi, feeling the blood drain from my face.

'Sorry. You knew? Sorry I thought you knew,' Rasi says.

'Oh yes. Of course. It's difficult for him,' I bluff.

'Especially, when so young. She's only four, isn't she?'

'Yes.'

Now I want to get away from Rasi immediately, to be alone. Tim is a liar, or certainly he is economical with the truth. I have to be alone and I don't want Rasi to know that I didn't know, especially as he may feel he's broken a confidence. I can't imagine why he even knows. Whatever am I going to do?

I toss and turn on my bed for what seems like hours. Finally, I come up with a plan. I've got Tim's mother's address, because he gave it to me. I write a proper letter to him so I can seal it. I don't want anyone to read my transcript for an email.

I don't want to sound angry – ever the same old Jo, not wanting to upset anyone else. But how could he not tell me that he has a daughter? It isn't exactly something you forget to mention.

Dear Tim,

I found out something today that I am very shocked by. Why didn't you tell me? Why didn't you? There's no shame in having a child, but to conceal it makes me wonder what other lies you have told me.

I don't know whether I can trust that you will be back but I really do want an explanation.

I don't want to lose you, but please, please tell me what other secrets you have. Are you married?

Jo x

I feel so tired but get up and shower. In an effort to cover up my puffy, red eyes I overdo the make up. I set off in search of Sahib.

'Is it today that you are going to Shimla?'

'Yes very soon. Can you be here ten minutes?'

'Yup. I'll grab some bread and I'll come with you. I need to go to the post office.'

I have to be so sure that this letter is sent.

253

Getting out of Jasanghari is the best thing I can do today. Sahib won't ask any searching questions and I can think, but the trouble is I just go over and over the same ground. All I really want to do is cry, so I close my eyes and try to sleep on the way down to Shimla.

'You tired, Jo?'

'Yeah, I haven't been sleeping well. I don't know why.'

We arrive in Shimla and Sahib parks in the usual spot. I leave him for an hour, queue in the post office and get an express delivery stamp so that he will get it quickly. Why shouldn't he know how I feel? Then I take myself off to a little café by the square and look around. As usual it is buzzing with people and plenty of noise, so different from being at Jasanghari.

The prospect of going back to Bristol without him, is bleak. My wonderful new relationship, which I thought was the best I'd ever had, is looking decidedly messy. Will I cope with heartache any better now than I did in my previous life? Do I really have this inner strength that Rasi assured me about?

When I get back to the centre, I try to avoid everyone, but Gemma catches me in the corridor.

'Hey are you coping OK without Tim?'

'Bit sad really. Just need to chill out alone.'

'Yes I understand. He'll be back soon though. He's head over heels.'

I give her a wry smile. I hope she's right.

After lunch every day I go straight to the general reception area to look at the post. My life suddenly feels empty. The place I was so happy in before Tim came to see me, now seems lonely for me.

I get a brief email note from Michael, thanking me for everything and telling me that lots has changed and Hannah and he are working it all out.

Six days running I go to reception, feeling more despondent each time. On the sixth day I find a letter addressed to me from Sydney, Australia.

254

Darling Jo,

I never wanted you to find out this way. Of course, I didn't and I'm so sorry I hadn't told you but I was scared that you'd think I had too much baggage and you'd ditch me.

I'll try to explain. I was with Celia for two years but only because she got pregnant when we were going out. There was never any thought that we would settle down together but we both felt that she should have the baby. So when Rosalie was born I moved in with Celia but it didn't work.

It's now 18 months since we split up and Celia is living with Chris, who is not a problem as far as Rosalie is concerned. I can see her when I want to and I spend time with her and take her to my mother's.

My mother has been ill – that was true, but it's not so serious. It was Rosalie I had to see. My mother told me she'd been crying about me every time she saw her and I couldn't leave it any longer. I love her more than anyone in the world, sorry - but I think you'll understand what I mean.

Please wait for me, Jo. I am coming back. I can afford to come back to India and go home with you for a holiday, but we may have to talk about you coming to live out here because I can't face living on the other side of the world from Rosalie.

There is a lot to discuss and decide and I wanted to talk to you about this face to face. We need to come to decisions together, and I was so worried that you might not want to consider this. I'm so sorry it happened this way.

Unless I hear from you I'm coming back on 4th September. Please wait for me. If you don't want me to, please send an email to tim.hewly@bigpond.aus or ring my mum's number which I gave to you. Otherwise, I will see you on Tuesday 4th.

I miss you more than I can say.

Lots and lots and lots of love and kisses, Tim xx

The feeling of doom lifts. It might not be easy, but he still loves me. I didn't imagine that we were so close, and he didn't actually lie. Tuesday is now only three days away.

Chapter 44

I get a ride down to Shimla to meet Tim with Anouk. Waiting on the platform on my own I'm surrounded by the snack seller, the juice man, the pakora woman, and all the others in their multi-coloured outfits. The train rolls in and my stomach rolls over. I stand and watch, trying so hard to maintain my cool. I see this big, tall dark haired guy striding towards me, smiling all over his face, and my heart leaps. All the anger and misgivings evaporate.

He puts his bags down and hugs me, holds me tight and kisses me. Some of the locals laugh and point and young boys dance around us singing.

'They obviously don't do this here.'

'Sorry, forgot. I bored my mum and sister to tears. They know you intimately now.'

'I hope not.'

'Well maybe not that much. They just know all about you. They could pass an exam on you.'

We walk back to Anouk and the van and for once I'm delighted that it's such a tight squeeze in the front. I feel so pleased to be back with my lovely man.

When we get back we have lunch and then sit in Tim's room. Before he unpacks anything we are in bed together, and then we lie chatting for what seems like hours.

'You'll love Rosalie, Jo. Here's a picture.'

I see a gorgeous little girl with curly brown hair. She is tanned and wearing a white dress.

'Do you forgive me for not telling you? Of course I was going to, but I wanted to wait until I got back.'

'Yes, OK. But please no more secrets.'

'Was it Rasi who told you?'

'He assumed that I knew and we were chatting generally about things. He mentioned you having children and I didn't want him to know he'd put his foot in it so I didn't say. I don't want him to feel unprofessional. Why did he know?'

'Well, I did have a session with him one day. I told him about my daughter - it just came out. I suppose I'm proud of Rosalie, but I recognise that it's not a great start to a relationship and I didn't want anything to spoil us.'

'As I said, no more secrets Tim, please.'

'No, OK. But you and I need to discuss what we are going to do. Look, I'd like you to come back and live with me in Sydney, and if you can't get a long enough visa to stay we can get married.'

'Wow. Tim.'

'Is that a yes?'

'It's a lot to take in, but let me think. I'm sure, well, yes. I want to be with you, Tim. But I need to go home first. Will you come with me?'

'Yes, but I think we should go soon. I can't spend too much time away. Look, apart from anything else I have a business to pick up, I need to earn money and I have to find us somewhere to live. We can't stay with my mum. I was renting before I left and I let it go.'

'So what do you suggest?'

'How soon can we go to the UK?'

'How long does it take to arrange? I don't know really.'

'Well when I've had a decent night's sleep, if I can possibly get one with you next to me, let's organise it. We can go to Shimla tomorrow, can't we? And we can go on the Internet and sort out some tickets.'

'Gosh. You do move quickly.'

'I am a fast mover, Jo.'

He pulls me towards him.

'Hang on a minute.'

I hold him at bay with my hand.

'Let's sort this out. We are going back to the UK – for how long?'

'How long do you want?'

'A week?'

'OK if we can be back in Aus by around the 20ᵗʰ that'd be ripper.'

'I see you've dropped back into the lingo.'

'Fair dinkum.'

I look into his eyes. His hair has grown enough now that there are little curls on top and at the nape of his neck. He seems more vibrant than ever.

I try to pull myself up, but he doesn't let me.

'No, Tim. I've got to get going now. If we're leaving soon I have to make some arrangements, check how much notice they want from me here. I'm a long term resident you know, and I'll see if we can get to Shimla in the morning, and I want to start saying my goodbyes. It's sad for me you know.'

'Come back here. We're not going in ten minutes.'

'OK, but there is a lot to sort out.'

'Don't forget the laid back lifestyle. If you're not careful you'll start getting stressed. Come here.'

'I'm excited and nervous and everything all at once. It's about ten huge steps all in one go. We've talked about being together, getting married, going to Australia, going home together, meeting Rosalie, giving up living here. It's a lot to take in, but I've always wanted to go to Sydney. One of my friends lived there for a while and said it was the most beautiful city in the world. So much to think about.'

'So you need to lie back and relax. Come on.'

He pulls me down.

'Leave me alone you Aussie brute.'

'I love you Jo. I have missed you so much. You'll love it in Oz.'

'I love you too. I really do and I've never felt so sure about anything in my life, but it's still a big change for me, more than for you. I know I want to do it, and that's really unusual for me.'

The next morning we go back to Shimla with Sahib. We walk up The Ridge to the Internet café, holding hands. We are so early that there isn't a queue, so we take a couple of seats in front of a computer.

'Right, mine is different because I have an open return so I only need to book the flight. And you need to try to get a single flight to Bristol, via Heathrow with Air India.'

'There's one here on Tuesday morning. What day is it today? Christ it's Friday.'

'Is it too soon?'

My eyes fill with tears.

'C'mon Jo.'

'It's going to be sad, but can't we look for one a couple of days later? Don't forget we've got to get to Delhi and that takes a day, so if we go on Thursday we will still be leaving on Wednesday won't we?'

'Yes OK. Why don't we try the deluxe bus? I was told that they leave every hour and they're only about 300 Rupees.'

'Yes I don't mind. We've both been on the Toy Train.'

'That's it then. Book it.'

'We can book them together but I don't have to pay, so let's see if that works. You know these websites, they might find that too much to cope with.'

When we've made our bookings at the café we wander around the Himachal Emporium looking for presents for our families. After a quick drink we get back to Scandal Point where Sahib is sitting on a bench, looking as if he has fallen asleep. I shake his arm. He looks startled and jumps up.

'All made?'

'Yes we're all done,' I beam at him.

'Thanks Sahib.'

As soon as we get back to Jasanghari, I search for Mira.

'I have news Mira. I am leaving. It's sad.'

She makes a pouty face, holds her arms out and hugs me to her big bosom.

'You no leave ever.'

'That's what I thought but I've got things to do, places to go, you know.'

'Man to go with?' she asks, her eyes sparkling as she cackles in her familiar way.

'Yes, Tim, the man.'

'He is good man. Big man. He can keep you safe.'

'I certainly hope so.'

Now I have three people I must talk to - Rasi, David and Gemma on their own. I don't want them, particularly David, finding out from someone else.

I run up the stairs to Tim's room. He's lying on the bed and pats it for me to join him.

'No, you rampant man. I need a bit of time and space to speak to my friends about it all, so please don't think I'm ignoring you for the next hour or so. I'm not sure I can catch them all today, but I might try.'

'You do what you have to. I can have you for the rest of my life. I don't have to be too selfish do I?'

He is such a welcome relief from Rob.

I put on my flip flops and go downstairs to the restaurant. My head is buzzing, but now it's happy. I am taking a huge leap of faith

261

and until I'd met Tim I had seen Jasanghari as an unending future for me, although in practice I had to leave some time soon. It is scary.

David is sitting on the terrace reading a book on his own. I'm pleased to see him first, and I take a deep breath.

'Hi David. Can I interrupt you?'

'Of course. What's up?'

'I really want to tell you first, but I'm leaving.'

He opens his mouth and looks at me.

'Why? Oh don't tell me, it's the Aussie?'

'Well, yes in some ways. I feel awkward telling you this.'

'No need. That's all in the past. Call it a temporary madness.'

He smiles so genuinely that I feel at ease.

'So what are you doing?'

'We are going home.'

'To the dreadful Greaves family?'

'Yes the very same, but I'm hoping they've got better, or at least my perception has improved.'

'Well you know my mate Michael is a new improved model, isn't he?'

'Yes and that helps incredibly. I gather others have changed too, so we'll see. But we're not staying long.'

'Ah?'

'I'm going to Australia.'

'Jo that's a big step to take isn't it? Are you that sure about Tim?'

'Yes I am. There are lots of things I have to get used to and new people and it may be tough, but I want to try.'

'Are you happy?'

'David I am. I'm really sorry about us, but I still treasure your friendship.'

'Me too.'

'Are you? Is it OK with Gemma?' I ask tentatively.

'It's good with her. We've had a lot of things to sort out and lots of rows, as you know.'

He chortles and looks away. Now my mouth feels dry.

'Sorry David.'

'Why sorry? You couldn't help it if I fancied you like crazy?'

'If you put it like that.'

'And things have worked out well for me really. I think Gemma and I are going to try to move out of here together and if it works who knows, we may have hundreds of little sprogs. How about you?'

'Well yes. I'd like to but..' I hesitate.

'What, don't tell me he's not up to it?'

'No, you idiot. I may as well tell you - he already has a child.'

'Really he's a dark horse then isn't he? He's never mentioned it.'

'No maybe not. He's not the kind of guy who goes around talking about himself much.'

'What, unlike me you mean. I see, the strong silent type. Is that your type?'

'Maybe. I wasn't having a go at you.'

'No I know. Anyway, this child. How old is he or she?'

'She's four and she's a girl and her name is Rosalie, and she looks lovely.'

'And the ex-wife?'

'Partner. Not wife. It was all a bit of a mistake and it didn't work out.'

'Well I hope he doesn't muck you around. Or he'll have me to answer to.'

'No, I trust him David.'

'Never ever trust a man, Jo.'

He laughs, and I raise my eyes to the heavens.

'You're hopeless aren't you? I have to trust him or I can't have a relationship with him, and also I have to trust my own instincts.'

'Well Jo. I've never been quite convinced about your instincts. They made a mistake with me.'

'Sssh David. Don't say that. You're with Gemma and you say it's good, so that is how it is meant to be.'

'Yes you're probably right. I'm just a bit jealous, I don't mind telling you. But I still want to be with Gemma. If I'd had my way I'd have both of you like some of these oriental princes who have harems.'

'Yes, yes. That would have been fun for us, I'm sure.'

I can't help giggling.

Gemma walks in wearing her white cap over her eyes and a pair of sunglasses. I feel guilty, but God knows why.

'Hey what would have been fun?' she asked suspiciously.

'I was just saying if we'd all stayed here forever. I came to find you Gemma to tell you that we're leaving. Tim and I. We are going to the UK for a week or so for me to get a visa for Australia, and catch up with family and I'm going to live in Sydney.'

'Jo!' Gemma says and takes her glasses off and grabs hold of me in a big bear hug.

'I'm so pleased for you. That's fantastic. Isn't it David?'

'Yes of course. Although, it will be different here.'

'Nothing lasts forever though does it?' Gemma says. 'And we'll be clearing off sooner or later. I hope you're going to stay in touch.'

Gemma sounds bossy.

264

'I want to know how you're getting on with your man and the family, although you'll be leaving them behind.'

'Of course. With technology these days you can be in touch wherever you are.'

'Unless it's Jasanghari,' David says.

'Well yes it's a bit of an exception though. I think Sydney might be a bit more connected to the world.'

'When do you go, Jo?' Gemma asked.

'Wednesday early.'

'No.' David looks shocked. 'I thought you meant in about a month's time.'

'We're flying out on Thursday and we're having a short time at home, but Tim needs to get back because of his work – he owns this surfing business and it's coming up for the season over there, and..'

'And?' David asks.

'And he has a daughter over there.'

Gemma's eyes open wide.

'Really? I never knew.'

'No it wasn't common knowledge, but he has a four year old girl.'

'So you'll be a step-mum.'

'Yes I suppose I will. I hadn't thought of it like that. Anyway I'm going off to see who else I can tell. I need to see Rasi.'

'Oh yes, Rasi,' David mumbles.

'I have to talk to Rasi. He's the one who got me sorted enough to be able to contemplate all this.'

'No, Jo,' Gemma says, tapping me on the shoulder.

'You are the one.'

'Yes, OK Gemma, that is true.'

265

Outside it's not as warm as it used to be. I nose around the outbuildings and peer through the slats into the room where Rasi often sees people. I have to be discreet in case he is counselling someone. He is lying on a mat on the floor, so I open the rickety old door slowly and creep in.

I stand looking at him while he has his eyes closed. I'll miss him, but I don't feel anything more for him now. It was as he had said, an attachment I was making because he was my mentor.

He opens one eye and then another and turns his head.

'Jo? Sorry how long you been there?'

'Only a minute. I didn't want to disturb you, but I wanted to talk to you.'

'Is there a problem? Do you want to make reservation?'

'No not now. I just need to tell you what I'm doing.'

I sit down on the wooden bench by the window and pull back the blind to let some air in.

He gets up off the mat, moving in an agile way like a sleek cat, to sit beside me.

'The time has come Rasi that I am going to leave.'

'Oh Jo. You stay forever, no? I not to be attached to my clients, but Jo, I shall miss you. We have wonderful talks and you such a clever woman.'

'What would I have done without you? You've made me love my life. Thank you.'

'You did yourself. Don't think that someone else did. You are great person and you should notice that.'

'I do much more now, but only because you guided me. The greatest thing for me and I can't believe now that I've spent my life not knowing it, is that it's up to me to make my life good. I don't have to wait for it to happen.'

'I know the world is fighting and the money is a problem now, but we think life getting better. People getting more aware, more caring. We are all responsible for our world.'

266

'I hope so. I have a concept of something spiritual which I've never had before. I used to believe in God and heaven and it was all rosy and nice and when it went away I had nothing to replace it.

'But now I believe that God is in us – not a person sitting up there in charge in a red jumper – that was my childhood fantasy. And I want to find God in myself and I'm not even sure I want to call it God because that means a man with a red jumper!

'Since I've been here I've become more spiritual, not religious. You can look for enlightenment in your everyday life. I only hope I can find it.'

'It's possible Jo,' Rasi says. 'Just remember this journey we are on, it never stops.'

'Don't remind me. Even though I felt like I'd retreated from the world, Michael came along to remind me about the past and that was hard work, very hard work.'

He nods.

'And there have been other ups and downs with my friends here. Lots of those that I haven't talked about, and now Tim.'

'Ah the Australian man. You are leaving with him?'

'I am and what's more we are going to live in Australia, and of course I have to meet his daughter, and maybe, just maybe, we will get married.'

He put his hands into prayer position and moved them up towards his face.

'This news is so good. So good. He seems a good man.'

'Yes it's not been easy, because he has his daughter and he went home, and I didn't really know if it would work out. But he came back and we've decided that we want to be together. It feels just right. I know it's a risk and maybe I'm crazy, but my heart is dictating now.'

'Life is all risk. If we don't risk, what have we?'

'I suppose you're right. I can only go with my gut feeling.'

I tap my tummy so he understands, and he nods.

267

'And your family? What about them?'

'We are going back to see them first. In fact Rasi, we are going on Wednesday.'

'So soon?'

He puts his hands up in despair.

'No time for party?'

'Sure this weekend if you think we can.'

'Of course, we have music and dancing. We have to say goodbye to our long staying people and you Jo, how long has it been?'

'Six whole months. A lifetime Rasi.'

'And you are happy with Tim?'

'Things are good, but he doesn't always tell me everything, you know. I'm not sure I really know all about him yet.'

'I was concerned, but I know you didn't want me say anything that you not know about daughter. Very wrong me to say something.'

'You did me a favour. How did you know I didn't know?'

'Your face. It tells a lot of stories. This getting to know it takes long time – 30 years maybe. He is man Jo. It's not natural to talk about feelings – that is for women. These men who are so, you know, what do you call it?'

'Macho?'

'Yes macho. They grow up in macho cultures – Australia you know. Where you don't talk about feelings. You go hunting wild animals, and the women, they sit talking!'

He grins broadly showing an array of white teeth.

'Australia is quite civilised,' I say laughing.

'Keep talking to each other,' he says wagging his index finger at me.

'It's important.'

'I'll certainly try. I know it may not be so easy, particularly as he already has a child. I won't be first in line, but I just feel it's the right thing to do. I've always been a bit non-committal before – do you know what I mean?'

He shakes his head.

'I didn't want to make commitment – I was a bit half-hearted, not really sure.'

'I see,' Rasi nods. 'Yes I know.'

'And you with your four children and your lovely wife. How do you manage? Are you as nice to your wife as you seem? Of course out here it's different.'

'It different. Women do not have great power, but my wife she is strong lady.'

'You mean in her mind. She's a nice small lady I know, but we call it feisty.'

'Fystee?'

'Yes like that. Knows what she wants and stands up for herself.'

'Yes you are right, she fystee.'

I get up.

'I am going now, but of course I will see you before I go. We will say goodbye on Tuesday and I perhaps will cry.'

'I, too.'

'I'll never forget what you've done for me. You are very special.'

This time Rasi has tears in his eyes as I hug him.

Chapter 45

Beth and Mark were in the lounge sipping tea. There was a strong smell of polish, two vases full of flowers and the room had been decorated.

She noticed her dad looked much older. The past few months had taken their toll.

'It will be the first time we've been together for so long,' Beth said.

'What do you think? I'm all nervous about Mum and about Jo really.'

'You don't need to be nervous about Jo do you? She's your daughter.'

'But I haven't seen her since you know, since all this happened with your mother.'

'Well I gather she's madly in love. I doubt she'll give you a hard time. Anyway Dad if we're having a do I want to bring someone.'

'Who?'

'Don. I met him at Rob's party last month.' Beth's legs were jigging up and down as she spoke.

Mark sat forward.

'Was he the one who didn't take your phone number? What happened?'

'It didn't occur to me at the time but Rob has my number so he got it from him. I've been seeing him every weekend since and I really like him. He's unattached and available and he's wonderful.'

'Good. I'm glad you're happy dear. Beth can I go to meet your mother at the airport on my own?'

'Yes I suppose so. I do want to see her though.'

Mark had made up the spare room bed but was hoping it wouldn't be needed. He had been on his own now for six months and after his initial attempts he had not even tried to touch a woman. He wanted Maggie back.

He put on the jacket she had bought him a few years earlier and splashed on one of her favourite after-shaves. He looked in the mirror. He scrubbed up quite well, but there were lines under his eyes that hadn't been there before everything changed.

He was leaning over the barrier at Heathrow, when a woman with short hair and baggy clothes walked up to him pushing a case on wheels. He was wondering why, when he realised it was Maggie.

'Hello,' she said and bent down to fiddle with her bag, giving him no opportunity to kiss her.

He put his hand on her arm.

'It's great to see you. You look, well, different, but good. Really tanned. You've lost a lot of weight though.'

She pecked him on the cheek in a perfunctory way.

'Come on – give me the case and some of your bags. I've got the car in the short term car park. What do you want to do? I can make you a meal when we get home.'

'That would be great. I could do with just being at home. I'm tired. I was up all night before we flew out.'

He put her bags in the boot and opened the door for her. She seemed friendly enough, but formal as if they didn't know each other well. She let down the back of the car seat, leant back and closed her eyes.

'There's a lot to tell you really,' Mark said. 'Jo's got a new boyfriend and she's bringing him home next week.'

'Oh that's fantastic,' she mumbled, still with eyes closed. 'I can't wait to see her. There's so much to tell her. What's his name, this boyfriend?'

'Ummm, now is it Jim or James, I can't remember?'

She groaned and made him feel like a disappointment already.

271

'And Beth, how is she?'

'Believe it or not she also has a new boyfriend.'

'Not married I hope.'

'No, he's apparently available. Beth seems to have changed. She's got quite friendly with Hannah.'

'Really? Sounds like an odd match. How come?'

'There's so much you don't know - Michael went out to India, to see Jo.'

'I knew that before I went. How was it?'

'He hasn't told me much about it but he seems so different. So cheerful. And I gather,' he hesitated.

'Yes.'

'That things are much better between them – Hannah and Michael. It seems,' he hesitated, 'That absence made the heart grow fonder.'

He glanced over at her to see her reaction. Her eyes were closed and her face was devoid of emotion.

'How do you know?' she asked lazily.

'Well he said that it was great to be home, how much he'd missed Hannah and the children. And that they were trying to make a new start. She has got a job.'

'She has what?'

Maggie suddenly sat up, eyes wide open.

'Yes. It's hard to believe and they're selling up. Buying somewhere cheaper. And another thing I was particularly surprised about.'

'Yes?'

'They're sending Stephen to state school. Michael told me he'd never been bothered about private schools but Hannah had insisted, but she's changed her views.'

'It sounds really different. And this is because he went away?'

'Yes. And you've been away.'

'I have and now I'm back for six weeks,' she said.

Mark plummeted.

'It sounds too good to be true,' Maggie said, laughing. 'I can't wait to see them all.'

She shuffled down into her seat.

'It's odd being in a car,' she mused as much to herself as to him. 'Particularly one like this.'

'Why?'

'I haven't been in cars. Occasionally in jeeps or trucks but usually sitting in the back, without all this luxury.'

She chortled. He wondered if she really was Maggie, or an impostor.

For the rest of the journey she dozed and he listened to the radio. It was all so awkward. Here was the woman he'd known for nearly 40 years and he didn't know how to talk to her.

He swung the car into the drive and parked outside the front door. He'd left all the lights on so it would be welcoming. He jumped out quickly and opened the boot to get her bags. Maggie yawned and climbed out. She fumbled for her key and opened the door.

'Nice smell. What is it?'

'It's chicken casserole, just in case you were hungry.'

'Mmm, yes.'

She walked into the kitchen and had a look round. Then she went into the lounge.

'Expecting somebody?' she asked, but not sarcastically.

'Some very nice flowers. I see it's changed – you've redecorated the walls, and that picture. Is it new?'

'No,' he answered, so pleased that she'd noticed everything.

'I had it in the office but I remembered you liked it so I put it up.'

She looked in the study and dining room and saw a large pale blue oriental rug. Where had that come from?

Upstairs was much the same as normal. She put down her things in the spare room and glanced in her own bedroom. It was so neat it looked unlived in. She noticed he'd even pulled the curtains back properly which he never used to do.

Mark put some potatoes in a pan and stuck the broccoli in the steamer. He felt desperate to talk to her, but made himself be patient.

'The house is nice and clean,' she said walking back in.

She'd changed into a pair of jeans and a T-shirt, which showed even more how thin she'd become. She took the casserole and peered inside,

'Gosh that looks good. Is cooking your new hobby?'

She laughed and he cheered up.

'Well I decided as a man on my own that it was time I developed a few culinary skills, became a bit domesticated. I can look after myself. I've had to.'

He wished he hadn't added that bit.

'A glass of wine, my dear?'

'I'll probably get drunk. I haven't had any wine since I left here.'

He opened his eyes wide, but made sure she couldn't see.

'It doesn't matter if you get a bit tipsy does it?' he asked. 'You haven't got to go anywhere. We've got all the time in the world.'

He wondered if he was coming on a bit too strong. He didn't want to put her off.

After dinner she showed him some pictures of the children in the village and some of the fellow workers.

'That straw hut over there. That was my little home and I grew to love it.'

'You've obviously enjoyed – not the right word, but you've obviously found it fulfilling.'

'I have, very fulfilling.'

'Makes coming back here a bit boring I suppose?' he asked tentatively.

'It can't be boring when you've got family to see. Particularly when you tell me what they've all been up to. I'm really quite excited. But I'm very tired. I'm going to have a bath and an early night.'

'There's plenty of hot water.'

She felt like a guest in her own home. It was very much his home now.

'Thanks for the meal. I appreciate the flowers – they're lovely.'

She helped him clear away and went upstairs. He wanted to run up after her and try and guide her into the bedroom, but he knew he had to play it cool. He could piss her off straightaway if he started being pushy, and besides it was her house too.

Maggie spent an hour in the bath. Mark sat watching television wondering what she would look like now she was much thinner. If they had a normal relationship he could have just gone upstairs and sat on the edge of the bath.

When she eventually got out of the bath he heard the door to the spare room open. He walked slowly up the stairs and knocked on her door.

'Yes. Hold on a minute.'

It was like having one of his daughters staying.

He opened it slowly and peered round. She was in a pair of pants and a short top. He couldn't believe the size of her. She looked the same shape as she'd been when he met her.

'Do you want anything?'

'No. I'm fine. I'm really tired.'

She climbed into the bed.

275

'Do you want any company?'

'No Mark, not tonight.'

With that she turned off the light and rolled over to face the wall.

Not tonight, he kept thinking. Maybe another night. He poured himself another glass of wine and watched *Have I Got News For You* to cheer himself up.

Chapter 46

My stomach is on edge all the time. The idea of my new life is exciting, yet it's daunting. Saying goodbye to all my friends at Jasanghari is heart-breaking. This is the place I've come to love and think of as home, where I turned a corner and became stronger, and where Tim and I have formed a deep relationship.

I've been through so many ups and downs with David and Gemma but I am still very fond of them. I seem to have set something in motion. They are going to travel together for a while and then decide what to do. Toni, Patrick, Nicola and Alain are all leaving a few weeks after me. The place is completely changing – there is a new influx of people arriving and it feels different. It is the right time to move on.

It's the night before we take the bus back to Delhi, and we're having a big party in the restaurant. For the first time in six months, alcohol is going to be available. I hope David can cope.

'I don't want a hangover tomorrow. I haven't had a drink for months.' I tell Tim.

He throws back his head and laughs.

'You'll have to get back in the swing of things now in the real world. You know the reputation us Aussies have.'

'I had heard. I'm sure I'll get back into it, but maybe not in such a habitual way. That's maybe a good thing.'

I didn't need to be concerned as there wasn't a lot of alcohol at my party, and it soon ran out. I'm a bit relieved as we have to get up so early.

We're eating a quick breakfast at 5.30 in the morning, but no-one is around.

'Strange. I thought they'd all be up to say goodbye. Maybe they're all hungover today!' I muse to Tim.

'We had our goodbyes last night. You can't expect miracles.'

Tim grabs our bags, and walks towards the door.

'Come on, my darling. We've got to go.'

We walk through reception and I take a long wistful look at all the pictures and deities around the room that I've become so used to. Sahib is standing in the doorway holding the keys to the truck. He holds open the heavy front door of Jasanghari and we walk outside.

I can't believe my eyes. There's a big line of people, including the staff, friends and other residents.

I gasp and put my hand over my mouth.

'Wow! I feel like the queen, or something! How amazing.'

Rasi, David, Gemma, Patrick, Alain, and Toni, Deepika, Mira and so many more people. I kiss and hug them all, choking back the tears, hardly able to speak.

Gemma and I put our arms round each other and have a long hug.

'Keep in touch,' I say to her my voice wobbling.

'I want to know what you're doing. You've got Tim's address and my mum's, but when we're all back on our phones we can talk or message all the time. We can support each other. I hope everything goes well.'

David looks uncomfortable, and his eyes look moist. He hugs me and perhaps we both briefly think of what might have been. Tim is hanging back while I say my goodbyes.

David shakes Tim's hand and says,

'Look after her mate. She's very special.'

'I will. I will.'

It's just overwhelming. We have to go so I climb into the front seat of the truck and turn to look at them all, waving until we turn a corner and I can't see them anymore. Tears are pouring down my face and I blow my nose.

'I'm sorry Tim. I knew it would be hard. I feel like I've been here forever.'

'We all so sad. We like Jo very much,' Sahib tells Tim.

278

'I understand Sahib. I like her quite a lot too.'

We all laugh, relieved for a light moment to break up the tension. I feel shattered and the motion of the truck makes me fall asleep on Tim's shoulder. When I jolt awake I found that we are winding our way into Shimla. Sahib parks up and insists on taking as many bags as he can, but Tim keeps hold of his rucksack.

We get to the bus stop and like everywhere in this wonderful country there are people everywhere. The ticket enables us to cut through the queue.

'Now going, 11.15 Delhi.'

'Come on quickly,' Tim calls.

I catch up with him, turn quickly to Sahib and kiss him on the cheek. His head wobbles, he beams and puts his hands together in *Anjali Mudra,* the prayer position.

'Thank you so much for everything,' I say.

I feel so sad but happy, so excited but miserable so I don't say a lot as we wend our way down from Shimla. It is a different route from the rail track, but we drive through beautiful forests and turn corners and see views of the mountains I have grown to love. I vow to come back one day.

'You're very quiet,' Tim says. 'Are you tired?'

'I'm so sad, so happy, and it's difficult.'

My top lip trembles, and I look away.

'I know,' he whispers, patting my hand. 'I just want you to be happy with me. I want to make your life so good that you never want for anyone or anything.'

'It's a lovely thing to say, but I have to do that for myself. You can't make me happy unless I want to be.'

'And do you?'

'Of course I do. But I have to get to know Rosalie and that may take time. She may not like her Daddy having someone else.'

'You may be right, but she'll grow to love you. Who wouldn't?'

It's late in the afternoon as the bus struggles through the traffic and people on our way into Delhi. Although it's steamy hot huge clouds are rolling in as if there's going to be a downpour. We walk round to the hotel where we first met.

'I wanted to take you back to this romantic place where we met,' Tim says smiling. He looks the picture of happiness.

'Yeah right. Shall we go out on the town so to speak? I'd like to go the bazaar, buy a few more presents, get the feel of India once more before we leave.'

'Why not, darling? Your wish is my command.'

'Good I'm glad we've got that settled.'

I giggle and he pokes me in the ribs, so we burst in the door like a pair of crazy kids.

'A double room please.'

The Indian lady behind the desk looks at us.

'You stay before?'

'Yes some months ago. How do you remember?'

'You came to the desk and I noticed your pretty face. And now you are with this Aussie man. That's good. Where are you coming from?'

'Near Shimla. We were in a lovely palace retreat – Jasanghari.'

'Ah yes but where are you coming from?'

'Oh I see. Sorry. Me, England, and he is from Australia.'

'Long distances. Oh dear.'

'No it's OK.'

'Come on, Jo,' Tim mumbles under his breath.

'Thanks,' I say to the woman. 'We'll find our own room.'

Tim grabs my big bag and we go to the stairs.

'Next you were going to tell her all about our relationship and how long we've been sleeping together.'

'Don't be silly.'

'It was getting a bit much.'

'Sorry.'

He strides up the stairs and opens a door to a bedroom.

'Huh, what's this? Two single beds. I'm not sleeping apart from you.'

Tim pulls out the chest of drawers from between the beds and pushes them both together. There's a massive fan on the ceiling whizzing round to give some relief from the heat, but it's so hot compared with where we've been that I need a shower already.

Tim lies down while I go in the shower.

'I think I'll have one too,' he says. 'I'm not sure we'll have much fun in here tonight. It's stifling.'

I come out with my towel wrapped around me and see he seems to have dozed off. I lean down and kiss him but before he can grab me I dodge out of the way.

'Come on Tim. Let's get moving. Have your shower.'

'You're asserting yourself a lot young lady.'

'I just don't want to waste the small amount of time we've got here.'

We go outside at 4.30 and find it's pouring with rain, but still steamy.

'Grab a rickshaw,' Tim suggests. 'Here's one.'

He waves his hand at it, it stops and we climb in.

'Main Bazaar please,'

The man nods and starts peddling while we are shaken around in the back. When we arrive it's stopped raining.

'What if we lose each other?'

'Go back to the hotel, that's best,' he says.

We are surrounded by rugs, material, curtains, some of which are tatty and some of which are so good and so cheap.

'I can't buy any rugs,' I say as much to myself as Tim. 'I've had to leave one in my room but I've already bought a couple of blouses in Shimla. I'm going to make that the theme for the presents I get everyone. I'm not sure I can see my Dad in one of these, but who knows? And Michael, well he's got used to it all now so I'll get him one. I've got something for Beth and my Mum, so I just need Hannah, Charlie and Stephen now.'

'Come on Jo. Hurry up. I've almost had enough.'

'Shopping, huh. It's not something we've done before. Are you going to be impatient?'

'There are lots of things we haven't done before. Shopping isn't my favourite hobby. I tend to prefer what we did back in Jasanghari.'

'You can't do that all the time.'

'Can't you? Want to bet? Come on anyway. We need to get back so we can go out for dinner and have a reasonably early night. For once I mean to sleep. I think we've got to be up early.'

'6 ish to get to the airport.'

He groans.

'Not again.'

It's dry now and warming up even more, with steam coming up from the pavements. I finish my shopping, rushing a bit so I don't annoy him and we walk back to the hotel, fighting our way along the pavements past the stalls, the kids begging and the general movement of humanity. We both have to change and shower again.

'Let's have a good curry because it will be the last authentic one for ages,' I suggest.

'Until I cook you one.'

'Something else I don't know about you.'

'You know what. Let's go back to the first night restaurant. I want to remember how I met this beautiful girl there and I wished I could see more of her, and here I am embarking on the rest of my life with her.'

I sigh happily.

He seems to remember the way so we walk briskly along holding hands and chatting. I'm feeling hot again and we step into the restaurant, and it seems like years ago since I came here, yet it's only six months. The aroma of spices greets us as we walk in and the air-conditioning is a welcome relief.

'So how are you looking forward to meeting the Greaves?' I ask him as we sip our Tiger beers.

'From what you've told me, I'm terrified.'

'No seriously. I hope you can put up with them and you won't run a mile. Can you cope with the British way of life, and the weather?'

'I've been before you know. I know about pohms and all their weird habits, like leaving their money under the soap.'

I kick him under the table.

'Shut up you Antipodean. I hope they've improved or you'll be meeting the most dysfunctional family on earth! But I can assure you they do wash.'

'Well aren't they all dysfunctional? Mine's not brilliant. As long as I'm with you I don't care.'

'I've learnt so much while I've been here and I shall never forget it. And I've found you.'

'And you won't get a chance to forget me.'

It is so hot at night that we end up lying on our own beds.

'It's a good thing we don't live here. It wouldn't help our sex life,' Tim says as he leans over and gives me a goodnight kiss.

'There are plenty of children born in India. I guess you get used to it. I feel so uptight about going home. I hope it's not too awful.'

'It will be fine. They might have all undergone transformation – like you have.'

'Fine chance of that!'

283

'Don't worry, darling. And something I never thought I'd hear myself saying, but I'm so pleased it's cold in England.'

My night is not particularly good with visions of Jasanghari, Gemma, David, Michael, Mum and even Rob flashing across my waking hours and in my sleep. What am I going to do about him? I really owe him an explanation. Hopefully no-one has told him I'm going back.

I get up about three times, shower myself down and get back into bed without drying. Being wet is the only way to get back to sleep, with the fan making me feel cool for a short while.

Chapter 47

'Mum, I know how much you want to see Jo. But let me pick them up. It will be easier for Tim because I've met him. You can see them the next day.'

'Michael,' she reproached. 'I can't wait to see her.'

'You will but they'll be wiped out and tired, and it's daunting for him.'

'All right then. How much everything has changed. I love you, Michael.'

Maggie hugged her son and he held her close, surprising himself.

On the way to the airport he felt little ripples of excitement. He got delayed by traffic, and saw Jo standing with a big tall guy he recognised.

Michael shook hands with Tim and gave Jo a big hug. She looked very healthy and relaxed and was still dressed in her loose Indian clothes.

'Tim's going to change some money. Shall we wait here? I'm glad you didn't bring a welcome party. I'm not in a hurry to dump the whole family on him. Step by step I think.'

'I'm afraid you have no choice. Dad has booked a room for Sunday lunchtime at The Bear. You know Mum's back do you?'

'No, I didn't realise. I haven't really heard from anyone. Is she OK?'

'She's amazing. And Beth is bringing a new man. God knows what he'll be like. So I'm afraid you're in at the deep end. And it's someone's birthday.'

'It's yours. I nearly forgot. When is it? Monday? I've lost all track of time.'

'Yep. 38.'

'Oh, and by the way we've got you and Tim a great place to stay.'

'Yes you said. How come?'

'I'll explain but Hannah arranged it.'

Suddenly I hear a sound I've hardly heard in six months, a beeping sound. It's my phone. I look at it and there are about seven messages.

'I feel like I've been out of the land of the living, and now I've got to go back to all this communication. One from Mum, two from Beth, another from Susie – who told her?'

I scan the names desperately hoping that there isn't one from Rob. No, thank goodness.

'I need to decide what to do about Rob. If I should explain things to him, what's best, or to leave him alone.'

'I don't know what to say, Jo. I suppose it was a bit shitty what you did, but I don't know the ins and outs of it.'

'No, that's because I haven't told you.'

I give him a wry smile and see Tim coming back.

'Sssh, don't say any more.'

When we get out to the car Tim says,

'You go in the front, Jo. You can catch up with your brother and I can have a snooze.'

We speed down the M4, as I update Michael on all the news of what has been going on in Jasanghari.

'And Gemma and David, they're back together, going travelling.'

Michael glances in the back and says quietly.

'I thought, well I know, that he really liked you.'

'Yeah, well. How about you, tell me all about it?'

286

'You won't believe it Jo. Hannah's been so fantastic. When I arrived she had the house on the market without asking me. But I wasn't annoyed. At first I was shocked and then really pleased.

'She always wanted to live in Frecombe but if we move to Gresham we can downsize and keep some money over, but even more surprising - Hannah has decided that we can get Stephen into Gresham High and that's a state school.'

'She doesn't mind that then? I thought she was set on the Royal Grammar School.'

'She was but it seems that she met one or two people whose children were at Gresham and they think it's first class. It is a pretty big change and I don't understand it. I haven't dared question it too much, but it suits me fine. She did say that my going away put things in perspective and she thought that keeping the family together was more important than a big house and the best school.'

'How nice.'

'We are getting on so much better. After having nearly lost them, you know, I really appreciate them. Until you've got kids you can't really know what I mean but I enjoy them much more now. And you should see the difference in them. They are flourishing now that we aren't tearing each other's eyes out.'

'They've always been great kids.'

'Yes. And – you might be surprised – Hannah's got a job at Hardwick's estate agents so she's bringing in quite a bit of money. She gets commission and she's really good at selling houses. She seems to have the right personality for it. And that's how we've got you a little house to stay in. She arranged it with her boss.'

'That's really nice of her,' I say in a sleepy voice.

'What is particularly good,' Michael continues. 'Is that I am able to pursue the career I want. I've got a job at an environmental company and am going on a course for a week once a month up in Wales. There's loads to learn but it's really interesting. But of course the pay is nothing like I used to get.'

I've never heard Michael talking so much and so enthusiastically. I drop asleep a couple of times, but keep pinching

287

myself to stay awake, and saying, 'Mmm' every now and then so that he knows I'm listening.

'Of course the housing market isn't what it used to be. Not sure how much you know about it, but it's gone right down, so she may not earn as much as she would have done in the good times, but it's just great having her bringing in some money. We have a smaller mortgage and will eventually have only one lot of school fees.'

'You're not moving Charlie?'

'It wouldn't be fair as she's been there for three years now. Stephen's quite happy. As long at the school is big on football he's fine, and some of his friends are going too.

'I like this job much more than anything I've done before. The whole ethos there – it's so different. Less focus on making money, but of course we have to do that, but real emphasis on making a better world. I work damned hard but I'm not expected to sacrifice everything for a huge salary. I only earn about half of what I used to get, but I'm doing what I want to do.'

'Sounds great.'

I can't help it but I let out a huge yawn.

'Sorry I'm going on a bit. Have a sleep. You must be tired.'

'Exhausted.'

It feels so cold now the sun has gone down, so I pull my jacket round me wishing I could cuddle up to Tim in the back. I start to nod off as Michael finally goes quiet. He switches on the radio and sings quietly to himself and I don't remember much more until I wake up and see that we're near Bristol.

'You OK? You've done all the driving. Sorry I didn't stay awake.'

'It doesn't matter. You're tired.'

We draw up outside a little house in a district I've hardly ever been to before. Michael picks up his phone and rings Hannah.

'She'll only be about five minutes.'

We sit in the car.

'It isn't anywhere palatial, Tim, but it's available and empty,' Michael says turning round.

'Jeez, we're just grateful for anything,' Tim says. 'Really kind of you. It looks fine.'

Hannah arrives looking slim and smart in a short black skirt and jacket.

'Hi Jo,' she says in a warm voice, which I've never heard before. She clutches me and gives me a real hug for the first time ever. I'm completely taken aback but try not to show it. She puts out her hand to Tim.

'And you must be Tim. Welcome. I hope this place is all right. It was quite lucky because it's between sales and the owner has given us carte blanche to use it before it's done up. We've got to sell it but he said he'd like someone to look after it.

'The market's flat and nothing's selling that quickly, so it might take a while. Anyway the owner told Jonathan, my boss, it would be fine for someone he knew to stay here for a short while.'

'Anything's great,' Tim says. 'It's really kind of you.'

'It's nothing.' She flashes him a big smile.

Michael takes my bag out of the boot and Tim gets his own. Hannah unlocks the back door and we all traipse upstairs. It's really old-fashioned but has a lounge, kitchen, bedroom and bathroom.

'Here's the kitchen,' Hannah says turning on the light and walking in.

'It's all quite clean and nice, but not very stylish. We do have more modern kitchens in this country Tim, in case you get the wrong impression.'

'Doesn't bother me,' he drawls.

'Michael's told me what a great time he had when he was with you Jo, and I can honestly say it's done him the world of good. I expect you want to relax now. How long was the flight?'

I'm about to answer but she's distracted and opens the fridge.

'I've put some food and milk, etcetera in here.'

289

'We must pay you back for that,' I say.

'No I won't hear of it. My gift for what you've done for us. I've made up the bed for you so you can sleep. I expect you're really tired are you?'

'Pretty much. Thanks so much.'

'Think nothing of it. I expect you'll want to get to bed so we'll go.'

'She's great,' Tim says as soon as the door was closed. 'I don't know what you were talking about.'

'Honestly Tim, she's completely different. I have never seen her like this. She hugged me properly. She used to give me an air kiss. It's great for Michael. He seems so happy.'

'From what you've told me it sounds like they've made a few compromises,' Tim says. 'It obviously works. Is that what we'll do Jo, make a few compromises?'

'Are you talking about living in Australia?'

'I guess so. It's quite a sacrifice living in someone else's country.'

'I know. But we'll manage won't we? Cup of coffee?'

'Yes please. And then let's go to bed. I want to make love to you in England to see what it's like.'

He clutches me round the waist.

'I think it will be the same. Get off.'

I skip off to the kitchen.

'We might be too tired for all that.'

'You bet.'

Chapter 48

I roll over and look at my watch. I've slept well but it's only 5 a.m. My body's time clock is all out. Tim is sound asleep, looking peaceful. He has a couple of days' stubble on his chin and his soft black hair is quite long now and flops on to the pillow. He has the longest eyelashes I've ever seen on any man or woman. When I told him that the other day he just said,

'Yes, so I've been told.'

I sneak out of bed quietly, and pull back the curtain. It's a beautiful sunny day. A voice comes from the bed.

'Hello. What's it like? Raining as usual?'

'No it's not. You can cut the sarcasm. It's a beautiful day. We can go for a walk.'

'Walk? I want to stay under the covers with you. I'm so tired.'

'I'm going to get some tea. Want some?'

'Come here.'

'Not yet, be patient.'

I wander into the kitchen and put the kettle on. It feels funny not going down to the restaurant and having all this space to ourselves.

Tomorrow is going to be a real test for me. Hopefully I can cope with everyone now that I'm stronger. And now I've got Tim too, it's like extra armoury. Will Beth flirt with Tim like she did with Rob? I wonder if he knows I'm back, or if he has heard about Tim. Maybe Beth has told him. I still feel guilty but it's no longer overwhelming.

I carry two cups of tea back to the bedroom. Tim's got his head propped on his hands and is watching me.

'You can imagine flying geese on the wall here,' I laugh. 'It's great to have it, but it is a bit 20th century!'

'Flying geese?'

'It's just something that old people used to have – ceramic flying geese.'

'Well, I'll believe you. Thousands wouldn't.'

We left our bags on the floor last night because we were so tired, and there are clothes strewn everywhere. I tiptoe gingerly around them so as not to spill the tea. I find a couple of coasters and put the mugs on the bedside table.

An arm comes round me immediately.

'Come here,' he says in a deep husky voice. 'You've been ages. I want to keep you in here all to myself all day.'

'All right. I'm here.'

I climb into the bed and snuggle up close and my phone rings.

'Don't get it,' he moans.

He moves on top of me pinning me down.

'Come on, don't be silly. I have to answer it. I don't know who it is. Please.'

'They'll call back.'

I try to push him off.

'Come on Tim, it might be someone.'

'Of course it's someone. No Jo. You can't.'

He kisses me again and the phone stops.

'They'll ring back.'

Two seconds later it starts ringing again.

'I can't ignore it. It might be Mum or Dad.'

'Frigging 'phones. It's much better in Jasanghari.'

I sit up and find my mobile in the open case. Standing naked I take the call.

'Hello.'

'Hello darling,' my mother says. 'I can't wait to see you. Can I come round this morning? I can't wait to meet Tim and tell you all about what I've been doing. What time suits you?'

'Hi Mum, I've got a few things to do. Make it ten, Mum. I'll look forward to it.'

I sip my tea.

'Got a few things to do have you?' Tim says, pulling me down towards him.

'It's ten to nine now so we've got under an hour until she comes. OK?'

'Mmmm.'

He puts my face in his hands.

'I love you Jo Greaves. I'm so pleased to be here with you.'

Ten minutes later the phone rings again.

'For f's sake.'

'Tim!'

The phone's disappeared so I rummage around in my clothes and find it.

'Can't wait to see you Jo,' Beth's voice says.

'And you'll meet Don. He's just .. well you wait. He's the best thing that's happened to me. And how about Tim? I hear he's gorgeous.'

'Who from?'

'Hannah told me. She sounded quite envious,' Beth chortles.

'Do you talk about things like that with Hannah?'

I can feel Tim kissing my back.

'I do now. There's lots to tell you. I have completely changed my opinion about her. She's OK, Jo. We never really knew her properly.'

'I'll have to go Beth. See you tomorrow. Oooh, I'll have to go.'

293

'Sounds good, whatever it is you're doing. Bye, see you tomorrow.'

'Tim, you're incorrigible. Look at the time.'

'Is this what it's going to be like Jo? Will you spend your whole life on the 'phone?'

'Not if we go to Australia, the calls will be too expensive!'

'Sorry Tim, Mum's coming soon.'

'Then we'll just have to be quick. I'll have to tell these Greaves that they're ruining our sex life.'

On the dot of ten the doorbell rings. I'm just out of the shower so I call out.

'Won't be a minute.'

I pull on my jeans and a top, brush back my wet hair and open the door. In front of me is a thinner, younger version of my mother with short cropped hair. I could have walked past her in the street and not recognised her.

'Mum. You look great, but not like you.'

'I am me and I feel great.'

Mum holds out her arms and wraps them around me. First Hannah, now Mum. I'm gobsmacked, so much so that I don't really reciprocate. I don't remember touching her like this since I was 11 or 12 years old, partly because I never wanted to and also because Mum never made the effort. I obviously need some time to get used to my new mother.

Tim looks a bit embarrassed so I turn to him.

'Sorry, Tim. This is my mum, obviously.'

'Hello Tim, nice to meet you.'

'Hi, Mrs Greaves.'

He holds out his hand.

'Good to meet you too.'

'Not Mrs Greaves. Call me Maggie. We're not formal in our family.'

She sits down, gets out an iPad, and starts flicking through pictures.

'I've been teaching these kids in Ethiopia. These lovely children, whose parents have died of AIDs, or who've been abused, and nobody wants them because they are tainted.'

I'm feeling quite strange. Here is my mother talking from the heart about something she's never mentioned in the past. It's odd that she's launched into it but I can also see that it's great for her. She seems so different.

'Mum. It must have been distressing, but also so rewarding.'

'When I go back I am going to be teaching a whole new school of children from nine upwards.'

'When you go back? What about Dad?'

'Yes. What about Dad? Good question. I don't really know the answer. For years I was in this marriage just thinking that whatever I did I had to hold it together for your sake, you know for the sake of the children – you know how everyone says that?'

'I am one of those children, don't forget. For us? You stayed for us?'

'Let me finish, dear. There are many reasons. I didn't have the confidence to do anything else. And also, there were three of you - young children. You can't just give up on a marriage because it's not going very well. I used to blame your father. I resented him.'

She gasps.

'Oh, I'm sorry. You may not know anything. Do you know about what was going on, do you?'

'Michael told me.'

'Yes well you know then. Sorry, Tim. This must be very boring. I was so angry and hurt that I took it out on him. Always moaning, always criticising. And really I was just a typical housewife victim. I did nothing about it. I didn't ask him to stop seeing, to stop seeing her.

'But all the time I was trying to get back some fantasy relationship that I thought we'd had, I was overlooking my own needs. Now I've been away I realise that my first duty should have been to myself, not to the marriage. I don't mean you are selfish but unless you are feeling confident and have your own self-esteem you can't really keep a relationship together can you?'

I nod but I've got tears in my eyes. I can hardly believe this is my mother talking, well burbling on really. It is non-stop and a bit too much. I feel embarrassed that Tim's here listening.

'You'll find out, dear. When you have children you two. Sorry, that's a bit presumptuous.'

'It's OK Mum.'

'Well, when you have children it's so difficult. The wife, even if she has a career, becomes less powerful. She doesn't go out any more and the man can do as he likes. He has all the opportunities. The wife is tired and exhausted and doesn't feel like, you know, like pleasing him.'

I glance at Tim. This is a bit of an avalanche for a first encounter. Now I'm bothered about how he feels hearing all this when he isn't with Rosalie.

'What I'm really saying is it changes the balance of power,' Mum carries on. 'You aren't very equal and even if you go back to work you end up feeling somewhat inferior.

'I didn't stick up for myself. I didn't say anything and I resented him rather than speaking out. That's not his fault. Maybe I could have asked him to stop and made an ultimatum. But I didn't dare.'

'I never knew.'

My eyes are brimming with tears now.

'It's OK now. That's what I'm trying to say. I feel great now. I've rediscovered myself and become a person in my own right. And that's very important to me so I don't know if I want to be in a conventional marriage again, but nor do I want to get divorced. So we'll just have to see.'

'Mum. Can you stop a minute? I just need to tell you something. Is it OK Tim?'

Tim nods.

'Tim – he's not been married, but he's had a previous relationship.'

'Well is that surprising? I'm not completely naïve.'

'Please listen, Mum.'

'I have a little girl,' Tim intervenes. 'That's what she's trying to say.'

'Oh. I see. How old is she?'

'She's four. Here I'll show you a picture.'

He gets up and goes into the bedroom.

'He's ever so nice darling,' Mum whispers to me. 'Much better than..'

'Sssh.'

'Sorry.'

Tim walks back in and hands Mum the photo.

'What a lovely little girl. What's her name?'

'Rosalie.'

'Lovely name. Do you miss her?'

'Very much, that's why, well it's hard, but we'll work something out.'

'Good. OK, I suppose I ought to go. Things are different now aren't they? Lots of people have children and don't stay together. I don't mean that's normal but it happens so much. I suppose we live in a very different world. Is your daughter OK? Does she understand?'

'It's tough on her, but children are so resilient. Her mother loves her a lot, and she's with someone else, and of course when I'm there I try and see her a lot.'

'Yes I see.' Mum nods and continues,

'Everything has changed since I was a child. The man always used to rule the roost – with my parents and Mark's. And often the man was the sole breadwinner, but everything's changed. Your expectations are different from ours. We were told "You've made your bed and you have to lie on it".'

'Look I'm sorry Jo. I haven't asked you anything about where you've been – the Himalayas I mean, and what you did, apart from meeting Tim of course. Michael mentioned kayaking and yoga. I can't imagine him doing either quite honestly.'

'He did the kayaking, I can vouch for that,' Tim says.

'Tim was an instructor. But he didn't do yoga. No that would be stretching things a bit too far, if you pardon the pun.'

We all laugh. Mum looks happy, that's it. I don't know if I've ever seen her like this before.

'Look Mum, it would take hours to explain it all. Suffice to say it was just incredible – life changing I suppose. I feel different, as if the person I was before wasn't really me. I did so many new things, Mum. I learnt to meditate.'

'So have I. Sorry, carry on.'

'Muuum,' my mouth drops open. 'What is going on with you?'

'It's not exclusive to the young is it? Carry on. I know I interrupted.'

'Yeah well you know how good meditation is, I obviously don't need to explain. I just sorted out so many things – we had a lot of personal development too and I talked and talked about myself, my life, my relationships. And mindfulness too. Do you know about that too?'

'I think I get what it's all about, and it's possible to practise being mindful in every way, isn't it?'

I nod and glance at Tim. Is he feeling comfortable with this? He looks attentive enough but perhaps he is being polite.

'I did masses of yoga and can even stand on my head. I learnt to cook Indian food the proper way - taking health into account, did creative writing, and I learnt Sanskrit.'

'That's a bit strong Jo,' Tim scoffs.

'Well I started to learn Sanskrit. It's a beautiful language – it's phonetic and there are just 50 sounds. It's supposedly the language of the gods – mantras are in Sanskrit. And Ayurveda. Tell me mum you surely don't know what that is?'

'I've heard of it, that's all I can say. Is it some kind of herbal medicine?'

'In a way.'

'Sounds terrific. You must tell me more when we have time. I'm back for six weeks.'

Tim gets up and moves towards the kitchen.

'Anyone want another cuppa?'

Finally, Mum leaves and it's almost lunchtime.

'I'm sorry. You won't believe me but she never used to be like this. She'd have been friendly to you but talking like that when she's just met you. It's quite embarrassing really. She never even spoke much before – just moaned. Now she's the complete opposite. I thought she'd never stop speaking!'

'I can see where you get your personality from. She's great. I'm beginning to wonder if you've been telling me porkies.'

'You haven't met Beth yet. You wait.'

'If she's anything like the other harridans you told me about, I'll be pleasantly surprised.'

'I didn't make it up Tim. It's odd. I go away and they all undergo personality change. Perhaps my going away did them good. Did you feel awkward, especially when she was talking about marriage and children?'

'No. I just felt you needed to be left alone for a bit, so that's why I went into the kitchen. But no, she's great. Come on let's get lunch. I want to see what sport's on TV today.'

'I liked it much better in Jasanghari where there was no TV.'

'We'll have to live in India then. That's settled.'

He opens the fridge.

'What can we have for lunch? I'm going to make you a proper Aussie sandwich, a BLT.'

He makes the sandwiches and carries them on a tray into the small living room and turns on the TV.

'Look, the Wallabies are playing. This is heaven, Jo. Come and sit down.'

'I'm not mad about rugby. It's so uncivilised.'

After the sandwiches, I decide to try and tempt him away from the rugby.

'Later, later. Sssh.'

He puts his hand on my knee but I can tell he's on the rugby pitch not with me.

'I didn't know I'd have to compete with sport. I've never known you say no before.'

Chapter 49

Having breakfast at the little kitchen table we look out over the neighbours' gardens. Each one is very neat and they all have little sheds at the back of the perfectly mown lawns.

'I've looked out of the window numerous times expecting to see the mountains – they're in my being. I feel all jittery about today. Do people normally change like this? It all seems a bit too good to be true? Hannah, for instance, I wonder if it's real or if she's putting on an act.'

'Seemed genuine enough to me,' Tim says nonchalantly.

'Yes but you really don't know how bad she was, Tim. I know I sound unkind and bitchy.'

'Never!'

I look at him – is he joking?

'Look. I know you're not bitchy. I couldn't stand you if you were. I believe you, but obviously it's difficult because I didn't know her that way. I'm sure she was as bad as you say.'

He gets up and lobs a couple of pieces of bread into the toaster.

'It's hard to take in. I saw Michael changing because I was with him but Hannah. Is she really so nice? Maybe she decided she really loves Michael, when she thought she was going to lose him.

'But all she ever used to think about was how much he earned and what house they lived in and now she's working and seemingly giving up all these things which were so important to her.'

'Maybe she has had an affair,' Tim intervened. 'I can imagine that wouldn't be hard for her.'

'Tim! Do you fancy her?'

'She's a looker Jo, but not a patch on you.'

'Had to say that didn't you?'

'No. I love you. Look, I don't even know Hannah, but no-one can deny she's a looker.'

'Yeah, I suppose,' I have to admit. 'And of course Michael was probably difficult to live with. He certainly had a lot of baggage to get rid of when he was with us. I can imagine he was hell and probably very cold. Maybe she decided to take what she could get. Who knows about people? Deep down we all want the same don't we?'

'You mean love don't you? Talking of which.'

He moves over and puts his arms round me. I lean on his chest, and think about the time at Jasanghari when I began to feel lonely and thought it was time for a relationship again. I'm so glad I waited.

'Seriously though, I am having trouble believing it about all of them. I went away to change my life because I was so fed up with my family. The ridiculous thing is I come back with you and they're all fine. It's like I'm a liar isn't it?'

Suddenly there is a loud pop and two pieces of toast jump out of the toaster.

'Hell, I nearly forgot them,' Tim yells. 'At this rate I'll be able to do an exam on the Greaves' family.'

'Sorry, if it's boring.'

Tim spreads the pieces of toast piling on loads of butter.

'Maybe your going has been a catalyst which has made them all sit up and re-evaluate their lives,' he says while concentrating on spreading the butter.

'I think you could be right. I didn't expect it or even think about it. I just wanted to get away. I knew I had to go and it seems that they've all – well I'm not sure about Dad – but most of them have got their lives together.'

'Do you think your little sister will have been transformed?'

'Michael, who never had any time at all for Beth, says she is much better. Apparently when he was in India, Beth went round to their house and became really friendly with Hannah – having always

302

loathed her before - and a week or so later she took out the children. That was what I used to do, and I'm not sure she ever bothered much before.

'But of course she has a new man now.'

'That's bound to do her a lot of good. Look at you. Ha.'

'Shut up you. We don't all need a man to feel good you know. Most of Beth's men are no hopers but by all accounts this one isn't married, hopefully not gay or a heroin addict, and sounds OK. We'll find out soon.

'I can barely remember Mum ever having been that cheerful. When I think of all those years she must have been so miserable, and who can blame her when Dad was doing what he was doing?

'I get the impression that she decided enough was enough and pulled herself up sharp. Going off to Africa took some guts. Some people think it's too late to do anything at her age.'

'I don't,' Tim says. 'My grandma started having boyfriends in her seventies.'

'She didn't?'

'She did. They were men of her age who were lonely or in dreadful marriages – just one or two of them. She fell in love and completely changed from being a fairly miserable person to being cheerful and loving. She obviously discovered something she'd never found before, and I don't mind guessing what that was.'

'Don't talk dirty about your grandmother! There's hope for us all yet then!'

'I'm not waiting that long darling. Talking of which. Come on.'

'There's no time, Tim.'

'Nonsense.'

He pulls me towards him.

'I love you.'

'I love you too, but I'm going to get ready now. I'm going to have a shower.'

'I'll join you.'

'What in this tiny shower? You'll find that difficult.'

Chapter 50

Mark glanced out of the window where an array of bright clothes were flapping on the washing line. There were reds and oranges and browns and greens, all colours he didn't associate with Maggie, and they looked like African clothes.

Maggie was sitting in a chair in the conservatory reading a book. It was only 8.30 and she was fully dressed.

'Morning. Want a cup of tea?' he asked.

'No I've got one. Thanks.'

She didn't look up from her book.

He found a sieve full of blackberries when he went to get some water in the kettle.

'Oh you've been out blackberrying. Where did you go?'

'I went down to the river and along the path. It was early.'

'Why didn't you tell me? I'd have come too.'

'I enjoy doing things like that on my own.'

He felt instantly snubbed. Years ago she used to ask him to walk to the river, to pick blackberries and he never wanted to.

He put on the kettle and walked back to where she was sitting. He pulled up a chair.

'Can we talk?'

'About what?'

'Us.'

'What do you want me to say?'

She put down the book and placed her glasses on the table nearby.

'What's happening with us? Is it over? Would you not give it another try? For goodness sake Maggie, I'm a man. I want you back – it's that simple.'

'It may be to you Mark. What about my feelings?'

'What the bloody hell are they Maggie? You never say.'

'I don't know. I just don't know. I am enjoying my new life. I don't really think about us that much.'

'Thanks.'

He started pulling his fingers as if he wanted to stretch them.

'Well it's the truth. I don't actually want to get divorced though,' she said calmly.

'Divorced? I was asking you if you wanted to be with me. Not if you wanted to get divorced.'

'I'm telling you. I don't want to get divorced, but I don't know if I want to be with you. Give me time.'

'How much time?'

She looked out of the window.

'How long is a piece of string? I don't know Mark. I need time. I'm sorry.'

'Would you like to go to a cottage in Devon for a few days?' he asked.

'Well, that's nice. Where?'

'Near Salcombe. It's beautiful down there. We could go for long walks and maybe long talks!'

'As long as that is all. I want my own room.'

'All right. We'll see how things go.'

'I'll go. Why not? Haven't been there for years.'

'I'll book it tomorrow. OK?'

'Yup.'

She picked up her book and carried on reading as if nothing had been said. He watched her – she didn't seem at all ruffled.

Chapter 51

'Dad hasn't rung me and I don't know why. Maybe he's worried about my reaction and I'm worried about it too. I can't get over his deceit.'

The doorbell rings.

'Come on. You'll be fine. The taxi's here.'

We ride along with Tim holding my hand and although I feel very happy, there is nervousness too. I hope today goes OK and they like Tim and everyone behaves themselves, which of course is not usually the case with my family. And, I don't know how they're going to take it when we announce what we're doing.

Maggie and Mark arrive at the restaurant first. Stephen and Charlotte run in.

'Where is she?' they call. 'Where's Jo?'

'Not here yet,' says Maggie. 'Be patient.'

'I can't be. Has she got this gorgeous man with her?'

'Yes. He is rather,' says their grandmother. 'But he's taken, Charlotte.'

'I know,' she whines. 'He's too old for me isn't he?'

Charlotte turns round and sees a man coming into the room. He has black wavy hair and a large smiley tanned face.

The first person I see is Charlotte and I shriek,

'Charlotte,' and move forward to hug her.

'How are you, you lovely girl? I've missed you.'

I turn to Tim,

'Sorry, this is Charlie.'

'Hi,' Tim says and shakes Charlie's hand.

She looks like the cat who got the cream.

307

'Tim, this is my…, this is Mark,' Mum says to him.

Charlie whispers to me,

'He's cool Jo.'

Stephen is standing impatiently by us awaiting his turn. He gives me a very brief cuddle, and eyes Tim.

'I'm going to a new school next year and where we've moved I'm in the football team. Midfield. Are you going to come and watch? Is this Tim?'

'Yes. Meet Stephen, Tim.'

'Do you play football?' Stephen asks.

'If you want someone to talk about sport to, he's your man,' I tell him.

Tim shakes Stephen's hand.

Dad is standing back watching. I look at him – he looks so sheepish.

'Dad.'

He holds out his arms, and I fall into them. My lovely Dad. I have missed him.

'Hello,' I hear, before I see Beth walk in with a tall blond man who looks a bit petrified.

'There she is!' she cries, pointing at me. She swoops over and gives me the briefest of kisses on the cheek. She hasn't changed at all. Beth turns her eyes on Tim and looks him up and down.

I put out my hand to Don.

'Hi Don. This is Tim. You've both got to put up with our family for the first time I guess.'

'How was India?' asks Don.

'Fantastic. We were at a palace that was a retreat. It was up in the Himalayas and it was pretty heavenly. Wasn't it Tim?'

'Yes. Mind you, I wasn't there for long. Jo knew it inside out so she's the one to tell you about it.'

'They run stress management courses at the company I work for,' Don says. 'And absenteeism has gone right down. I went on a course and was quite surprised that I enjoyed it.'

'Come on everyone,' Mark says loudly, waving his arms towards the large oval table.

'We need to sit down and order.'

It's all a bit cramped so the first to sit down have to squeeze in before the others can. I've got Dad on my left and Tim on my right.

'I want to hear all about it Jo,' Dad says. 'What have you been getting up to there? Michael told me some things but they didn't sound quite my cup of tea.'

'No Dad. Probably not, but that's not to say you shouldn't try something new.'

'Maybe, darling, maybe.'

When we've ordered I nip out to the ladies. As I'm washing my hands the door opens and Beth walks in.

'He's gorgeous Jo. Is he the one?' she probes.

'Well maybe. He's just right for me. Yes he's lovely.'

'Tell me do you ever argue, or does he just act adoringly all the time?'

I tug at the towel to dry my hands. I'm not sure if I like the line of questioning.

'He certainly stands up for himself if that's what you mean. He's easy going to a point but not a pushover. How about Don?'

'He's quiet in company, but he's very self-assured. He's just what I need. I can't run him round my little finger and on the plus side he doesn't treat me like men normally do. You'll be proud of me. I hadn't been out with anyone until I met him last month. I gave up Jack.'

'So I heard. Was it difficult?'

'Yeah. But what was he offering me? I hate to say you were right but I was better off without him. He'd never have left his wife,

309

and I don't think I really wanted him, if I'd got him, if you know what I mean. I think he was a nice fantasy.'

'How did you meet Don?'

'At a party of Rob's.'

Beth goes red, and I catch a flash of something on her face like guilt. I bet I was right, I bet something happened between them. She quickly says,

'Sorry. I didn't mean to bring him up.'

'It's OK – he knows about Rob. I wouldn't want him to meet him, but I don't mind you going to Rob's party. Now I think of it I might have met Don before if he's a friend of Rob's.'

'He told me you were a lovely girl so I assume so.'

'I thought I recognised him. I'm sure he didn't know me well enough to say that. Perhaps Rob has been talking. Is he happy? Rob, I mean. I feel bad about him, but I'm so relieved to be out of it.'

'Rob's Rob. He's after Heidi and I don't know if she's still keeping him hanging on.'

'I thought she fancied him.'

'Perhaps that was in Rob's imagination. She's been a good friend to him and I think he wants more out of it. So he's OK. Guess what though? Susie was there with a man, would you believe?'

'Yes, Michael told me she had a man.'

'Michael, how does he know? Has he been snooping around her again?'

'No. Someone he knows works with her or something like that. I can't remember. Anyway what's he like, Susie's man?'

'He was really nice actually. I was amazed.'

'Beth, that's mean. She's a lovely girl.'

'Bit boring though. I can imagine her preferring a cup of hot milk before bed instead of a good session in it. What's Tim like in that department?'

'Shut up Beth. I wouldn't tell you in a million years. Suffice to say he's a lovely man in every way. What's going on with Mum and Dad? Are they together or what? I saw Mum yesterday and she seems very content with her new life.'

'I don't know.'

A look of despair comes over Beth's face. She continues,

'I don't know what will happen. I was so upset with him, but now I feel a bit sorry for him. Jesus, he's been pathetic, but he may have pulled himself together. I think he's trying to get her back.'

'Come on we'd better go back to the table. They'll wonder what we're doing. You know what Dad and Michael always say about women in the toilets.'

'Where on earth have you been?' Michael asks on cue.

'You know,' Mark responds. 'Women in the toilet. Natter, natter, natter.'

'We knew you'd say that Dad,' Beth moans. 'You're so predictable. We had a lot to discuss.'

'What do you talk about all the time though?'

'Men!' pipes up Charlotte.

'We're flattered,' says Mark, guffawing.

'Don't be, it's not usually that good, believe me,' quips back Charlotte. 'I know.'

Hannah looks at Michael and gives him a complicit smile.

Maggie is regaling Don with her experiences in Africa and the children are deep in conversation with Tim. Tim is explaining the rules of Aussie football, and Stephen is hanging on his every word.

As the desserts turn up Mark bangs his spoon.

'I've something to say. On Wednesday I'm taking your mother to Devon for a few days.'

Everyone looks at Maggie and she smiles and shrugs her shoulders, whatever that means. She looks younger, more contented, so unlike my mother.

311

Michael then taps on the table and stands up.

'I'd like to propose a toast to Jo. You've made a big difference to me and my life.' He looks at Hannah.

'I never realised it for all these years but I do now. I'm lucky to have a sister like you.'

Everyone looks at me and my eyes feel moist. I look at Beth to see if she minds what he's said, but she looks relaxed.

Suddenly Charlie gets up and rushes to the door, and I'm shocked wondering if she's upset. Michael's eyes follow Charlie, and there is a burst of

'Happy Birthday to you,' as a waitress enters carrying a big cake covered in sparklers.

Charlie takes it over to Michael and puts it in front of him. He looks absolutely thrilled and blows out the candles. My heart goes out to him, looking more contented than I've ever known him.

I mumble to Tim,

'May as well do it now.'

He nods slightly and I take a deep breath and get to my feet.

'Well, I guess it's my turn to say something. It's great to see everyone and Michael looking so happy on your birthday. But we've got some news.'

Mum and Beth both gasp – speculating a bit too much.

'Tim and I are going to live in Australia.'

'Really? When?' Dad asks. He looks absolutely crushed.

'Quite soon. And if I am to stay in Aus, I may need to marry him. That will be really awful – no I'm joking. Of course it's fine, but we're not getting married yet. And you'll all have to come out when we do.'

No-one says anything for a few seconds and then Michael speaks.

312

'You deserve to be happy, Jo. That's great but you'd better invite us out there soon. I've just found my sister. I don't want to lose her.'

'Perhaps we'll come out and visit too,' Beth looks at Don. 'What do you think?'

Dad looks like a man defeated.

'Oh no, we're going to be scattered all over the world, but you'll come back for holidays won't you?' Mum says.

'Well, we may not live there forever. It's just we have to choose one or other country and I'd like to try Australia first. Then we'll have to decide and see what happens. Dad?'

'Yes, yes?'

'You're not pleased for me, are you?'

'I've only just got you back and you're going again. I mean, when?'

'We're staying here for about a week, while I get organised and get a visa sorted. You can come out and stay.'

'A week,' he scoffs. 'It's not the same though is it? Being 20,000 miles away. The whole family's going to be scattered.'

He looks at Mum for moral support, but she looks at me.

'Oh come on, Dad,' Beth says. 'It's their life, and nowadays you can talk to people and see them which is just like them being here. Anyway, who are you thinking of now?'

I am shocked – this is not like Beth.

Dad looks at his wine glass, picks it up and swigs it back, almost choking. He surveys the table and sees expectant faces. He holds up the glass, swallows nervously and musters up a smile.

'You have my blessing Jo – and Tim. Beth is right. All we can want for our children is that they are happy, and this time, hopefully we'll know where you've gone.'

The room fills with laughter and fun.

Printed in Great Britain
by Amazon